# When We Collided

Also by Emery Lord

*Open Road Summer*
*The Start of Me and You*

# When We Collided

## EMERY LORD

BLOOMSBURY
NEW YORK LONDON OXFORD NEW DELHI SYDNEY

Copyright © 2016 by Emery Lord
All rights reserved. No part of this book may be reproduced or transmitted in any form
or by any means, electronic or mechanical, including photocopying, recording, or by any
information storage and retrieval system, without permission in writing from the publisher.

First published in the United States of America in April 2016
by Bloomsbury Children's Books
www.bloomsbury.com

Bloomsbury is a registered trademark of Bloomsbury Publishing Plc

For information about permission to reproduce selections from this book, write to
Permissions, Bloomsbury Children's Books, 1385 Broadway, New York, New York 10018
Bloomsbury books may be purchased for business or promotional use. For information
on bulk purchases please contact Macmillan Corporate and Premium Sales Department at
specialmarkets@macmillan.com

Library of Congress Cataloging-in-Publication Data
Lord, Emery.
When we collided / by Emery Lord.
    pages    cm
Summary: Can seventeen-year-old Jonah save his family restaurant from ruin,
his mother from her sadness, and his danger-seeking girlfriend Vivi from herself?
ISBN 978-1-61963-845-7 (hardcover) • ISBN 978-1-61963-846-4 (e-book)
[1. Love—Fiction. 2. Family problems—Fiction. 3. Depression, Mental—Fiction.
4. Mental illness—Fiction.] I. Title.
PZ7.L87736Wh 2016      [Fic]—dc23         2015011933

Book design by Amanda Bartlett
Typeset by Newgen Knowledge Works (P) Ltd., Chennai, India
Printed and bound in USA by Berryville Graphics Inc., Berryville, Virginia
2 4 6 8 10 9 7 5 3 1

All papers used by Bloomsbury Publishing, Inc., are natural, recyclable products
made from wood grown in well-managed forests. The manufacturing processes
conform to the environmental regulations of the country of origin.

For my family, sailing onward

# When We Collided

# CHAPTER ONE
## *Vivi*

I knew I was in love with Verona Cove on the first day, but I waited until the seventh day to commit. After one week here, I'm carving my name into a tree in the center of town. It's way harder than you might think, digging a pocketknife into ancient bark. Eleven letters have taken me hours, or it felt like that, anyway. Fortunately, before the sun rises, no one polices Irving Park—or anywhere, really. I'm pretty sure the worst crime Verona Cove has ever seen is someone dropping a napkin. The napkin dropper tried to chase it, I bet, but the wind swept it up, and eventually, somewhere, the napkin became litter.

And besides, I'd actually enjoy getting caught—clearly, since I implicated myself in jagged lines forever etched into a tree older than any of the 3,051 people in this town: *Vivi was here*.

When I'm done, I pat my handiwork because—okay, yes, I'm a nature vandalizer, but this is a crime of passion. I know the park doesn't mind because I love it here, and I think even the neatly trimmed grass and placarded benches can sense my affection.

I take the footpath out of the park, only now realizing how much later I am than usual. The morning sun has edged past the horizon line, casting shadows of the leaves like lace on the sidewalk. Flowers burst throughout every inch of the town—fuchsia roses crawling over trellises, forsythia blazing like yellow fireworks. As I walk down the sidewalk, the trees undress above me, dropping pale pink petals like a slow burlesque.

This is why I want to stay forever, not just for the summer. So far, my argument to my mom has been that Verona Cove makes Hawaii look like a floating garbage heap. I mean, I've never been to Hawaii, technically speaking, but I've seen pictures. Verona Cove is a tiny coastal town you might expect to find on the shore of Massachusetts or North Carolina, but instead it's tucked into a tiny notch on California's curved back. I've lived in a few towns, so believe me when I say that Verona Cove isn't one. It's Mayberry meets the rain forest meets Shangri-La. Each detail is so perfect that it feels like a film set, and I want to run my hands across the painted lattices, the retro mailboxes, the street lamps that glow like rows of white moons. Everything is clean but not totally pristine, like every inch of town is lived in and loved.

The shopping district is a three-by-three grid, and Main Street creates the center line. Every morning, I pass a handsome brick restaurant, a locally owned hardware store, and the bookstore. The storefront I'm aiming for is marked by a sandwich board with "Betty's Diner" in beautiful, chalk script at the top. Below, it reads in pink block letters: Voted Best Breakfast by the *Daily Gazette*, followed by the breakfast and lunch specials. Cove Coffee displays a similar certificate in its window: Voted Best Coffee by *Daily Gazette*. There's only one of everything in this town—a drugstore, a grocery, an art store—so each is the best by default, but I love that the town takes the time to honor each contribution.

Bells jingle on my way into the diner, and I'm hit with the smell of maple syrup and coffee and spicy sausage. I've come here all seven mornings, since there's nowhere else to go at this hour, and the excitement of a new town has been waking me up early.

Because I'm later than usual, Betty's is full up with octogenarians—white puffs of hair hovering like clouds over the backs of the aqua vinyl booths.

Betty herself is behind the register, punching at buttons. "Oh, hey, honey bun. One sec."

I think Betty keeps words like *sugar*, *darlin'*, and *honey* etched on a pair of dice in her mind. With each customer interaction, she shakes one or both dice to land on a single word or a combo: *honey pie, sugar darlin', doll baby*. I like to hear who I am each day. The term of endearment is like a fortune cookie at my favorite Chinese restaurant; it's not why I go there, but it makes the experience a touch sweeter.

She comes out from behind the counter, surveying the packed diner. "Might be a quick minute before a table frees up."

But I've already spotted my in: an older man wearing a thin sweater. "That's okay. I'll sit with Officer Hayashi."

She looks at me as though I have just said, *I will tame a tiger now, and he will feed me pancakes with his paws.* "Uh, sweetie, he's a little particular about his alone time in the morning. And always."

"I'm not worried." I flash her a smile because I know something she doesn't: Officer Hayashi is no curmudgeon.

My third morning here, I was on my way into Betty's when I spotted a German shepherd—all sharp angles, nose, and ears—sitting in the back of a cop car.

"What are they bringing ya in for, cutie?" I asked through the cracked window. The dog stared back, proud and attempting the stoicism required for his job. "Not assault or battery, no way, you're too gentle for that—I can tell. Trafficking? Nah, not the type. Aha! Theft, I bet. What was it? A whole pizza off the table? A birthday cake right out from under a little kid? You look like the sweet-tooth type."

His long tail smacked against the back of the seat.

"Boneless wings with jerk sauce," a low voice behind me said. "That's her weakness."

A girl dog. I felt silly for assuming otherwise. And, of course, she was wagging her tail at the sight of her partner—a man with white hair and a navy-blue police uniform. When he got close enough, I read the name on his silver badge: *Hayashi*.

"But she's not under arrest. Yet, anyway." He took a sip of his to-go coffee from Betty's.

"Oh, I know she's on duty," I said. "I was just teasing her. Couldn't resist—I'm crazy about dogs, and she's a real gem. I can tell these things."

"Yeah, she's a good girl, aren't ya, Babs?"

"Babs?" I asked, bristling. What a name for a police dog! Honestly, all the male German shepherds get to be Rex and Maverick and Ace.

"Kubaba, actually."

Even more ridiculous, though I tried not to react.

"Well, nice to meet you, Kubaba," I told the dog, and, turning back to her partner, I held out my hand. "I'm Vivi, by the way."

He shook my hand. "You a law-abiding citizen?"

"I've never been under arrest." I smiled, coy about quoting him. "Yet, anyway."

But see, here's the thing: after that, I went home and searched the name Kubaba. And now I understand Officer Hayashi well enough to know he'll be kind to me.

"Hi!" I say, approaching his table. He's staring down at the crossword, printing neatly with blue ink. "Vivi. From earlier this week? I accused your K-9 unit of being under arrest."

He looks up, studying me as if I'm trying to trick him somehow. "I recall."

"Kubaba," I say, "was the only queen of Sumer in her own right. The only woman on the Sumerian King List."

A smile creeps onto his face. "You looked her up, eh?"

A world of male shepherds trained to rip out a criminal's throat, and he named his regal girl for what she is: their equal.

"Can I sit with you?"

He glances around, clearly trying to find another open seat he can dispatch me to. I just smile pleasantly, waiting for him to give in. Everyone does, eventually. His gaze shifts back to me. "Of course you *can*."

*Hmph.* Old-timer snark, after which I am supposed to correctly ask, *May I sit with you?* But instead I settle into the booth across from him, thumping my bag down beside me.

And the good officer does not know what to do with me.

"You sure you never been arrested?" he asks. "You seem like the type. Disregarding social rules."

I splay a hand on my chest, all drama. "Why, I would *never*."

My lips press together, trying not to smile. See, even if I did get caught marking up the tree, I know Hayashi is an old softie underneath. When he returns to his crossword, I open my sketchbook to the page I was working on last night. My inspiration word is scrawled at the top and taunting me. To represent *wabi-sabi*, I meant to draw a simple pink gown, raw silk with a sort of ripped texture at the bottom. But I got caught up, and now it's a girl wearing branches of cherry blossoms, pink petals fanning out as if she's spinning.

I start over on the opposite page, occasionally stealing glances at my tablemate. When Hayashi doesn't know an answer, he chews on the tip of his pen and scowls at the newspaper, as if the page will be intimidated into giving up the correct word.

"Hey, doll baby," Betty says to me, pouring coffee into my mug. I drink coffee for the taste, of course, since caffeine is the last thing I need. Most of the things I do in life are for flavor, not necessity. "On to the waffles?"

My first morning here, I ordered the first item on the menu—the Classic Omelet—so I just decided I'd try everything, in order. I've worked through all the omelets already. "Yes, please! Sounds positively divine."

"Here you are, Pete." She sets a plate in front of him. Sunny-side-up eggs and crispy bacon on warm biscuits. *Mmmm.* I haven't gotten to that column yet.

"So." He picks up his fork. "What's with the Marilyn Monroe thing?"

I touch the ends of my curls. "It's not a Marilyn thing. It's a *me* thing."

He's digging into his food, not even paying attention. "Okay."

Oh, honestly, can't a gal do something for the hell of it? I've gained some weight in the past few months, and the curves are new to me. So I thought, *You know, what better time to dye my hair platinum blond and cut it to a length between my earlobes and shoulder tops?* I spun big sections of blond into foam curlers and drenched the whole mess in home-perm chemicals. I don't even really know anything about Marilyn Monroe. But girlfriend was on to something with her short, curly hair. Bouncing on top of my head, it feels fun and light and like I'd be ready to roll if the forest pixies ever ask me to go dancing with them. And as long as my hair is going to be all Marilyn-y, I figured I'd try out some red lips and nails.

I've read that animal coloration can be for mimicry or protection or for signaling to a predator or a potential sexual mate. Ha! Perhaps my platinum dye and red lips and pink cheeks are all of the above. Or perhaps I just like plumage.

When the waffles arrive, I push my sketchbook aside to make room, and I dig in and *oomph!* Carb heaven, golden and buttery and dusted with powdered sugar.

Officer Hayashi is staring down at my sketchbook page. He uses a chunk of biscuit to mop up the last of his runny egg yolk. "*Wabi-sabi.* You know what that is?"

"As I understand it," I say, trying to sound academic, "it's an untranslatable word. *Wabi* can mean rustic or stark or transient. *Sabi* is like . . . faded. Or fad*ing*. Old. Together, I guess it's like seeing beauty in simplicity and nature. In fleeting moments and even in decay."

He tips his coffee back, emptying it. "Where'd you learn about that?"

"From my friend." Can I still call Ruby my friend? Her image invades my brain, her hot-pink lipstick and fringed black hair, and I'm sickened with missing her, with missing her whole family. "Last spring, her mom did this huge mixed-media show juxtaposing the Japanese aesthetics she grew up with and the Western aesthetics she studied in college."

Before he can add anything, I sigh, gesturing to the sweeping cherry-branch dress. "I'm trying to translate some of the concepts into couture, but I'm not sure I can mesh them with *my* personal aesthetics. I like inventive, bold fashion, so I have a feeling that once I finally get to Japan, I'll be more about the street style. Have you been?"

"I haven't, no. But I . . ." He hesitates, pulling cash out of his wallet. "I have always wanted to see Kinkaku-ji."

"The Golden Pavilion?"

He nods. "My mother spoke of it with awe."

"Why haven't you ever gone, if you want to?"

"Oh, you know. Life." With this, he tugs a worn baseball cap onto his head. He leaves our booth without another word.

I'm not far behind him, because my morning routine has one more stop before work.

Verona Cove sits above sea level, so if you walk westward on any street in town, you'll eventually hit the bluffs. Some of them drop off right above the ocean, and others taper downhill toward the shore. I think I imagined the California coast with surfers running headlong into the waves and with pops of colorful umbrellas. But it's quieter, just the whoosh of water and call of birds. I stand on the cliff with mist rising from the ocean almost straight below me, and, even after a week of this, it stuns me. The natural world makes the finest architects and designers and artists look like silly amateurs. I'm so lucky to stand witness to panoramic blue skies and white-tipped waves and the craggy earth beneath my feet.

I anticipated the few birds that scamper near me, which is why I pocketed some crumbs of waffle from my breakfast. They peck at the torn pieces on the ground while I dig into my purse for the thing I came here to discard. I have two neon-orange bottles in my purse, so I've got to make sure I find the right one.

The pills are smooth to the touch. I push my finger against one pill to slide it out. Once it's in my hand, I wind up because I've learned that you've really got to put some force behind the meager weight of a tiny pill. I fling my arm forward, hand opening for the release.

The pill soars over the cliff, and I imagine the tiniest *plink* as it hits the ocean's surface. Maybe a fish will spot it, and his round mouth will break above water to ingest it, and if he's been having some rough emotional ups and downs, he'll feel better! You're welcome, little guy.

Turning my back to the Pacific, I start toward the pottery shop. I can't imagine a better summer job. I don't have to wear a uniform, and I get to watch people create art, which is almost voyeuristic—a glimpse at the bare soul. Magic, I tell you. Magic.

I lucked into the job, really. On my second day in Verona Cove, I sat on the bench outside the shop hoping to entertain myself for a while once it opened. By the time the owner showed up—an hour after the posted opening time—I'd run my pencil down sketching dresses. The owner, Whitney, has the warmest energy and the best curls I've ever seen—thousands of them, tightly wound. I couldn't stop staring at her hair and thinking that God himself must have created it with a curling iron the size of a number two pencil. Her apologies flurried between explanations—that she got into this groove with her own pottery the night before, that she overslept again.

We sat for the next hour, me painting a bowl for my mom and Whitney organizing the glaze paints into rainbow formation. She kept apologizing, but I told her not to worry about it, that sleep and I are only casual acquaintances. She joked that maybe I should work in the shop some mornings so she could sleep in. *Actually*, I said. *I've been meaning to get a job.* That's when she stopped laughing and asked if I was serious, even though she could only pay me minimum wage. And, well, you can probably guess what my answer was because here I am, digging for the shop keys in my bag.

When I turn onto High Street, I see that the bench outside Fired Up is occupied. Sitting there are a little girl with pink sneakers and a guy about my age with dark hair. Even from a distance, I can tell his hair is not a styling choice but the result of a perpetually overdue haircut—kind of rumpled, with the start of curls. It's really great hair; if I had hair like that, I would never cut it or dye it or change a single thing.

They're talking as I approach, the little girl swinging her legs. The guy is seventeen or eighteen—too young to be her dad—but he almost looks like he could be *someone's* dad. I can see dark circles under his eyes, so maybe that's it. Or maybe it's his slouchy khakis and navy T-shirt with a pocket over his heart. This is not a cool outfit or an uncool outfit, just practical. Everything about him says he's too busy to even realize he's that cute.

"Good morning!" I say. They both stare like I'm a cartoon character come to life.

"Hey." The guy stands abruptly, and the little girl follows his lead.

"You here to paint?"

"Yep," he says. The girl bobs her head.

"Well, come on in." I motion to them with one hand while still rooting around for the keys with the other, and I give my most charming smile to spur them from their muteness. I'm not much for silence; it simply doesn't suit me. I'd rather carry on a conversation with myself than crawl the trenches of awkward nothingness. Since I'm not sure what else to say, my mind wrenches back to this morning's activities and my breakfast companion.

"Are you guys locals or here on vacation?" I hold the door open, and they walk inside.

The guy clears his throat. "Townies."

"Oh, excellent." The door shuts behind us, and I plunk my purse down on the counter. "Do you know if the Verona Cove police are strict? I mean, like, on first-time offenders. Who may have created some, ahem, unsanctioned art on the local plant life. Asking for a friend, of course."

## CHAPTER TWO
# *Jonah*

I'm going to murder my alarm clock one of these days. I don't use my phone as an alarm because there's a very real chance I'd chuck it out my attic room's window. Every morning the clock shrieks, and I mentally flambé the whole damn thing. Set it on fire in a huge saucepan. Laugh as it melts. On the rare morning that I feel almost awake, I give the alarm clock a stately Viking funeral in my mind. And there it is again, screeching.

My feet trudge down the stairs. Must. Find. Coffee. Then shower, load of laundry, unload the dishwasher, work. Before I can get to step one, I'm sidelined by a hopping motion in the kitchen.

"Jonah! Today, today, today!" Leah's feet hit the linoleum on every other syllable. She's already dressed, right down to her pink sneakers. I was eleven when she was born, and sometimes I still can't believe she's old enough to tie her own shoes.

"What's today?"

Her smile flatlines. "I get to paint pottery. I filled up my chore chart, and you promised."

Shit. I did promise.

She crosses her arms. "Last week, Wednesday or maybe Thursday, you said *Monday* you would take me. Today is Monday. That means we're going."

"You're right." I'm not awake enough to figure out how this will work. I have to be at the restaurant by eleven, and my older brother and sister are already at their jobs. But I really don't want to take the younger ones to the pottery place. There's a saying about people being oil and water, but Bekah and Isaac are like oil and a hot frying pan. Put them together, and there's hissing, spitting, and the occasional burn. They got into a screaming match yesterday morning over who'd get to sit in the recliner while watching TV. Bekah lobbed a pillow at Isaac's head, missed, and broke a vase. So I grounded them both. I don't really know what *grounded* entails for an eight- and an eleven-year-old, but it sounded authoritative at the time.

"So we can go?" Leah asks.

"Yeah, we can go."

"Yay, yay, yay!"

Lifting a mug from the cabinet, I turn back to Leah. "You want oatmeal?"

"I want peanut butter–banana toast, but Bekah wouldn't toast the bread for me."

"How about peanut butter–banana oatmeal?"

She makes a face.

"Fine. Toast it is." I redirect my hands toward a loaf of bread and then drop one slice into the toaster. I hand Leah the banana and a dull knife. She holds the knife in her right hand and braces the banana with her left, tucking the tips of her fingers under like I taught her. Our dad taught me, in the kitchen of his restaurant. He also showed me what would happen if I did *not* use this technique to protect my fingers from the blade. The demonstration involved ketchup as fake blood and a lot of dramatics. I was nine. It was the greatest thing ever.

When the bread pops up, I plate it for Leah. She smears the peanut butter. Smiling, she says, "I'm going to paint a coffee cup for Mom at the pottery shop."

"Good idea." I pour my coffee. Behind us, Isaac wanders into the kitchen. A chapter book eclipses his face. Isaac can walk while reading. Like, he can walk better while reading than the average person can walk while doing nothing else. He sidesteps street signs, climbs stairs, and dodges pedestrians. It's almost disturbing. He peers at us, and the refrigerator door is reflected in his glasses.

"Did you say we're going to paint pottery?"

"*We* are," I say.

"Yes, yes, yes!" Leah says.

"Cool! I'm coming, too."

"Nope. You're grounded. And look at the chore chart. Who has all their checks for every week this month?"

Isaac squints at the chart, searching for an angle to argue. "Well . . . only Leah. But that's not fair! She gets all the easy jobs because she's the littlest. Anybody can sort laundry and set the table."

Leah scowls. I resist pinching Isaac, hard. "Leah's only five. She does everything she can, and I never have to ask her twice."

Nobody argued during the days when my mom handled the chore chart, which is a laminated grid with our six names lining the left side. She managed our eight-person family's calendar of activities and events. She signed permissions slips. She made waffles every Monday morning to soften the blow of the weekend ending. She put away Christmas decorations on December 31. But that was before we became a seven-person family.

Everything about my dad was big. His height, his laugh, his personality. Now I look at pictures of the eight of us and, when I imagine him not there, the whole picture is off balance. And so are we.

My dad used to joke that he'd forget his head if my mom didn't sew it on every morning. I was too young to know the saying about forgetting your head if it weren't attached to your body. Instead, I stared at my dad's collar. I wanted to see Frankenstein zigzags across his neck.

Then he died, and it turned out my mom relied on him for basic function, too. My mom mostly stays in her bedroom now. Sometimes I wonder if she's whispering to her heart: *Beat. Beat. Beat.* To her lungs: *In, out. In, out.* Like it takes all her time and energy to exist.

On my way upstairs, Bekah calls for me from the room she shares with Leah. She's on her knees, digging through the lowest drawer of her wardrobe. "Have you seen my dark blue shorts?"

"No. Wait—maybe. They're probably in the wash."

"Uggghhh." Groans constitute at least half of Bekah's interactions with me. She's eleven, which I don't remember being nearly as difficult as she makes it out to be. "I wanted to wear them today."

"Then do your own laundry."

She moves toward her closet with another groan, stamping her feet. I take a sip of my coffee. It's moments like these when I savor the bitterness.

"What's wrong?" This is Silas's hasty response when I call his number. My older brother works at Cove Coffee as a shift manager, and I can hear the familiar noises in the background: whirring milk steamers and choppy voices.

"Is there *any* chance you can get off work early?"

"What? I specifically took the early shift so I could be home in time for you to leave for the lunch shift."

"I know. I forgot I have to take Leah somewhere."

"You can't take Bekah and Isaac, too?"

Sure, I could. I just might wind up leaving them on the side of the road like old patio furniture or a moldy couch. With a cardboard sign that says, Free: Take.

"I grounded them yesterday."

There's a pause from Silas's end of the phone. The silence communicates words we've exchanged many times before. *What if Isaac gets it into his mind to perform a science experiment or Bekah decides to meet up with friends at the pool without telling anyone? Would Mom even know? Maybe it would make her snap out of it. Maybe she wouldn't care.* Leaving them here could be the same as leaving two kids totally alone. But Bekah's eleven. "Then leave them, and just tell Mom. They'll be fine."

The line goes dead, and I dread my next stop. I don't know when I started to feel like the warden of an ailing shut-in.

I stand outside the barely cracked door for a moment before opening it. Since my dad died, my mom has spent more time behind this door than she ever did while he was alive. On the good days, I know it's a matter of time before she wakes up. On the bad days, I think I'm watching her die in slow motion.

"Mom?"

Her head lags over toward me. She smiles weakly. I'll never get over it—how seclusion has whitewashed her cheeks. They used to flush from laughing. From running around in the yard with Leah and Isaac. "Hey, pal."

"Hey." I step closer, but not near enough to sit on the bed. "I promised I'd take Leah to the pottery place. Silas is at work till ten, so it'll be Isaac and Bekah here for an hour or two."

"Okay." She rolls over so she's facing me. "Sorry I didn't get up to fix them breakfast. I'm just so tired today."

Today and every day for the past six months. Although she does get up for church most Sundays. These apologies are a pretense. So are the questions. *Would you mind packing lunch for the littles? Could you walk Bekah to soccer practice?* She always asks; she always says thank you. I'd do it anyway. She knows that.

"Don't worry about it, Mom."

There's no point in guilt-tripping. She can't make herself feel better. I can't make her feel better—none of us can. The least we can do is not make it worse.

"Thanks, pal." *Her smile is almost real*, I think. "What would I do without you?"

I honestly don't know. With all her professed gratitude, my mom must understand that we're doing her job. The three of us older kids are trying to make up for two parents, day in and day out. I'd probably try to shake my mom awake if she didn't look breakable.

I throw on the same clothes I wore yesterday and catch a glimpse of myself in the hallway mirror. Man, when did my hair get to looking like *that*? I guess I shouldn't be surprised. My last haircut happened when Candice Michaels pulled me out of the street and into her salon. Like a stray dog.

"Best behavior while I'm gone; I *mean* it. If I find out there was fighting, I'm going to walk back to the pottery shop and put *your* nail polish collection," I tell Bekah, then turn to Isaac, "and *your* favorite books into the kiln."

Bekah rolls her eyes. Isaac doesn't look up from his book. Leah dances around in my peripheral vision. She can't contain her excitement within her personal space. She has to spin it around the living room.

We have a van, but we only use it for trips out of town—to the mall for back-to-school clothes or to see movies at a big Cineplex instead of our town's tiny theater. My older sister, Naomi, uses the van to get to her internship most days. None of us mind because we can walk everywhere in Verona Cove. Leah skips twice for every stride I take. We pass Mrs. Albrecht and Edgar, a poodle that looks so much like her that I've wondered if they're actually related.

"Hi, kiddos," she says. We wave, and Leah pats Edgar's head. On our left, we pass a power-walking couple in Serious Workout Clothes, and they do not say hello. There are two types of people in Verona Cove: vacationers and townies. Leah and I, we're third-generation townies.

I'm not saying there's a turf war. That's an exaggeration. Townies rely on vacationers—we like them, even. And vacationers *loooove* Verona Cove. That's how they say it. But townies love Verona Cove like we love air. We don't have to say it or even think about it every day. It's in our lungs. It's what we're made of.

Leah and I stop at Cove Coffee—me for more coffee and her to see Silas in action.

"Hey," he says. He hands me a to-go cup of black coffee. "You got it figured out?"

"Left 'em. It's an hour or two. I mean, we'll see how it goes."

"I can't see!" Leah grumbles, so I lift her up. She loves a behind-the-scenes look at anything. Silas is topping a drink with whipped cream, then chocolate sauce, and Leah claps delightedly. He's worked here for a while, but she can't get over it. Her brother, behind the counter. Silas grins and slides a tiny cup to the end of the bar. Hot chocolate. Leah squeals with happiness, but Silas holds one finger to his lips, winking at her. She mimics him, winking in this overexaggerated way—closing her eye for too long.

Psychologists would probably say we spoil her because she's the baby of the family. But it's actually because she's so damn cute.

On our way to Fired Up, I drain my coffee and Leah slurps her hot chocolate. We settle onto the wooden bench outside the shop and talk about what we want to do this summer. I want to perfect my beurre blanc sauce, and I want to keep running on the beach so I don't die of a heart attack like our dad. But that's not how I put it to Leah. I say I want to try a few new recipes and become a faster runner. She wants to go to the library a lot and see that animated movie about ducks and build a sand castle bigger than the one we built last year. We're strategizing the latter when I sense a presence on our right side.

"Good morning!" The girl looking down at us has white-blond hair, and her lips are the color of maraschino cherries. She doesn't look like any girl in my school. She doesn't look like any girl I've ever seen in real life. And she's looking at us . . . happily. No hesitation to be cheerful in our presence.

"Hey." I nearly stumble in my attempt to stand up.

"You here to paint?" The girl cocks her head toward the storefront.

At my side, Leah nods, and I continue my verbosity. "Yep."

"Well, come on in." She grins, gesturing at us.

As we wait for her to unlock the door, I look down at Leah. I feel like we should know this girl—she *works* here. She must live here. But Leah is too busy watching her.

"Are you guys locals or here on vacation?" She holds the door open, and Leah and I walk into the store.

"Townies."

"Oh, excellent." She claps her hands as the door shuts behind her, and she sets her bag down. "Do you know if the Verona Cove police are strict? I mean, like, on first-time offenders. Who may have created some, ahem, unsanctioned art on the local plant life. Asking for a friend, of course."

I open my mouth to say—well, I'm not sure what, exactly. Instead, the girl laughs as she motions Leah forward. "Listen to me, getting ahead of myself. First things first! Painting! Come on down. You're this morning's lucky winner. As your prize for being an early bird, you get to pick any seat in the whole place. I'm so thrilled to have customers this early in the morning. I mean, don't get me wrong, I also enjoy spending time with myself. I'm pretty good company."

The girl keeps talking as Leah selects the only table that sits inside a square block of sunshine from the window. I follow her, watching the beautiful girl as she ducks into the back room. She looks like lemon meringue pie tastes. Sunny, tangy, sweet. After she emerges, she drapes a small pink apron around Leah's neck, then ducks down to tie it in a bow at her waist. "So, what's your name?"

Leah looks at me. She does this a lot, asking for permission with her eyes. I nod at her. I always nod at her. She doesn't need my permission to talk to people. When Leah stays quiet, the girl nods, too. "You're so smart not to talk to strangers; that's something I was never good at when I was little. Well, I'm still terrible at it, but once you get a job, they call it customer service. " Her red lips move quickly, parting and closing to form each syllable.

She holds out a hand to Leah. "I'm Vivi. I'm sixteen, almost seventeen, and I just moved here for the summer, and I live on Los Flores Drive. My favorite color is blue, and I love dogs and ice cream and laughing so hard that I *almost* pee my pants."

Leah pushes her lips together, crushing the smile that wants to form. The girl—Vivi—looks triumphant. "There, now I'm not a stranger anymore. You know all sorts of personal things and even one embarrassing thing about me. But you don't have to tell me your name if you don't want to."

"I'm Leah." She gives Vivi's hand a quick squeeze, not even really a shake.

"Hi, Leah. So very nice to meet you. And what about you, cutie pie?" Vivi tilts her head at me, and a few round curls bounce toward the ground and back. Did she call me cutie pie? The only person who calls me that is Betty. Betty is sixty-something and has known me since I was born. "Or are you also leery of strangers?"

"Jonah." I deepen my voice as proof that I'm a guy. Not a cutie pie.

Her laugh sounds like wind chimes. I don't know what I said that was funny. She stands on her tiptoes to slide an apron over my head.

"Oh, I'm not painting. I'm just the brother."

"Don't be ridiculous, Jonah," she says. She moves behind me, securing an apron around my waist as she did with Leah. I don't hate it. She surveys me in the apron, smiling, before glancing down at Leah. "I think the paints are calling your name. I highly recommend going wild with them. There are eighty-six thousand colors, and I bet you could use at least half of them. The more, the better!"

Leah selects as many paint bottles as her little hands will hold and then grabs two mugs. Apparently I, too, will be painting a mug. I dip a brush into some dark blue paint. Leah hunches over her mug, already committed to detail work. I swab a wide paintbrush against the mug again and again, methodically. When Vivi returns, she sets a roll of paper towels and a mason jar of clean water on the table. Then she sits down in the chair next to mine. I'm going to say something first this time. Maybe I'll decrease my chances of being such a dumb ass. "So, what do you think of Verona Cove so far?"

"Um, basically I'm in love. I actually expected ginormous beach houses and towering hotels, but it's so refreshing that nothing here is ostentatious or trying too hard or soulless. All the quaint houses and B and Bs. It's *charming*."

I shake my head, eyes on the mug. I'm filling the coarse porcelain with flat blue strokes. "Yeah, the city council won't approve zoning ordinances for any new single-family residences over three thousand square feet. They won't approve hotels either, just bed-and-breakfasts."

She blinks, taking in that information. Oh God, I am such a jackass. It's unbelievable. This girl probably speaks three languages. This girl probably has a cool older boyfriend or an acoustic rock EP. Or both. And I say the phrase *zoning ordinances*?

"That is fascinating." Her eyelashes have slowed. They're so dark, hovering over blue eyes. Wait, did she just say *fascinating*? Without a shred of sarcasm? "I'm so completely taken with the history of Verona Cove because it's not like anywhere I've ever been, and I just want to know how it's this way and why it's that way. Know what I mean?"

I want to say yes. I want to say, *Yes, beautiful girl, I know. I understand you to your very core. We are soul mates.* Instead, because of the aforementioned jackassery, I shrug. "I've lived here my whole life."

"Well, take my word for it. You're a lucky guy, like every-single-number-on-the-lottery's-winning-ticket lucky. Not many people get to have their whole childhood in a place so beautiful. Or so small and kind that you tell people your name once and they actually commit it to memory."

Holy hell, where does this girl live that people don't remember her? New York, probably. "So where are you from?"

"I've lived a lot of places. Seattle, last. And most. I was born there, then we moved to Boulder but back to Seattle after a year. From there, we moved to Utah, then San Francisco for a bit before going back to Seattle. Been there a while. Until we came here."

"Seattle. It rains there a lot." Well, this is going great. Conversationalist of the Year. I'll just continue to recite basic facts about US cities until she wants to go out with me.

To my surprise, she grins. "Yes, it does. It also *doesn't* rain there a lot. They don't tell you that part. That the rainy season is dreary, but the sunny days are more beautiful than anywhere."

"So you're on Los Flores? Which house?"

"The really modern one. Richard, the guy who owns it, is my mom's number-one buyer, and he's in China for the summer, so he offered it to us. He thought the seascape might inspire my mom, which it totally has." She leans toward me, covering her mouth with one hand. "Plus he's a bachelor, and between you and me, I think he's got the hots for her."

There's a tug at my sleeve. I glance down at Leah's mug, which she's holding up for my inspection. Shakily painted hearts in every color. The in-between surfaces are filled with mint-green paint. "Looks great, Leah. Mom will love it."

She smiles, but then Vivi starts in. "Oh *wow*. Are you an artist?"

Leah's brow furrows. "No . . ."

"Well, you're *very* talented, let me tell you. There are people much older than you who can't paint *nearly* as well as you, and I know because my mom is a painter as her job, so I can tell when someone has a gift for painting. Jonah, for example, does not."

This makes Leah giggle. Her cheeks are pink with pride. Mine are probably pink, too. I open my mouth to make excuses for my solid blue mug, but Leah gets there before me. "Your mom is a painter?"

The question startles me. At home, Leah will say what's on her mind. But in public, even around her friends from school, she sits in the backseat of every conversation.

"Oh, yes. That's why we're here—so she can paint the sun and the ocean."

Leah considers this. "So you don't know anybody here except your mom?"

Vivi shrugs. "Well, I've met *some* people. Why? Do you have any good friend recommendations? Or fun things to do? Or the best places to eat?"

"My house," Leah says. "That's the best place to eat."

"Your house?" Vivi grins.

Leah nods. "Jonah, can Vivi come over for dinner tonight?"

"Um . . ." Look, I'd love to go out to dinner with this girl. But not dinner at my house with my crazy family. They're both looking at me. Shit, I honestly have no excuse. We don't have any food? What a lie—I buy stuff in bulk to save money. The truth is too brutal: my mom is lost in a depressive episode, and I have five dysfunctional siblings. Vivi makes eye contact with me, and I mentally plead with her: *Please don't make me sit at our kitchen table and watch you take it all in. The bickering, the stark lack of a parent.* "Sure. If you want to."

Vivi claps happily, and Leah smiles. *You didn't have a shot anyway*, I tell myself. *So nothing lost.* Leah handed me a ticking time bomb of an idea, and I signed for the delivery. Now I'll have to let it blow up in my face.

"What are we having tonight?" Leah asks.

"I haven't decided yet. What do you want?"

"Pizza. But not the store kind. The kind you make." She glances at Vivi. "It's the best. You'll love it."

It's not a cheap meal to make, but I'll do it. Leah gets up to choose an additional paint color. When she's far enough away from us, I stoop my head down. "You don't have to do this if you don't want. Honestly, she'll understand."

"Of course I want to." Vivi narrows her eyes like I'm talking crazy. As if accepting a dinner invitation from a five-year-old is the most normal thing in the world. "Like I said, I'm new to town, and also, my mom doesn't cook, so I've eaten cereal for dinner for a week. Delicious cereal, actually, but I could use some hot food. Some sustenance, you know? So, what time should I come over?"

"Um . . ." I trail off. I'm calculating how long it will take me to get ingredients, walk home from work, and make the dough. And how long it will take me to clean up the house, persuade my siblings to be normal in front of Vivi, and figure out what, if anything, to tell this girl about my parents. Or lack thereof. I need two weeks, minimum.

"Here." Vivi grasps my wrist, pulling my whole left arm toward her. I feel wetness against my skin, the cool stroke of a damp paintbrush. When she's done, my arm displays ten digits in blue paint. Her phone number runs from my bicep, where my T-shirt sleeve begins, to the base of my palm. "Just text me when you know."

By the time we step outside, we've been at the shop for less than an hour. In that time, Leah made a new friend, and I got a girl's phone number painted on my arm. I look down at Leah. "That was weird."

She nods. "Good weird."

Now I have less than half a day to make my life seem normal—or at least normal enough that a pretty girl can come over and not run away screaming. I need a plan. And a haircut. And possibly tranq darts for my siblings.

Leah is walking on the curb like it's a balance beam. I watch her for a moment before asking, "How weird do you think our family is, on a scale of one to ten?"

"One hundred," she says simply. "But good weird."

Most days, I feel like I'm barely holding it all together. But if my littlest sister can believe that her life is good despite having no dad and a ghost of a mom, then it's worth it. *Good weird.* I know it doesn't sound like much. But it's enough.

# CHAPTER THREE
## *Vivi*

"Morning, Vivi!"

I look up to see Whitney bustling toward the front counter. Her hair frames her face with tiny tendrils, deep chestnut with a hint of red in the broad daylight. I'm immediately envious of the maroon skirt that wraps around her waist and falls all the way to the floor. "Good morning!"

"How's business today?" She sets down a small box of new paints.

"Pretty darn good. Fifteen customers in—what has it been, six hours? One person painted two things. Plus I made a new friend. Aaaaand"—I turn to her, making my eyebrows dance with intrigue—"I met a boy."

Whitney spins toward me, already grinning. "Oh, *really*."

I think back on Jonah, his messy hair, his dark eyes the color of a filled-up coffee mug when you stare into it—deep and brown and fading into black. Delicious, warm. "*Mmhmm.*"

"Would I know him? Is he a vacationer or townie?" Whitney rubs her hands together like she's waiting for me to bundle up my juicy details and hand them over.

"Townie. Jonah." His name is easy to overpronounce for bravado. *Jo-nahhh.* I love the *oh* and *ah*, and the *n* sound that requires tapping my tongue on the roof of my mouth. My name only needs lower lip and front teeth to say out loud.

Whitney's eyebrow ring moves up at least an inch, catching the overhead light. "Jonah Daniels?"

"I have no idea. Medium height, dark hair, has a darling little sister named Leah. Sort of has this distracted, overwrought vibe."

"Yeah, that's Jonah." Whitney has gone from excited about my hot gossip to perplexed by something. I can't tell which detail has thrown her off. Oh, heavens, if he has a girlfriend, that will be a terribly annoying hiccup—one I'll overcome, of course, but annoying nonetheless. It'll take a while to deal with, and I'm not made of time. I have plans, you know. Good ones. Whitney crosses her arms more tightly. "So he asked you out?"

"Well, not *technically*. Leah asked me to come over for dinner, and Jonah agreed to it. But I think he liked the idea—well, maybe I'm projecting that, but he'll like the idea by the time I leave the dinner table." I flash my winningest smile, but she still looks unsure. "Gosh, you're acting like he has leprosy or something. What is it? If he's an ax murderer, just tell me quick so I can decide whether to risk it for dinner tonight."

"No, it's just . . ." Whitney trails off. "His family has been through a lot in the past year. Everyone has been worried that—"

"You don't have to tell me," I say, cutting her off. "In fact, I'd rather you didn't. I don't mind being introduced to people's skeletons firsthand, in person. I more than don't mind it. I prefer to reach right into the closet and shake their bony hands and say hello for myself."

Whitney laughs. "You're a good girl, Viv."

"Why, thank you." I give a little curtsy. "Besides, it takes a lot to scare me off, especially when the boy is *completely* unaware how hot he is, which amplifies it, if you ask me. Like, the responsible-older-brother thing is pretty sexy. Don't you think?"

Whitney laughs. "I'm twenty-six, Viv. I don't evaluate the sexiness of sixteen-year-old guys."

"Well, then, take my word for it." I wink, laughing as I grab my purse from behind the register.

On my quick walk home, I'm sure of my choice to not know Jonah's secrets. I've been through a lot in the past year, too, and I would never want someone handing out my personal information like it's a flyer to a concert or a coupon for a new restaurant. Those are my truths to disclose in my own time, if I ever do at all.

None of that's very fun to think about, though, so by the time I reach Los Flores Drive, I've switched to thinking about my paintbrush gliding across Jonah Daniels's skin.

Richard's house is a mod beach bungalow that is very middle-aged-single man, all sleekness and hard edges. There are industrial-looking lights suspended over the kitchen island, and the couch rests on spiky wooden legs. Basically, the house is very chic, but the furnishings are not cozy. It's the newest-looking house I've seen in all of Verona Cove, which is a bummer, but house crashers can't be choosers, I guess. I hung strands of lights on every wall in my room here, trying to cozy it up and make it look as close to a Yayoi Kusama exhibit as possible.

I *do* give the house points for the floor-to-ceiling windows in the living room. They're not even windows, really—they're walls made of glass. They meet in the right corner, which points directly to the ocean. It's positively magnificent. When the sun sets in the evening, it sets across the entire living room.

Big curtains drop down with the push of a button, but my mom and I can't bear to use them because it seems like such a waste. At night we gaze over the ocean, and we can't believe the vastness or the blackness or how busy the waves are while the rest of the world sleeps. And oh Lord, the way the moon fills up the cosmos—there is divinity in this view, I'm telling you.

It makes me believe my mom when she says Richard may be a gajillionaire businessman, but he also has a very deep soul—like a tide pool with a drop-off you wouldn't expect from such a serene surface.

Inside, my mom is sitting at her easel, which is set up in the living room corner. She's the captain, steering at a glass bow that points seaward. She's been working on this same painting since she first set eyes on this glorious view, and my instinct is that it is almost done.

The painting is an abstract, like tangled ribbons of color all over the canvas. Most of her pieces look, to the untrained eye, like a total mess. A joyful, colorful, total mess. It is not so hard to see how she made me, too.

She twists around, finally noticing me. "Hey, chickie."

"Heya."

"How was work?"

"Oh, delightful, really."

When she stands up, she stretches her arms over her head. I'm sure she's been in the same position for a while. She looks at me, then the look turns more intense, and she steps closer—close enough to rest her soft hand against my cheek. "Have you lost a little weight?"

I stiffen, pulling away from her touch. "No. I don't know. No."

"Are you sure?"

I sigh because I hate this for two reasons: One, I don't want to go back to being a beanpole. Fuller hips look gorgeous on me, though I'm still hoping my chest fills out more. Two, I know what she is implying. "Well, Mom, it's summer in California, so I'm probably sweating more or something."

"Viv." She sighs, closing her eyes for a moment, like a tiny prayer for strength. "Please don't make me ask."

"I won't *make* you do anything." I glower at her. "How about you just *don't* ask?"

I hate to be reminded, and I hate that she still thinks about it. I don't think about it—at least, barely, because I don't see the point in reliving the bad parts of your life. Earlier this year, I got too low. And then too high. They put me on medicine that pulled me out of my rabbit hole, and one of the side effects was weight gain. That's why my mom is being suspicious and suggestive and *unfair*.

I try to do this thing when I get upset, when I start to float upward in a rage: I push all my anger down my arms. And then I snap my fingers, with both hands, trying to crush those feelings. The sound, the feel of that *snap*. Sometimes it brings me back to earth.

My mom follows me as I go up to my room. I look over my shoulder, snapping my fingers once on each hand. Nope, still furious. "I'm almost seventeen. It's *very* hurtful and insulting that you don't trust me."

We stop outside my door, and she looks sad—so sad, like she's helpless to silence what she's about to say. "Viv, tell me that you're taking your pills. Just say it, and I'll believe you."

I step into my room, then spin around to face her, my hand already steadied on the door to slam it. "Yes, okay? Yes, I am taking the stupid, fucking pills."

The door hits, heavy against its frame, and it echoes into the hallway. I burrow into my bed, angry enough to cry—which isn't a shock, considering I'm angry enough to yell the f-word in my mom's face. I don't even care, because I've asked her eighty thousand times to just not bring it up, and honestly, how hard is that? Avoiding one single topic in the entire, ever-loving world?

I let myself cry for a while, pitiful and sprawled out on my comforter, and I bury my head into Tannest's plush fur. Tannest has been my best stuffed-animal friend since I was little. My mom suggested that I name him Tanner because he is a tan-colored dog. But, since he is completely tan and I couldn't imagine him being tann*er*, I named him Tannest. He lives at the head of my bed with a pink pony named Rosabelle and a stuffed turtle named Norman.

I'm not sure how long I've been sniffling when my phone beeps.

*Hey. It's Jonah. From this morning.*

*From this morning*, like he had to remind me. Like I met another, more memorable Jonah in the past few hours. A smile sneaks across my face. How darling that he thinks

I'd forget him inside of six hours. I roll over onto my stomach, holding my phone in both hands as I type.

*Hi Jonah from this morning. Are you still making me dinner?*

*Pizza's on around 6 if you're interested.*

Hmm. Detached, totally nonflirty. Jonah, Jonah, Jonah—you are only encouraging me. It's like being at an animal shelter, where I want to be the one the most skittish dog takes a liking to.

*Oh, I'm interested.*

*Cool. 404 Seaside Street. Leah's excited.*

Oh, Jonah. Silly boy. I will *make* you flirt back with me.

*Just Leah? Not you?*

I spin the phone in my hand, waiting and smiling to myself. This is exactly what I needed for the summer—the sunshine, the ocean, some seriously blatant flirtation. And a little bit of a challenge.

Finally, my phone beeps again. *Of course me too.*

Ha—got him! That's all it takes to perk me up, and suddenly I can't bear to stay in my room and not make up with my mom. I shuffle downstairs, nibbling on my lip as I go.

She's sitting at the kitchen island when I turn the corner from the stairs. I cross my arms and lean against the door frame, sighing without really meaning to. I don't want to be the first one to talk; I don't know what to say, exactly. My mom senses my presence, and she gets up from the table to face me. Her eyes are a little red because she's a very sensitive person, like I am.

"You know I don't like bossing you around." It's true—she hates telling me what to do. My mom believes in the inherent worth of instincts, like self-reliance as a way of transcending. She encourages my creativity, my impulses, my *me*-ness. To a point, I guess. "I'm proud of the person you are, and I do trust you. But I have to watch over you because you are my baby, and I will always need to protect you, even when it makes you mad at me."

"I know that." My voice is quiet—the murmur of a child who apologizes to get out of the time-out chair. I tug my left sleeve instinctively, covering the long scar. "I'm sorry I yelled. I just hate to be reminded of it."

"I know. But we have to communicate. Dr. Douglas said that we—"

"Can we not talk about it anymore? Please, I just . . . it physically hurts in my chest to think about, and—"

"Okay. Okay." She pulls me into a hug, though I keep my arms across my chest, cradling myself even as she cradles me, too. I rest my head on her shoulder, and we stay this way for a little while, under Richard's light fixtures, which probably cost more than my life.

When my mom pulls away, she keeps her hands on my arms. "I was thinking of ordering sushi for dinner. What do you think? Philly roll and a spider roll? Some sashimi?"

I love sushi more than any other food on the planet. This is her olive branch, and I'd normally take it in a hot second. "Sounds perfect, but can I get a rain check?

I forgot to tell you I'm going over to a friend's house for dinner."

"Oh, that's fun!" My mom claps her hands together. Just like that, she is my best friend again, not my nagging mom. She slides onto a nearby stool, and I resume my position leaning against the door. "At Whitney's?"

"No, this is a brand-new friend. Two, actually. This little girl came into the store this morning—seemed shy but warmed up to me, and she invited me over for dinner, since we just moved here. She said the best place to eat in town is her house."

My mom laughs. "That's precious. So you're dining with a kindergartner?"

"Yes . . . *plus* her much older brother, who has no idea how severely cute he is."

"Aha." She grins. "Well, that sounds great. Much better than sushi with your old mom."

"Mom . . ." I roll my eyes because she knows I love hanging out with her, which is why I do almost all the time.

"I'm just teasing you," she says. Then she reaches over to hold my hand in hers, looking a little sad again. "We're okay, right? You'd tell me if we weren't okay?"

She means: you'd tell me if *you* weren't okay. I nod, squeezing her hand. "Yeah, we're okay."

# CHAPTER FOUR
## *Jonah*

The restaurant is called Tony's because that's what it is—my dad's. It feels as much like home as my own house does. I know every scar in the wood floors and baseboards. I know every ingredient in the kitchen. I know that you have to pull the freezer handle up and over at the same time if you ever want it to open. When my dad bought the building, it was a pizza kitchen. He and Felix redid most of it years ago, but the old brick oven remains. Both before and after my dad.

The menu consists of things my dad liked best when he opened the restaurant two decades ago. Most entrées are inspired by the Italian cuisine my dad learned at home or the French cuisine he learned in culinary school. Chicken piccata, steak au poivre, pesto tortellini, that kind of thing. He made the simple classics so well that they tasted brand-new again.

When working lunch prep, I have the same routine: wash and tear lettuce, dice tomatoes and onions, grate cheese. I like the ritual of it. But today I can't focus. Bad news for someone wielding several types of knives. All I can think about is dinner. I scrubbed my hands in the industrial sink but didn't touch the blue-paint phone number on my arm.

My shift is almost over by the time Felix busts in through the back door, carrying two cardboard boxes. I can't see his face, just his tanned arms on either side. "*Hola, amigos!*"

Everyone grunts their hellos. In a kitchen, you call the chef "Chef." It's protocol. I mean, football players don't call their coach "John" or "Eric." They call him "Coach." But my dad was Chef for almost twenty years. I thought it was his first name until I was four. Like, I thought he became a chef because he already had the name. There couldn't be another Chef at Tony's. Felix insists that we still call him Felix, even though he's the head chef now.

Felix is my dad's best friend. Was. No—is. I never know which tense is right. When someone dies, that person no longer *is* your best friend. He *was* your best friend. But when you're the person left here, like Felix is, you're still in the present tense. Like I am. Tony Daniels was my dad. But I *am* his son.

"Got yourself a tattoo, Maní?" Felix glances at my arm as he places the boxes on the counter near my work space. My dad called me Peanut when I was in elementary school.

It embarrassed the hell out of me until I made him stop. Never thought I'd miss it—never in a hundred years. So I like that Felix still calls me that, but in Spanish.

"That a phone number?" Felix leans closer to see the marking. "A girl's phone number?"

I try to sound all casual. "Oh. Yeah."

"No way." He waits for me to surrender, to admit that I'm lying. When I don't, he punches my arm. "It is? You asked a girl for her number?"

Gabe, one of the prep cooks, overhears this. "Oooh, Daniels. Got yourself a lady?"

He dances a little, thrusting his hips as the other guys whoop. But I'm actually glad they razz me. After my dad died, they could barely look at me. The whole kitchen was so quiet.

"Nice moves," I tell Gabe, who is still doing his stupid-ass dance. "Had plenty of practice humping nothing, huh?"

He flicks me off, grinning while the others start in on him. Even Felix laughs. It's a big, round laugh like my dad's. Their friendship spanned so many years that their personalities melded together. Felix uses a lot of the same words and phrases from inside jokes. Sometimes he inflects a word the way my dad would. Or maybe it's that my dad sounded like Felix sometimes. On the good days, he makes me feel closer to my dad. On the bad days, he makes me miss my dad until it feels like my ribs are splitting apart.

"Get out of here, then, Maní," Felix says as he heads into the office. The office is really a broom closet with a desk and shelf shoved in. My dad, tall as he was, always looked ridiculous in there. "Go call your girl."

I return home with two grocery bags of supplies for my usual pizza menu. One pizza will be simple, for Silas, Bekah, and Isaac—the pepperoni purists. And for Vivi, if she's a meat eater. If not, she can have some of the artichoke, spinach, and feta cheese pizza. My mom loves it, and so does Naomi, because she's a vegetarian. I hope Vivi wants that one because it's my most inventive pizza—the impressive one. I'll also make a small cheese pizza for Leah. She hates any other toppings to even touch her pizza, and she barely likes tomato sauce. Basically, it's round cheesy bread. I'll eat whatever is left over because I like them all.

When I turn onto our street, I see Silas on the front lawn. He's pitching a Wiffle ball to Isaac, who swings and hits nothing but summer air. Bekah laughs from the infield, and Leah doesn't notice. I think she's supposed to be playing outfield, but she's dancing around in the grass instead. By the time I'm near them, Silas's pitch connects with Isaac's bat, and Silas misses the catch, pretending like he made an honest effort. Isaac stumbles toward first base, which appears to be a flattened cereal box.

They only ask Silas to play Wiffle ball these days, not me. When I stopped coming home in my uniform last spring, I told them I'd stopped liking baseball. That I hadn't gone out for the team again because it wasn't as fun as I thought. The truth was that I had to be home with them. Naomi was at college, my mom wouldn't get out of bed, and Silas couldn't do it on his own.

"Hey, guys," I say. There are several responses at once. Isaac demands to know if I saw his hit, Bekah asks what's for dinner, and Leah wants to know when Vivi is coming over. "Yes, I saw the hit, and it was awesome. We're having homemade pizza for dinner, and I told Vivi to come over around six."

"Who's Vivi?" Silas asks, recovering the Wiffle ball that Isaac hit.

"My friend!" Leah says.

I make eye contact with Silas. "I'll tell you later."

That's all it takes for me to become old news. Isaac begs Silas to pitch again, and Bekah argues that it's her turn. I'm not dealing with this noise. No way. I've paid my dues for the day.

Inside, I assemble the ingredients from the store with the ones I already had at home. I use my dad's pizza sauce recipe, which he altered from my grandmother's recipe. She was born in Sicily, so that piece of paper is Italian gold. Not that I need the recipe card anymore. The trick is a little bit of honey and some marjoram. A little sweet, a little spicy. *Like me, eh?* my dad would say, narrating from behind the kitchen island. My mom would mutter *uh-huh* and roll her eyes even as she smiled.

I shift into my cooking trance easily. When my mind is juggling all the steps in a recipe, I can't think about anything else. Well, I guess I could, but I'd screw up the food. Every time I finish one task—mix dough so it has time to rise, defrost pepperoni—my mind adds another task onto the end of the list. My hands have to move to keep up with the ongoing tasks. I like making a whole meal at once because it's even more complicated than just an entrée. Tonight, I'll make a salad and a dessert, too.

In the kitchen, my dad is still everywhere. In the wooden handles of the knives, in the heavy pizza stones. His hands touched these things a thousand times. I know it's lame, but when I'm cooking, I can remember his voice most clearly. *Jonah, try the julienne for those onions; good work, kid. You know what they say, son—a watched pot doesn't boil, but an unwatched pot makes for soggy pasta. Keep an eye on that thing.*

I'm not sure how much time passes as I finish prepping the pizzas and mixing the salad. Eventually, Bekah and Isaac bound into the living room to play a video game, and Silas leans on the kitchen island. I glance up at him from pitting cherries for black cherry cobbler.

"So, Leah really invited a friend over for dinner?" he asks. I knew he'd be surprised. We both worry about her.

When I nod, he says, "That's awesome. Did she run into someone when you guys were out this morning?"

"Um, sort of. Met someone new at the pottery place."

"Even better."

"She's . . . a little older than Leah."

"Like Isaac's age?"

There's a knock from the front of the house. I lean back to look out the storm door. Vivi's standing there, waving and holding what appears to be a bottle of wine. She's almost an hour early. Shit. She wasn't supposed to know how much effort went into dinner. It was supposed to appear effortless. Like a feast at Hogwarts. Wait, no! I don't want to be Dobby in this equation. Jesus. "No. Like the age of that girl right there. Because that *is* her."

Silas glances at me, waggling his eyebrows as he moves to open the door. "You're going to explain this to me later."

Vivi's wearing the same thing as she was earlier, short shorts and a loose sweater that is a useless shield for the bathing suit top beneath. She introduces herself to Silas and says something about not realizing I had a brother. Then she laughs when Silas tells her there are six of us total. I probably should have warned her this morning. Maybe she scares easy. If she does, she won't last through the salad course.

"Hey, Jonah," Vivi says brightly. She sets the bottle down on the counter. "I've never been early to anything in my *life*, but I thought I'd come over and hang out for a while before dinner, just because I kind of needed to get out of my house. And I brought some sparkling grape juice because I thought it would be fun, but that was before I knew that you have five siblings. So I guess everyone can have about as much as a shot glass can hold."

She laughs again, that trilling sound. Silas stares between us, looking for the missing link in this story. Before I can respond, Leah turns the corner, almost crashing into Vivi's bare legs.

"Vivi!" Leah cries. "You're here! Hi! Do you want to see my coloring books?"

Without missing a beat, Vivi nods in amazement. "Of *course*! How did you know? That is precisely why I came over early."

She winks at me as Leah tugs her by the arm, and my face is probably turning the color of the tomatoes. When they're out of the room, I return to my pitting. I can feel my brother's stare boring into me.

"Jonah, don't lie to me. How did you get that girl to come over to our house?"

"What? I don't know. What does that even mean?"

"Did you adopt her? Or hire her in some way?"

I make sure none of the littles are looking before giving Silas the finger with both hands.

"Chill." He hits the back of my shoulder. "I'm just impressed you invited a cute girl over."

"I didn't. Leah did."

"I get it now," he says, pointing at the island. "Why you busted out the black cherry cobbler. Nice."

"Shut up." God, I'm a loser.

I used to be good at talking to girls. Or at least not bad. With three sisters, I know girls aren't that mysterious. They're just people. I used to talk my friend Zach through this like, *Dude, just ask her questions like you would anybody. What's she interested in? What does she care about? It's not that hard.* So I think I'm just rusty.

Leah and Vivi settle onto one of the benches at our huge farmhouse table. There are single chairs at each end, one for my mom and one for my dad. I always found the benches annoying during family dinners. You can't shift around without making two of your siblings move with you. But now, I'd do anything to have a table filled with eight people. One of us always sits in my dad's chair and another in my mom's. It's awkward, and it feels wrong. But it's better than staring at two empty chairs.

Armed with a whole stack of coloring books, Leah explains every picture.

"See," she tells Vivi. "This is where she goes out in the snow and wears the green dress."

I try to keep focused on the dessert, but I can't help eavesdropping on Vivi. She's asking Leah about all of us, about how old we are and what we like to do. Vivi's a snake charmer, making words rise out of Leah's mouth. My sister chatters on—three bigs, three littles, but thankfully no mention of our parents.

"Smells great, Jonah!" Vivi calls when the pizza is hot enough to melt the cheese.

"Thanks." Back to my cobbler. Because my talking-to-her track record is at crash-and-burn, screaming-as-we-plummet status.

Vivi squares her shoulders back toward Leah. "Okay, I think I've got them all. Naomi, Silas, Rutherford, Bekah, Isaac, and Leah."

Leah dissolves into giggles. "No! Not Rutherford. *Jonah*."

"Oh, right." Vivi smacks her forehead. "Duh, Viv. Okay, tell them to me one more time."

Taking a big breath, Leah recites all our names. "Naomi, Silas, Jonah, Bekah, Isaac, and me."

"Naomi, Silas, Jonah, Bekah, Isaac," Vivi repeats, "and me."

The giggling starts all over again. "No, *me* . . . Leah!"

"My name's not Leah!" Vivi says. "It's Vivi!"

Leah's a goner, sideways on the bench with laughter. I feel myself smiling.

"Sounds like a party in here." Naomi appears in the kitchen doorway, work bag on her shoulder. She stops short when she sees a stranger at the kitchen table. "Um. Hello."

"Hello!" Vivi says, sitting up straight. "You must be Naomi."

Naomi stiffens. Maybe it's the surprise of an unexpected addition who somehow knows her name. Maybe it's that Naomi is not exactly a warm person to begin with. Maybe it's that Naomi is perpetually tired from the commute to her internship. But whatever it is, my sister is not thrilled. "And you are . . . ?"

"Vivi," she says simply, as if her name is an explanation in itself. And, as I'm coming to find out, it sort of is.

"She's my friend," Leah announces, lifting her chin up.

"Leah invited me over for dinner after she found me wandering around Main Street like a stray cat, with no one around to feed me. Does that sound about right, Leah? *Meowwww.*" Vivi glances at my little sister, who nods confidently through her giggles.

"Umm . . . okay." Naomi's not even fake smiling. "Jonah, I think we have some soda in that garage refrigerator. That'll be good with pizza. Help me carry it?"

She's giving me an intentional look. In response, I throw a glance at Silas. I don't have to—he's already lifting himself off the couch. We each play referee for the other two. Silas and I rarely fight, but we'll both get into it with Naomi every once in a while.

When we're all three in the garage, my sister turns with her hands on her hips. "In the future, I'd appreciate if you didn't invite total strangers into our home."

"She's not a stranger. And Leah invited her—not me."

"We *agreed*. We agreed to keep things quiet around the house for Mom."

"Yeah, and look how far that's gotten us. Besides, I like her. She's . . . sunny."

She snorts. "I'm shocked. You like a girl who looks and dresses like that."

Okay, as if I wasn't pissed already. That'll do it. My face goes hot. "You know what, Naomi? I don't really give a shit what you think."

"That's just *charming*, Jonah. Very mature."

"You're not even here most of the time. I don't know why you think you can move home for the summer and start telling everyone how it is. We did this for *months* without you."

Her eyes narrow. "So my opinion no longer counts because I have to be in college some of the time?"

"Hey, you said it, not me. This is our full-time reality. You get to come and go."

Naomi recoils. Her voice becomes a scary whisper. "I come home *every* chance I get. Most kids my age go on spring breaks and study abroad, and I'm here. Do you know how insane my commute is?"

"And I dropped baseball to be home with them after school." I gesture to include Silas. "We get up at the ass crack of dawn; we help with homework and school projects. We—"

"Enough." Silas's voice is quiet. "We're not playing the game of who has given up the most." Naomi and I both open our mouths, still arguing our cases. Silas holds up his hand. "Stop. Jonah, you don't get to disregard Naomi because she was at school most of the year."

She looks vindicated, but Silas keeps talking. "And Naomi, you don't get to make unilateral decisions because you're the oldest. Jonah's right. I'm okay with anyone who can make Leah laugh like that."

Naomi's eyes burn into me. "*Fine*."

"Fine." My jaw clamps after I say the word.

We come back in, holding the soda as our excuse. Vivi has made setting the table into some sort of game, and Leah's so delighted that Isaac and Bekah wander into the kitchen, too, wanting in on the fun. I give Naomi a look, like *See—this is a good thing*. She avoids me.

When Vivi's not looking, I poke Isaac's shoulder and hand him the plate of food for our mom. He turns to take it upstairs without a word. We do this every night, even though she only sometimes eats it. Other times, she shuffles downstairs to the kitchen at odd hours, searching for anything appetizing. If one of us sees her, she startles like she's a burglar caught red-handed stealing our food.

"Oh! I almost forgot!" Vivi leaps up as everyone else assembles around the table. I've set all the food out to be passed around already, so I don't know what she forgot. "The sparkling juice! Jonah, do you have some little glasses for it somewhere?"

"I think so." I dig around the hutch until I find mini champagne glasses that must have belonged to my grandmother. There's a pop as Vivi opens the bottle, and she pours a bit of sparkling juice into each glass, passing them out to my siblings.

It's a holiday. It was not a holiday five minutes ago.

Vivi climbs back onto the bench with Leah. I nestle in between Isaac and Bekah. Silas and Naomi sit at the ends of the table—their natural places as the oldest.

"Thank you so much for welcoming me into your home," Vivi says, lifting the little glass. "I don't have any siblings, and I'm so glad to pretend to be a Daniels for the night."

A Daniels is not something anyone in Verona Cove has wanted to be for six months now. Her ignorance is a relief. Like we don't have to fit into our New Life of Mourning as long as Vivi is here. We can breathe easy in our stiflingly sad house.

"And thank you especially to Jonah for the most beautiful meal I've seen in ages. I swear to the Man in the Moon, if it tastes half as good as it looks, I'm going to come meowing back at your front door for table scraps." She winks at Isaac. His cheeks redden beneath the rims of his glasses. "So . . . cheers!"

Vivi holds up her glass and clinks it against everyone else's. Leah looks like she's been invited to a tea party with Alice in Wonderland.

Bekah scrutinizes Vivi's face, in awe of her. "So, your mom lets you wear that lipstick?"

Oh God, kill me. Someone. Anyone. End it. My sister is going to grill Vivi about her appearance. And parents.

Vivi smiles. It makes her lips look like an apple slice. Red Delicious. "My mom is a painter, so, really, she can't get mad if I paint my lips, now, can she?"

"Cool," Bekah says under her breath. She's resting her left hand in her lap, the way Vivi is.

"Oh my God," Vivi says, swallowing her first bite. "This is the best salad I've ever had in my life. Literally. What is *in* this thing? Like, manna or something?"

"What's manna?" Leah frowns down at her bowl. "This cheese tastes like barf."

"Leah," Naomi snaps. "That's not nice."

Vivi just laughs. "Manna is the food they eat in heaven. And stinky cheese is delicious cheese; you just don't realize that until you're older. Trust me, though. Someday, you'll eat this salad again and realize, holy moly, it's sprinkled with magic."

I clear my throat. "It's just lettuce, Gorgonzola, honey-glazed pecans, and diced pear. The dressing is a plum vinaigrette."

"He makes the dressing himself," Bekah says. I'm pleasantly surprised that she'd brag about me.

"It's kinda more of a fall salad," I say, "because of the—"

"Oh no." Bekah groans, glancing at Vivi. "I got him started. We're gonna have to hear about food for the rest of dinner."

Okay. No longer pleased with Bekah.

Vivi launches into a story about how she once ate armadillo by accident, which has everyone cracking up. Even Naomi wants to laugh. I mean, she's not *actually* laughing—she's ripping pieces of her pizza crust off and chewing them mercilessly. But I can tell she *wants* to laugh. Once my sister decides to be grouchy, she never changes her mind.

My gaze moves clockwise, taking each person in. The kitchen feels warmer, fuller. Vivi teases Silas and Isaac, who seem sheepish and delighted by the attention. She compliments Bekah and asks Naomi questions about her internship. My siblings are locked into her, rotating in her orbit. I am, too. It's like I can't look away.

"Oh my God, Jonah, look at this dessert. Are you kidding me?" Vivi stabs at the cobbler. "Black cherries are my life. I'm serious. They're my absolute favorite fruit; I'm totally obsessed, like can*not* stop eating them the past few weeks."

"Jonah and me are obsessed, too!" Leah says. "We eat cherries every day over the summer, but we know how to spit out the pits, so it's okay."

Silas shoots me a look, impressed that someone coaxed Leah that far out of her shell.

After dinner, Vivi announces that she'll hang around to color more with Leah. I bus the table with help from my brothers, and Naomi disappears upstairs, still annoyed with me. Bekah sits on the couch pretending to read while still watching Vivi like she's a unicorn in the wild. My hands dunk dishes into warm sink water, but I keep stealing glances into the living room. Vivi is lying on her stomach, coloring alongside Leah on the floor. Their knees are bent, feet swaying up in the air. My eyes follow Vivi's body from her red toenails, up her legs, tiny shorts. When she laughs at something Leah said, it's loud and happy and changes the whole shape of her face. The knife in my hands clatters into the metal sink.

"Jonah!" Leah yells. "Come look!"

I glance away so Vivi won't realize I was already looking. God. I once saw a video online of a dog crashing into a screen door. Over and over. He couldn't figure it out. This is me and trying to be cool in front of Vivi.

"Come look at my picture!" Leah demands.

Fortunately, I have a master's degree in Leah's Art Criticism. I say everything looks beautiful and ask the artist lots of questions about her color choices. She loves her princess coloring books so much that I'm surprised she's letting Vivi use one.

"Wow! Your mermaid looks just like in the movie," I tell Leah. Then I steal a glance at Vivi's coloring page. Her princess has purple hair, thick-rimmed glasses, and a lip ring.

Leah examines Vivi's drawing, too. "Belle doesn't have purple hair. Or glasses."

"This isn't Belle," Vivi says. "This is her twin sister, Claudette. She goes to a university where she's studying marine biology. She has to wear her glasses because she's farsighted and because she reads a lot of textbooks."

"But why is her hair purple?"

"Because she goes scuba diving sometimes, so she's seen how many colors there are underwater."

"Like fish?"

"Like rainbow fish and coral and underwater plants and all kinds of things. She can't just go down into that kingdom with mousy-brown hair, you know? She'd be out of place."

Leah nods as if this is totally sensible. "Cool. What's it called? Marinabology?"

"Muh-reen bi-ol-o-jee," Vivi says. "What do you want to be when you grow up?"

"A teacher." This is Leah's stock answer to something a lot of adults ask kids. Also, this might be the only profession she knows other than chef. "Maybe. I don't know."

Vivi presses her for more. "Okay, clear your mind. Like, totally blank—are you picturing nothing in your head? Nothing at all. Infinite black space."

Leah pinches her eyes shut. "Uh-huh."

"You can be *anything*, anything in the whole world. Imagine the entire blue-and-green planet with swirly white clouds—the way it looks from space. Out of everything on this enormous Earth, what do you most want to be?"

Leah considers this. "A peacock."

I almost choke on my laugh. She's the funniest, most creative kid in the world. "You'd be a peacock?"

She nods, eyebrows pulled down. I know that look. It says, *You better not be teasing me.* And I'm not. "They're blue and their feathers are the prettiest."

Vivi stares at her, totally serious, with her lips pursed in curiosity. "What makes you think you can't be one?" She says this like she truly doesn't understand why peacock isn't a profession.

"I guess . . ." Leah's little face creases between her eyebrows and beside her mouth. "I guess I don't know how."

"Oh." Vivi shrugs. "I do."

"You do?"

I try to imagine Vivi turning my sister into a peacock, but the image won't come. Maybe if I turn my head away, Vivi would shoot sparks at my sister with a wand, turning her into a peacock. It wouldn't surprise me that much at this point.

"Of course I do. We'll work on it soon, okay?"

"Okay!" Leah's excitement leans into a yawn.

"Bedtime, sleepyhead," I announce. "You too, Bekah."

"I was going upstairs anyway," Bekah says, flipping her hair as she gets off the couch. Leah, however, gives me a murderous look, like I'm embarrassing her.

"Jonah," she howls. "Noooo."

Vivi slides in easily, climbing to her feet. "Leah, if you don't go to bed, how will we hang out tomorrow?"

Leah turns. "We'll hang out tomorrow?"

"Sure. If you want."

Leah hugs Vivi's legs, squeezing quickly, and then bounces upstairs.

I shake my head as Leah disappears around the corner. Now it's just me and Vivi, and I'm not sure what to say. I'd rather flirt by making her really good food. "A peacock. Leah's a riot sometimes."

Vivi shrugs. "She was probably a peacock in a past life. Her spirit is still part avian."

I feel my eyebrows rise. "You believe in reincarnation?"

She gives me the eyebrows right back. "You *don't*?"

Um, no, I do not. "So, what have you been in a past life?"

"It's not what; it's *who*," she says. "I've been a dolphin and a ballerina, probably in the 1920s or so, and I used to be part of a pack of stratocumulus clouds. Those are the only ones I know for sure."

Either this girl is certifiable or she's saying this for my entertainment. But the craziest part is that I can imagine all those things. I can picture her above the waves in the slick body of a gray dolphin. I can imagine her in a tutu or floating above the stratosphere as a puff of cloud. I feel oddly out of touch with my own self, that I don't know what I used to be. Or, apparently, *who* I used to be. "I must be new to the world."

Vivi shakes her head vehemently. "No, no. I can always tell when this is someone's first life. This is Bekah's first life, for example, so you should cut her some slack because it's really hard to figure things out without having some preexistence instincts."

"So, who did I used to be?"

She tilts her head, and the curls on that side fall toward the ground. Her eyes are looking through me. She places her hands on my chest, palms warm. I tense up so any muscles there will be more pronounced.

"*Hmm*," she says. "In your last life, you spent many years as a tree—oak, I think. Somewhere in the Great Plains. It's why you feel deep roots in this life, here with your family. Your tree life was so long that you still have strong instincts to shelter little ones. You may not remember it, but your shoulders do."

She slides her hands over my shoulders, but I know she means it to be clinical. An examination, like she's diagnosing me with former lives. I'm not sure where to look, so close to her face. Skim milk skin, dark eyebrows. My mom used to watch all those old black-and-white films. I never understood them, but the first dirty dream I ever had was about Brigitte Bardot. *No! Think about . . . cooking. Vegetables. Parsnip! Parsnips are hideous.*

"Wow, the tree life is still so present for you." Her laugh warbles in my ears. "It's also why you can be a bit . . . immovable."

I frown. *Immovable?* Does that mean boring? She touches the tip of my nose like I'm a small child. "The best part is that before you were a tree, you were a sea captain. And before that, an otter."

"Why is that the best part?"

"Because it's still in there!" she exclaims. Her fist knocks on my chest. "All of it. First you were an otter, the most playful creature in the *world*. And then you were born as a human boy for the first time, and you became a sea captain because the water called to you from your otter days. But it's all still in there, Jonah. The tree stuff is more recent, but there's an otter in there dying to make a Slip 'N Slide in your backyard and spend the whole day doing nothing else."

Wow, that's a lot of weird information. "Okay. When do you think I was a sea captain?"

She shrugs. "It's hard to say specifically. Turn of the twentieth century or a little before, I think."

"Maybe I sailed to New York City, where you were performing as a ballerina."

Her air intake is sharp, almost a gasp, followed by a brilliant smile. "Yes! Maybe you watched me dance."

To demonstrate, she backs away from me and lifts to her tiptoes. She moves her arms in graceful lines, then drops her limbs back to the ground, smiling. "I took lessons for a few years because I missed my former ballerina life so much that I needed to relive it a little."

I play along, smiling. "Yeah. I'm *sure* I've seen you do that before."

She steps toward me, delighted, and bubbling over with energy. "Maybe you came backstage after you saw me dance. Maybe I took you underground to my favorite Prohibition spots, and we drank bathtub gin together. Then maybe we got stupid drunk to jazz music and stumbled back out onto the cobblestone streets to my apartment and made love the whole night, sweaty because there was no air-conditioning back then. I bet if we smelled juniper, we'd remember pieces of that night; don't you think so?"

Now, what in the hell do I say to *that*? Did she say *make love*? I'm not sure which is more confusing: that she'd use that phrase like someone's mom or that she just casually suggested maybe we were doing it in another life? There can be only one response. "Maybe."

"Well, I should get going," she says. "Are you busy tomorrow morning? I'm off work."

"Not busy. Just home with the other three."

"Good. I'll bring supplies."

"For what?"

"A Slip 'N Slide." She flashes me that strawberry smile. "God, Jonah, keep up."

## CHAPTER FIVE
### *Vivi*

I don't know if you've ever sprawled out in a wide-open field and stared up at the blue sky and felt the planet humming all around you, but that's what my days feel like here. The world moves a few paces slower—so slowly that my movement feels like zipping, like crackling energy through the streets.

When I met Jonah Daniels yesterday, there was a magical shift in the trajectory of my summer. He's the ring to my Frodo, the wardrobe to my Lucy Pevensie. His presence in my life sets me on my journey, and I can feel it, a vital mission pulsing in my bones. Here is a boy who *needs* me. That's why I bought supplies at the hardware store and headed over to his house: because I knew he'd be surprised that I meant what I said.

They're already in the backyard, each little kid squealing with joy as Jonah points the hose at them.

"Vivi!" Leah calls. "Hi!"

It doesn't take us long to set up the tarp on a slight downslope in their lush backyard. We blow up a baby pool at the end and fill it with water. Jonah checks underneath the Slip 'N Slide for rocks—of course he does—and calls out, "All good!"

The world smells like cut grass and beach air and hose water, and my stomach tightens with excitement.

"Who's first?" I ask, popping open a mega-size bottle of dish soap to line the plastic runway for maximum slippage and slideage. I look magnificent, if I do say so myself, in my wide-brimmed sun hat and the leopard-print leotard that I'm using as a bathing suit. The leotard is super formfitting, so I don't have to wear any underthings, and it has long sleeves to cover my scar. Isaac brings out a retro radio and sets it to the oldies station, and I shake my leopard-print hips around in pure glee.

Silas dives onto the plastic runway—what a ham—and crashes into the baby pool at the end.

"Bravo!" I yell from the top.

Bekah holds up four fingers on each hand. "The judges give it an eight out of ten."

"Go 'head, Leah," Isaac says. It seems like he's being a considerate big brother, but I think he's a little nervous to try it himself.

Jonah jogs down to the end and gives her a thumbs-up. You can't really catch someone once they go flying, but Leah doesn't know that.

Leah nods, sitting down at the top. She slides gently, bouncing right into the pool and giggling herself silly. I go backward, saluting just for the laughs, and the other littles follow behind me, shyly at first and then wildly, fearlessly. Our squeals attract some neighbor kids, who rush back home to put on their bathing suits.

Everyone has taken at least two turns before I get Jonah to try it. I spray him square in the stomach with the hose. "C'mon, sailor. Your turn."

"All right, all right, I'm going." He peels off his T-shirt, and my thoughts about this are as follows: *Um, hello.*

He sits at the top of the tarp and turns back to me. "Give me a push?"

*Hmm.* I figured he was a run-and-dive type, but whatever. I set the hose at the top so it gushes downward, and I place my hands on Jonah's shoulders.

Before I realize what's happening, he grabs me with him, and we're both sliding, and I'm shrieking with laughter. We're a tangle of limbs, slick against the soap, whooshing so fast from the velocity from our combined weight. We roll through the baby pool—shockingly cold—and past it until we land on the grass. I lie faceup, crying from laughing, and I lean my cheek against the blue plastic side of the pool.

"You guys okay?" Silas calls.

"Yeah!" Jonah's voice is right beside me, and then he's looking down at me, his face blocking the sun. The beams make a halo around him. "Viv? You okay?"

"Perfect!" I gasp out the word, still laughing. "Never been better. I *told* you. Otter."

His hair falls across his forehead, and he smiles down at me. Not a shy smile, not that hesitant, lips-clamped thing he did all of yesterday. No, this is a real grin, the first he's given me.

You wouldn't believe the things I'd do to get this world-weary boy to smile like that. Today, it took a Slip 'N Slide, and tomorrow will be something different. Oh, my—do I have plans. I'm going to spend my whole summer changing the expressions on Jonah Daniels's face.

∞

The next morning, I go about business as usual: throw a pill into the ocean, feel the breeze on my face, and thank the constellations that I can *feel* things. But then, as I'm taking out my keys to unlock the pottery shop, my gaze catches on the bench outside the store. There's a brown paper bag sitting there, with my name on it in black marker. Intrigue! I glance around, looking for conspirators, before I settle onto the bench. The bag has a bit of weight, a square shape pushing out the bottom. I'm hesitant in unrolling the top, ready to lean back if something explodes out. But it's a restaurant to-go box, it seems.

Inside, a sandwich with layers of juicy tomato, soft mozzarella, and fresh basil, on thick sourdough bread.

Or maybe something fancier I don't know the name of—focaccia? Ciabatta?

Jonah.

I stare down into this little cardboard box like it's a trunkful of jewels glinting back at me. He . . . packed me lunch?

I can imagine his hands, delicate on the knife with sure movements of his wrist, slicing through red tomato, white mozzarella. Stacking them into restaurant-perfect presentation. Golden potato chips settled around the sandwich. And a homemade cookie, slid into the side.

Was this some attempt to woo me—foodie flirtation? It must be, right? Even though making a lunch is something a parent does for a child? I don't want to be another person he has to care for. I want to be someone he cares about.

I flip this around in my mind all morning. When it's time to eat, I peel back the bread as if the sandwich will reveal the answer. Are you a romantic Roma tomato? Or is this a platonic plate, a kindness between friends?

"I ran out of the lavender paint."

"Huh?" I blunder, looking up at the customer. I almost forgot I was at work. "Oh. Sorry—there's more in the back. Let me get it for you."

The first bite reveals a bit of balsamic vinegar somewhere and a sprinkle of salt, against the near-sweet tomato and the freshness of the basil. It's heavenly and hearty and somehow creamy. And I feel . . . cared for. Like part of a family. What a simple need, to eat—and to have someone prepare a meal for me with such care, such love? It's like I can taste it.

Like it's not just the meal that fills you up, but the feeling.

On my way home, nearly bursting with that feeling, I stop by the restaurant, which is homey and like seeing another big piece of the Daniels family puzzle. Here, in a well-loved brick building—beautiful but with untapped potential, outdated decor, worn edges—I understand a little better.

"Hello there," I say, extending my hand to the man making notes behind the host station. "Is Jonah Daniels in?"

The man stares at me for a moment before an amused smile forms. "Sure is. Come on back."

He leaves me in the hallway outside the kitchen, and I bite at the red lacquer on my nails until Jonah emerges in an apron, over a plain white T-shirt that's tight around his arms. Teasing voices call out to him from the kitchen, and he glances back at them, grinning, as the door swings shut.

"Sorry about that. Bunch of idiots," he says. His hands are clearly just washed, wet and held up like a surgeon's before an operation, and I wonder what I pulled him away from. But he looks happy to see me, more relaxed than at home. "Hey."

"Hi," I say, not smiling. "You made me a sandwich. Why?"

"Why? Um. I don't know. I was packing lunch for Naomi anyway? I thought you might want a sandwich at work? And the shop is on my morning running route?" He studies me, unsure now. "Did it keep okay? Tomato can make the bread a little soggy, I know, but—"

I step into the space between us, grab the neck of his T-shirt, and I plant my lips on his, a kiss that is quick but sure and determined enough to leave a red smudge across his mouth.

"It was perfect," I say. "See you tomorrow."

Two faces appear in the kitchen door's porthole window, making wooing noises. Jonah slaps his hand against the plastic, hard, and smiles at me. "See you tomorrow."

There's a flutter in my chest and wet handprints on my shirt where he touched my waist, and this warm, glowing sense that I'm not nearly as in control of this situation as I believed. The feeling rises in tiny champagne bubbles, fizzy and sweet and full.

# CHAPTER SIX
## *Jonah*

My mind has been like a cement mixer for the past three days. If I stop thinking about Vivi for too long, my life might harden into the gray slab it's been for six months. So while I was making lunch for Naomi yesterday, I was thinking about Vivi's loud laugh. About the way she's not intimidated by our family or by anything else. The sandwich just happened. Then I spent most of my shift at the restaurant like, *Great job, asshole. Make a girl a packed lunch like she's off to her first day of kindergarten.*

Until she showed up at the restaurant, kissed me, and left.

Movies make it seem like the first kiss is the big deal, and it is. Hell yeah, it is. But they never tell you about the pressure for the second kiss—all that time to think and build up expectations. What it will be like when you see each other again. So, if there's a second kiss, it's gotta be me, and it's gotta be good. I thought about it all through breakfast.

The littles have been fed, and they're outside playing with some old squirt guns we found in the garage. I scoop out the last bowl of oatmeal and sprinkle it with brown sugar and pecans.

Upstairs, I'm surprised to find my mom out of bed. She's on the floor, surrounded by a pile of books near her shelves.

"Thanks, pal," she says as I set the bowl down on her dresser. "I've been thinking I should declutter my room a bit. Lots of books that I won't read again to give away, so I can make room for the ones I have sitting on the floor."

"Great idea!" I sound too eager. But this could be her breakthrough. There's a book in her hands, one of her favorites by Gabriel García Márquez, and she examines it. I hear the first hiccup, a repressed cry, a gasp she can't keep in.

I take the book from her, but not before I see my dad's handwriting on the inside page. *For you, amore mio. Of course.* I set it on the shelf and pull my mom up, guiding her toward the bed.

"I'm sorry," she whispers. "I'm so sorry."

I leave her curled up on the bed, shoulders shaking as the bowl of oatmeal goes cold. She always seems to feel worse when we see her upset, so it's better this way. In the kitchen, I sit down on a stool and press my forehead into my hands. I'm not sure how long I'm there before I hear the door, but I don't bother looking up.

"Hey," Vivi says. Her voice is a full decibel lower than normal. She already knew something was wrong. So much for the impressive moment of seeing someone after a first kiss.

"Hey." The word comes out defeated.

She sidles up on the stool next to me. "The littles were playing in the front yard and said you were in here. You okay?"

I want to brush it off. But I'm too tired.

So I shake my head from its place between my hands. I haven't exactly told her what's going on with our family because I don't want anything to change. "My mom's not feeling well today."

Vivi walks to the stove. Fills the kettle with water and correctly guesses the cabinet we use for coffee and tea. One cup of tea for me, one for her. She sets them in front of us and sits back down beside me. We sip in the quiet. When we're done, she pours more tea in a new mug and sets it in front of me. I take it up to my mom, who apologizes for crying earlier. I almost duck back out, to give her privacy. To not keep Vivi waiting. But somehow I know she won't mind. So I tell my mom all about our Slip 'N Slide day, even though I know Leah already did.

By the time I come back down, Vivi has washed all the dishes from this morning's breakfast and loaded them in the dishwasher. I wait for her to give an excuse—some reason to sprint away from my complicated family. I wait for her to ask questions. Instead, she holds out one hand to me, the other clutching scraps of paper.

"Scavenger hunt clues," she says.

This is where I can't keep up. This is where I see that our summers will be too different. That our lives are too different. "I wish I could. But I have to grocery shop today. We're almost out of paper towels. And I need stuff for dinners this week. And—"

"Well, give me a minute, why dontcha?" she says, smiling. "Do you have a pen?"

The edited scavenger hunt leads the littles to Patterson's grocery store and keeps them occupied while I fill the cart. When I'm done, I find them in the seasonal aisle. Vivi spots me and the full cart. She snatches a Hula-Hoop from off the rack and announces, "To move on to the next clue, one of you must dive through this Hula-Hoop like a dolphin!"

"Me!" Isaac hurls himself forward, stumbling a little as he lands on the other side.

"You move on to the next phase!" Vivi announces, as Leah claps. "The clue is . . . in the grocery cart! You have to help Jonah load everything onto the conveyor belt or you'll never find it!"

They barrel toward me—even Bekah, who usually acts too cool for things like this. Vivi gives me an exaggerated shrug and a smile. She's making this up as she goes.

At home, Silas gets caught up in the scavenger hunt, too. We spend the day following clues around town and then catch a late movie at the theater in town. Vivi pays, insisting that it was the scavenger hunt prize. When we leave the theater, the world has gone dark around us.

"That," Leah announces, "was the best movie I've *ever seen*."

She says that after every movie.

"Me too," Vivi says. "It had everything! Adventure! Sword fighting! Magic! Romance!"

We wander home, stomachs stuffed with popcorn and soda. The littles are pretending to be characters from the animated movie—a knight, a princess, a sorceress—and Silas is egging them on. Without warning, Vivi jumps on my back, urging me forward like a steed in the film. The others gallop beside us, laughing.

At the edge of town, we pass Officer Hayashi, in uniform but without his dog. We all stop running. Isaac pushes his glasses up, and Silas stands up straighter.

"Good evening," he says evenly.

"Good evening," we mutter—all but Vivi, who says, "Evenin', Officer!"

He looks at Vivi on my back, his mind calculating something. "You taking up with this troublemaker?"

Shit! He thinks I'm a troublemaker? My eyes go wide, but Vivi scoffs behind me, offended.

"Oh, am *I* taking up with *her*?" I sputter. "Yes, sir. I am."

"Careful there. Full of mischief, that one."

"Yes, sir, she is." How does he even know her?

"Yeah, yeah." Vivi laughs a little, her chest pulsing against my back. "See you tomorrow."

When we're out of earshot, I whisper to Vivi, "You'll see him tomorrow?"

"We eat breakfast together sometimes."

Before I can even ask, Bekah jumps in front of us. She pretends to cast a spell on Isaac, who dodges.

"I want to be the sorceress!" Leah exclaims.

"You can't be the sorceress. You're the princess. Now, silence!" Bekah moves her hands in a billowing motion, as if calling magic against Leah.

"Silas!" Leah shrieks. "It's not *fair*! She's being mean!"

I wait to feel Vivi slide to the ground. Because, really, who wants to spend their summer listening to this? Who wants to witness Silas try to break it up without tears? But Vivi only tightens her hold around my neck, shimmying her legs up higher on my waist. She stays.

## CHAPTER SEVEN
## *Vivi*

Here is something I never expected to feel: love at first sight for an entire family. But life surprises you. It tells you to close your eyes and blow out the candles, and then sometimes smashes your face into the cake before you can even make a wish. But! Sometimes, every once in a while, you get your wish in. You wish for a boy to spend the summer with, and instead life gives you his whole beautiful family.

It's a good thing I'm so crazy about them because they're always, always around. In the week since I kissed Jonah, we've been alone together exactly once, and it was not the right time. Now, as he smiles over at me, hitching the beach bag up on his shoulder, the sun feels even hotter on my face.

The second our feet hit the beach, Leah and I take off running, kicking up sand. We squeal as we hit the water, and I lift her up and spin her so that her toes skim the ocean in big circles. When we get too cold, we turn cartwheels in the sand with Bekah. Jonah's setting up the beach umbrella, which Isaac has planted himself beneath, already reading his book.

"Hey!" Jonah calls from our little camp. "Sunscreen."

The troops report back and assemble, Bekah digging into the cooler Jonah brought. She examines the Popsicle packaging, looking for the colors beneath the white paper, dark berry and tangerine.

"Do you think they make mango Popsicles? Passion fruit?" I ask, smearing more SPF 100 onto my arms and legs.

"Or pomegranate?" Bekah examines her pineapple Popsicle. "I bet Jonah could make them."

I look back at Jonah, my eyes hidden by big cat-eye sunglasses. Leah's rubbing sunscreen onto her nose while Jonah gets the back of her arms. He takes out her low ponytail, gathering her hair into a little bun at the top of her head. It's sloppy but second nature, his hands twisting the hair tie. The sweetness aches somewhere in my ribs. It could wreck a girl—this handsome guy, shirtless in the summer sun, making sure his little sister's neck won't get burned.

For most of the day, his eyes stay on the littles—watching Leah splash at the edge of the water, supervising the sand-castle construction, and anticipating fights. He's always reading their moods and needs, and it's only once in a while that I catch his eyes on me. But when I do, he gives me a slow smile, like we're both in on a secret. Jonah Daniels and his gaze are enough to make a girl feel like she emerged from a huge seashell in the middle of the ocean, like the painting of Venus, surrounded by sea foam. And maybe I did; I don't remember being born, and I wouldn't put it past my painter-mother to pull it off.

Also, I'm not going to pretend like I don't look fabulous in my bathing suit. It's a polka-dotted one-piece that covers up an ill-advised tattoo, with a halter top that does my chest a serious favor. I wear a thousand bangles on my left wrist for panache.

We splash and we reapply sunscreen and we cover Isaac in sand, sculpting a mermaid tail for him. Our hours at the beach melt together like the box of sticky Popsicles, and when it's time to leave, I walk a few yards away to finish the last item on my beach to-do list. Using a small branch Isaac found for me in the banks between the shore and cliff line, I spell out careful letters in the sand—*Vivi was here*—even though I know the tide will rip my memorial away.

"Another one?" Jonah's by my side, admiring my handiwork. I guess he's seen me do this before. Earlier in the week, I convinced Jonah to plant more flowers in the backyard of his house. We helped the littles dig with spades, and I told them about biology and sunflowers and sprouts, and I made some of it up, but that's okay. On our last seeds—zinnias—I took a scrap of receipt paper from my purse and scribbled *Vivi was here* on the edge. Then I buried it in the dark soil alongside the brand-new almost plants. Once they grow, I'll still be in there somewhere. We were so dirt-covered when the plants were finally all in the ground, but we took turns under an outdoor shower that Jonah said their family hadn't used in years. An *outdoor shower*—beach living at its magical, practical best. Like making a rainstorm whenever you want one.

"Viv." Jonah nudges my arm with his elbow, bringing me back to him. "Why is that? All the you-were-heres?"

"Because it's all so fleeting, isn't it? The ocean existed so long before us and will stay long after us—most trees, too, and some animals. Isn't that crazy? My dress collection will live longer than I ever will." I can't help the sigh that slips out. Oh, how I'd love to be eternal in one life. "I'm just looking for some kind of permanence, so my mark will linger on the world once I'm gone, in the places where I found joy. Does that make any sense?"

He places his hands in the pockets of his swim trunks and rocks on his heels. He's wearing black shades, but I can tell he's still studying the ridges of each line, each letter. "Yeah. I've just never thought about it like that before."

There. Right there. Some kind of pain is pressing itself into Jonah's skin—a cigarette burn for each time he thinks of it—and I am ready to know what it is. The anticipation of being alone together grows like steam in the air. But that heat is not why I need to get him alone—at least, not at first. It's because I want to know if he's ready to tell me about the pulsing sadness that I feel in this beautiful family, an undercurrent beneath us.

By the time we walk home, the sun is descending into a sherbet sky, and I have a plan. Leah is asleep on Jonah's shoulder, little mouth hanging open a bit. Bekah and Isaac are tiny, exhausted zombies lumbering toward their own front door. I love the Daniels residence, which is tucked back from the street, surrounded by low trees that are so deep green they look almost blue. When I asked, Jonah said the house is a Craftsman bungalow, but all I know is that it's white and homey. Especially with fireflies hovering around the yard, the image that comes to mind is a magic cottage in a fairy tale.

"There you guys are." Silas leans against the open front door. "I was starting to think the ocean swallowed you up."

Isaac ducks in, and Bekah's behind him, setting our huge beach bag in the foyer. When Jonah sets Leah down, she stands on her own but keeps her eyes closed. Silas chuckles, scooping her up, and he turns to go inside.

"Let's not go in." I catch Jonah's hand in mine. He startles a little, like I've broken a barrier between us. "Silas and Naomi can take it from here. Let's go get ice cream for dinner, just us."

"Okay." He smiles, but it's a halfway smile because he's tired. I know he's tired, that he is *weary*, and I want to know even more. "Silas! Vivi and I are going out to eat."

He knows Silas won't mind because we've had the littles with us all day long, and he's overdue for a break. After a week of life with the Daniels family, I'm starting to learn the expected give-and-take between three teenagers who seem in charge of their whole family. As we start down the street, Jonah keeps a hold of my hand, and I'm lost in thought of their little world.

I'm in love with Leah, of course, and her limitless imagination and infectious giggle and the unselfconscious way she plays with my hair. I love Isaac and his obsessions and tiny glasses and spiky hair, created with some sort of gel clearly stolen from an older sibling. I'm in love with Bekah and her preteen moodiness and eye rolls, the way she's still a carefree child until she catches herself and slips back into sulkiness. I'm in love with Silas—his immature jokes meshed with responsibility for the littles. Even Naomi, obstinately making me earn her friendship, and I'm failing so far, which only makes me try harder.

And Jonah. Oh, Jonah. That boy did me in that first night at his house—seeing him in his natural element, cooking and surrounded by his rambunctious family. Such a precarious balance and yet he let me right in. What a heart! And since he can be so serious, I nudge him with each slow afternoon, with hip bumps as we walk along, with looking over at him right this very moment and biting my lip as if it is a random tic. Which it is not.

Jonah is so stuck in his weariness that of course he doesn't realize anyone else sees him. When we walk down the street together, girls always glance over quickly at him. Once we pass, they turn around to get another look. Of course they do. Jonah is a truly beautiful boy—that gorgeous hair and olive skin and strong arms from carrying groceries and his little sister. He has those deep, dark eyes that show he carries a lot of heavy things inside himself, too.

In town, we order two ice-cream cones—mint chocolate chip for him and rocky road for me. We came here earlier this week to eat banana splits, and Isaac ate so much that he almost puked, which was sad and also hilarious.

"Thanks, Patty," Jonah says to the woman who hands us the cones. Then Jonah holds the woman's eye contact, gesturing toward the staircase. "Do you mind?"

"Nah." She winks at him. "Just be careful."

I trail behind Jonah as he moves up the stairs at the back of the shop. The upstairs floor looks more like an old house than an ice-cream parlor. There are a few framed paint-by-numbers, a door with a glass handle—a bathroom, maybe—and another door, which Jonah opens. It goes out onto a flat tar roof, which seems sturdy enough.

This view is spectacular, a front-row seat as the neon sun dips her round belly into the ocean below.

"Wow," I breathe, settling next to Jonah on the edge of the roof. We both dangle our legs off the edge, and I'm disappointed to find a fire escape right below us. If we fell, we would be fine, which is a shame—ice cream, cute boy, and sunset on a roof? The only thing missing is a little buzz of danger.

This is probably the longest I've ever been quiet in my life. We walked the whole way here in the quiet, and now I look at this boy, whose eyes seem burned out behind the smoke screen of warm brown irises. "Oh, Jonah. You look so tired."

His smile is wry. "I *am* so tired. I've been tired for months."

"Well, we fit together like mint ice cream and chocolate chips, Jonah, because it takes me a while to get tired. All night long, I dare the stars to outlast me, and I'd say the score's about even during the average week. So you get some extra sleep, and I'll stay up for both of us; how about that?"

He glances sidelong at me, not fully committing to a *look*. "Can I ask you something?"

"You can ask me anything, Jonah."

I knew he'd open up, if we were alone and I was quiet enough. So I kick my legs against the gutter, happy to wait. The wind off the ocean tousles his beautiful hair, like the cold front knows all my dirty thoughts and will exploit them. I am so crazy about Jonah's thick almost-curls that even the atmosphere knows it.

He stares down at his ice-cream cone instead of licking it, even though the mint is softening by the second, threatening to drip. "Why haven't you asked about my parents?"

I've noticed the lack of parent in the Daniels household—of course I have. They've said enough that I know their mom is upstairs and maybe ill. The littles use the phrase *my dad used to*, but I don't know if he's dead or if he left or if something else prevents him from being around. Maybe he's institutionalized or deployed. Jonah doesn't watch me while I think; he eats his ice cream and stares out at the waves.

"Well, let's just say I have my own personal fun facts that I keep close to the vest." I take a lick of my rocky road, rotating the cone in my hand to smooth the ice cream into a rounder shape. "If there were things you wanted to tell me, I figured you'd tell me in your own time."

"Oh." He looks genuinely relieved. "Okay, good. I thought you didn't ask because you already knew—like someone in town told you."

Come to think of it, Whitney did mention something the day I met Jonah. She made him seem haunted, followed around by ghosts who tug at him in the silent spaces.

"My dad died. Six months ago. That's what they would have told you. Heart attack."

I take this information like a knee to my gut, an *oof* sound almost escaping my lips. It knocks the wind out of me, despite the breeze pushing extra air against my face. I imagine the sweet faces of this beautiful boy and his siblings, and I nearly have to gasp for breath. "Oh, Jonah."

"I don't like to talk about it. I mean, I'm not good about talking about it." The ice-cream cone droops from his hand, nearly dropping to the fire escape below. "And my mom is—I don't know. She pretty much stays in bed. We keep thinking it'll get better, but I'm not sure how much longer we can keep it up. Silas is supposed to go to college in the fall, and . . . I don't know. I can't take care of the littles by myself."

He swallows, his Adam's apple making a barely perceptible shift at his throat. Then he lifts his hand as if to shade his eyes and instead rubs a tense space of forehead, massaging right above his eyebrow. "She does have good days. She usually goes to church on Sundays. Sometimes she gets up and showers, and sometimes she even goes to the grocery store. We've tried to get her to a therapist, but it just makes her cry when we bring it up. Naomi keeps saying it's clinical depression, and she needs to be on medicine, but my mom won't hear about it. God, this all sounds so crazy. I hear myself saying it, and it sounds crazy."

"Jonah, I swear on my favorite vintage dress that what you're saying is not crazy by my standards. Sad? Difficult?

Yes. But there is nothing crazy about that kind of grief, especially when it's totally justified and normal."

"You call it *normal* to be despondent for six months?" With a snort, he finishes his waffle cone and dusts off his hands.

"Maybe." I shrug. "I can't really say. I've never been madly in love with someone for two decades and had six babies with him and made a life with him and then had him ripped away from me in one instant. So I'm not sure what's 'normal' for that."

He winces, taking that in. "Well, now I feel like an asshole again."

"Again?"

His hand goes back to the spot on his forehead. "About a month after my dad died, Felix reminded me there's a difference between grief and depression. His son has dealt with depression, so he would know. And it's like you said—my mom's grieving. I know that. I just think it maybe slipped into depression. How can you even tell? Six months seems like too long to stay in your room."

I almost say that I think it's a good sign that he said she still cries, but I close my mouth because that seems like a cruel sentiment. But what I mean is, depression, it settles like a shadow over your body while you sleep, and it mutes every frequency into blankness, into fog. Everyone thinks you can't laugh when you're depressed, but I couldn't cry either, because I couldn't *feel*.

Instead, I put it back on Jonah. "Are you mad at her?"

"Yeah." He looks up, guilty and bewildered at the sound of his own voice, like the word slipped out of his mouth without his mind's permission. "I've never admitted that before. I've never even thought it before. Maybe I'm not mad. I know it's not her fault. I just hate this. I hate it for her, and I hate it for me, and I hate it for Leah and for Isaac, and . . ."

"You're doing everything you can, you know. Taking care of everyone, shouldering all the responsibility to give her time to grieve?" I pat his leg. "You're doing everything."

Jonah bobs his head, as if he hears me but doesn't quite believe it. I'm overwhelmed with sadness for him, but I still feel a sense of wonder up here beside him. We're on the rooftop of the world, and I think of kids like us somewhere in Madrid or in Sydney or Hong Kong, and I wonder if they spend their summers getting as close to the stars as they possibly can.

"Well," he says, sighing. "Am I a beach day buzzkill or what?"

"Oh, you stop that." Then a sigh catches in my throat, too, because I don't like what I have to say next. If I hate thinking about it, then I *loathe* talking about it. But I'll do it for him. "I know I act like I don't have a care in the world . . . but, Jonah, I've prowled the dirtiest back alleys of sadness, okay? And I know what it's like to fight for your life on those mean streets. So if you need someone to vent to or someone to be quiet with or someone to talk your ear off, I can be that person. I'm not scared of the dark places."

"Thanks, Viv." He does look relieved, leaning back against his arms, so his chest rises toward the sky. "I thought you might bail if you knew. It's . . . a lot, my family right now."

"*I'm* a lot, too, Jonah." Then I lean back, matching his posture exactly so that we're stomachs up to the setting sun. "And you don't have to worry about things like that with me. If I met a boy who was perfectly whole, in mint condition with no dings . . . well, I swear to God, I think I'd fall asleep on the spot. And you *know* that's not easy for me."

His eyes watch me from their corners until a sly smile creeps onto his face.

"What?"

"Nothing." He can't shoo the smile away. "I'm just . . . really glad you're here now."

"I'm glad you're here now, too, Jonah."

So we stay there above the town, being here and being now, until the last possible moment. Until the last scrap of sunbeam lights our path back across the roof and through the door and into whatever happens next.

∝

Later that night, I'm wishing Jonah had kissed me on the roof, even though we were talking about sad things—things that could wrestle your soul and pin it to the ground. It's late, technically, but not by my standards—maybe 1:00 a.m. or so—and I'm working on sewing projects in my room because, well, what else am I supposed to do at this hour? I'm ripping a hem on an old dress, prepping it to become much shorter and cuter, and this can be fairly boring work. So I entertain myself by imagining *many* different scenarios in which Jonah is a sexually aggressive person, and it's just getting good when my phone beeps. Oh, I hope it's Jonah, and it is. He's asking if I'm awake, which of course I am. Beep again. *Look outside?* I'm glittery with anticipation as I push my window up, and sure enough, Jonah Daniels is standing below, on the driveway.

"Hey." Night wind shifts his hair, and he shoves his hands in his pockets—as if he walked all the way over here and chose *this* moment to get sheepish.

"Hey." I try to sound casual, which is difficult when you're yelling down to someone. "What's up?"

"I can't sleep. Even though I'm exhausted. So, uh, do you want to go on a walk? Down to the beach?"

"With you?" I ask, teasing him. He shoots me the look that says: *Give me a freaking break, Viv, I'm trying here.* So I grin. "Always. Be right down."

I'm wearing a navy-blue nightdress with thin straps and little edges of off-white lace. It covers as much of me as any daytime summer dress, so I figure it's just as well. I pull on an oversize cream cardigan, and I close my eyes, trying to decipher how it feels. It feels like I rolled out of bed and pulled on a sweater to walk to the mailbox. Close, but not exactly right. Faux pearls. I layer strands and strands of chunky, costume pearls around my neck, and yes, precisely—I am a girl who rolled out of bed to have an impromptu beach date with a boy.

I prance down the steps and see my mother's form in the glow of the TV. She's watching a French film with subtitles, one hand cradling a glass of white wine. Her head turns, and she finds my gaze over the back of the couch. A knowing smile twitches at her mouth. "Where do you think you're going?"

"I'm sneaking out," I say, ruffling my curls. "Can't you tell?"

"Oh, yes. Very subtle." She examines me. "Same boy? Jonah?"

"Yes, same boy," I huff, wounded.

"I want to meet him, Viv. I mean it."

I turn fully, horrified. "What, like now?"

"Is he *here* now?"

"*No.*" It's a flimsy lie—too reactionary. I'm usually better than that. "Maybe. Yes. We're just going for a walk. He couldn't sleep."

"Then, yes, I'd like to meet him now." When I don't move, she pulls herself up, lengthening through her spine. "I'm sorry if you don't like it, but Dr. Douglas said—"

"Fine," I snap, unwilling to hear another *word* about it. I turn toward the front door, but I think better of it, swiveling back to my mom. "Can you . . . not ask about his parents?"

Her head leans slightly to the side, long hair pooling in her lap. I see her gathering the fragments: I spend all this time with his siblings, no mention of parents. He's here late at night, unable to sleep.

"It's really hard," I say quietly. "And recent. Okay?"

She nods, the determined-parent expression falling a little. Jonah isn't the opponent now—a possible threat to her daughter. He's another child, as I am to her.

Jonah stands in the driveway with his hands still in the pockets of his khakis, which are rolled up to his ankle. I like this—that even when he dressed himself and left his house, he knew for sure he'd be taking me to the beach. I grin as I walk gently across the asphalt, leery of rogue pebbles. There's just no ever-loving way that I'm wearing shoes on a night like this; it's bottom-line insulting to the gorgeousness of a summer night.

"Hey," Jonah says, before I can reach him.

"Hey. Perfect timing; I was just thinking about you." I clutch his hand, pressing my lips together. "But, just one thing. My mom wants to meet you."

"Oh. Um. Now?"

"Yeah—I know, she's being so weird. Do you mind coming in really quick? I swear she's not going to interrogate you. She just wants to see that you're a normal, functioning person, and then we can do whatever we want."

"Sure." I can see it in his eyes, though, that this is not the evening he had in mind. Ugh, Mom! This would have been so romantic without interference.

Inside, the French actors are discussing something passionately on the TV. My mom rises from the couch, wine still in one hand. I forget, because I'm with her all the time, that my mother is sort of a presence. She has waist-length, '70s-queen hair and this sweeping way of walking, in flowy blouses.

I can almost hear Jonah swallow. "Mom, this is Jonah."

"Hello, Jonah," my mom says, taking him in. And I can guess what she's thinking: *Huh. A guy in khakis. No half-shorn hair or visible piercings or tattoos*—not that she minds those things. Jonah's just the first . . . unadorned guy who's made it to "meet my mom" status. I can't tell if she's disappointed or impressed.

"See?" I present Jonah like he's a prize on *The Price Is Right*. "Normal. And cute! Good job, me. Let's go."

I grab his hand and try to tug, but his feet stay planted.

"Nice to meet you." He reaches his other hand out to my mom. "Sorry—Vivi just told me outside that I had to be normal. I haven't had adequate time to prepare for this role."

My mom smiles genuinely at this, amused as she shakes his hand. "Nice to meet you, too. I'm Carrie. Vivi tells me that she's been spending time with your *five* brothers and sisters."

"Oh. Yeah." He glances at me, almost sympathetically, as if I do not *adore* every moment with them. "There are a lot of us."

"And where do you fall in the lineup?"

*Is this really more important than me walking on the beach with this very cute boy?!* I ask my mom in an attempt at telepathy. *What are you doing to me?!*

But Jonah's already answering the question, perfectly comfortable standing here while I am clenching his hand like, *Let's go.* "In the middle. We separate it into three oldest and three youngest, bigs and littles. I'm the youngest big."

"Sounds like fun. I'm glad Vivi found you all. Okay." She smiles at Jonah, then at me, dismissing us. "Thank you for indulging me. Not too late, Viv. Just a walk."

"*Hmph*," I say, my back already to my mom, while Jonah calls, "Nice to meet you!"

There's a path of worn wooden steps down to the ocean, and we take it. Jonah tells me about working at the restaurant, about the bustle and the customers and the funny line cooks who work with him. When we reach the part of the beach that is littered with driftwood debris, he bends his knees, offering himself for a piggyback, and I climb on. He hitches me up and steers us until we hit the shoreline, and I clamber down from his back and press my feet into the sand.

A single yellow flag beats against the ocean wind, and the sky stretches for every mile of ocean, and then longer and farther. We're the only people as far as the eye can see, and all the world feels like a private show, screened on the endless black sky. The universe is unfurling its whole self to us, arms wide and beckoning.

My feet veer toward the water. "I just have to touch it, you know? It's the former dolphin in me."

"Careful." His voice is soft, a warning in the warm air. He's such a dad, I swear to God; it's like he can't stop himself. "The riptide can be really strong."

I know this, of course. That's what the yellow flag is for—to notify vacationers that the water at night can be grasping and ironfisted.

"I've always loved that the tides are caused by the moon," I explain. I give him my most enticing grin, trying to melt him into a more relaxed version of himself. "So far away, but so beautiful. So powerful. I can always feel it tugging at me, too."

"Umm . . ." He laughs, but he's not mocking me. No, I'm not sure if Jonah could ever really mock someone, not the way that other people do.

"Maybe you don't feel it yet because you weigh more than me. But I feel it, as real as a lasso around my waist." I hold my arms up, as though a rope has a hold on my midsection, and I follow it toward the water, toward the moon. It's cold, the water, but I'm up to my calves before Jonah speaks up.

"Don't go too far . . ." he warns. "It's not like Verona Cove has lifeguards."

I throw my sweater onto the sand so it will be dry for the walk home. "Oh, Jonah. Lifeguards are such a myth."

"What? Lifeguards are not a *myth*. We just don't have them here."

My knees are wet now, and I spin to look at him, talking louder so he can hear. "Do you really think that a lifeguard—one single person—could stop the universe from taking you if it really wanted you?"

"I mean, I think that's why they have mouth-to-mouth resuscitation." He emphasizes the last word like he's making his point with a five-syllable fancy word that he clearly misunderstands.

"Well, sometimes the universe gives you back, when it doesn't want to take you yet—it just wants to remind you that it *could*, if it wanted to." The water hits the hem of my nightgown, and now my whole lower half feels supported. Ah yes, my soul knows this feel of submersion, of fluidity and bottomless freedom.

"Vivi, you're getting soaked. And you can get in serious trouble for being in the water after the beach closes."

He has waded in ankle-deep, but I'm up to my waist, and we have to raise our voices to hear each other. It's freezing cold, but I can't even really feel it because I'm loving this way too much.

"Jonah, for God's sake, you used to be an otter. Give in to that instinct." I fling my arms out, and they reflect pale moonlight, with dark freckles like pinholes on my skin. "Give in, Jonah Daniels!"

He makes it up to his knees, and I am so confused by his reluctance. I'm telling you, these beach townies, they simply do not appreciate the majesty that sidles up to their backyards. I can practically see Jonah's brain clicking away: Must. Calculate. Risk. But I want him to shed the grown-up parts that he needs to care for the littles, and, just for tonight, do what makes him *feel* something.

But I like the way his dark hair whips in the summer wind, so I'll forgive him for his pragmatism. I move toward him so I'm only thigh-high in the water, and I press my wet palm against his dry forehead. A drop of salt water slips down his nose, and I say, "Jonah Daniels, I baptize you in the name of the God of Midnight Swimming, may he—"

"The God of Midnight Swimming?"

"Well," I say, "you may know him as the Moon, but he has many formal titles that I don't want to get into right now. What was I saying? Oh, right. May he protect and guide you so you'll stop being such a goddamn buzzkill and start acting like the supernova that you are."

Jonah looks at me like I'm absolutely off my rocker. Or maybe it's a look of amazement, like I'm a whole galaxy, glittering and vast and unchartered. But then he smiles in this way that makes me feel known. And now I can't think of anything but snacking on black cherries at the beach earlier today. The way he licked the juice off his lower lip.

I close my eyes a split second before he kisses me, and I clutch the hem of his T-shirt to stay planted against the swaying waves. His hands are on my neck, pulling me in, and the ocean floor drops out from beneath us and the Moon himself whispers, *Damn.*

It is nothing like that first, quick kiss where I was moving on impulse. This is an exchange, intentional and charged: yes, we are doing this, yes, yes. The difference between a happy summer day and a hot summer night. We're knee-deep in the ocean, and I'm starting to think I'm in over my head.

So I throw my arms around him and hang on, kissing him wholeheartedly but without the *Where is this going?* and *Does he like me?* and *What does this mean?!* And I know there are people who would judge me for this. Even Ruby once asked, *Gosh, Viv, do you keep track of how many guys you kiss?* Nope! Because listen here, sisters: it's summer and this boy is handsome and kind, and, frankly, I want to kiss anything that makes me feel so seen. How do you like them cherries?

When we finally move apart, we're breathing faster than when we started. Jonah's eyes are more open than before—but not in height or width. In depth. Like he's more awake. Mouth-to-mouth resuscitation indeed.

I expect to feel triumphant, but all I can do is stare back, clinging on to him still. My vision tilts, perspective shifting like everything I see is now one degree different—finally clicked into place. Like an opera singer onstage who believes she is the performer, only to find the orchestra—its earnestness, its unexpected soul—nearly moving her to tears. You mean to give, and find yourself taking and taking, soaking it in.

"All right, *fine*." Jonah grins as he takes my hand, and we run into deeper waters, gasping at the cold and the beauty.

## CHAPTER EIGHT
# *Jonah*

I don't like running, but I do it any time Silas can be home in the morning. My feet plod along the sand. Really, it's a fast-paced slog. I have an old iPod with shitty battery life, but it works. When running along the beach, I listen to metal. I used to hate the sound of all that screaming, but now it helps. It usually drowns out my thoughts, but not today.

Vivi has been by my side for almost two weeks now, but I needed to angst alone this morning. My worries woke me up early, pestering me like Leah on Christmas morning. I crept through rare silence in our dark house, left a note, then drove the car a few miles down the coast. I didn't want to run in Verona Cove, down Main Street or along the beach path like I normally do. I needed to run in a place where memories don't fill my peripheral vision, the ghosts of who we used to be watching me like marathon spectators.

I'm following a trail of questions down this long stretch of sand: What the hell are we going to do? Will Silas really defer college? Do I finally tell Felix that I think my mom needs real help? And my dad's heart problem—I know it was genetic. Can I even get checked for that?

After my dad died, I looked up the most heart-healthy foods. Now I make oatmeal almost every morning for my brothers and sisters. They seem to understand that I have to do *something*. So I invent flavors to keep it interesting—peanut butter–banana oatmeal, maple syrup–walnut oatmeal, strawberry–powdered sugar oatmeal. When they demand pancakes as a change of pace, I use a recipe that includes oatmeal and chocolate chips. I'm not sure if shoving the maximum amount of oats down all my siblings' throats is the best heart-health plan, but it's better than nothing.

My dad was naturally big. Not round, but tall and wide. Vivi would say he was descended from redwoods. All of us kids have my mom's build—medium height and lean. Naomi and I have my dad's Sicilian dark hair and eyes. The rest of my siblings have the lighter coloring from my mom's side. Ever since he died, I've been looking for my dad in Silas and Isaac, watching their faces for his nose, his expressions, his eye crinkles. Felix says I'm more like my dad every day, but I don't see it.

Vivi relieves me of these thoughts. She lives in overdrive, and I have to work to keep up. It takes so much energy that I can't concentrate on my own crappy life. She fills everything with new memories so that my life feels like more than "exactly like it was only minus my dad." She makes me drive an hour to the nearest Target so we can ride the bikes up the aisles, and Leah can play with the bouncy balls until the manager asks us to leave. She writes a play with Isaac about an old-timey baker named Paunchy Paul and the many critters that sneak into his bakery late at night to eat his bread. In the one-night-only performance, Isaac played Paul, complete with our dad's chef hat, a pillow stuffed down his shirt as a fat belly, and a mustache drawn with Vivi's eye makeup. Vivi was costume director, lighting director, and Head Mouse. Bekah played a mouse in one scene and a raccoon in another; Leah played the squirrel that persuades Paul to bake them miniature breads stuffed with acorns. I baked bread to use as a prop, and Silas and Naomi whistled as they bowed. My mom didn't come down. But the next morning, the littles reenacted their parts in her room. She laughed at their silly happiness until she cried. I hustled them out the door and left her in peace.

The memory makes my legs push harder against the sand until they burn. Vivi never gets weird when I'm sad or frustrated or pissed about the state of my family right now. I don't know much about dating, but I know enough to be grateful that Vivi doesn't push.

I dated a girl named Sarah last year, my longest relationship ever, and she pushed like a wrecking ball. I still like her as a person, but not as a girlfriend. She's tiny and feisty, like a little Yorkie dog. I liked that she was in charge of about half the clubs at school. When we were little, she was the girl who got every colorful Girl Scout badge and outsold everyone in the tristate area during cookie season. She thinks success is a quick one-two punch of deciding what to do and doing it.

In the first days after my dad died, Sarah was nice to have around. She's prepared. Just, as a lifestyle choice: prepared. For any situation. She does things like pack a whole purse full of tissues when she attends your dad's funeral. She even had a bottle of baby aspirin, like she knew my sister would cry until her head throbbed.

But then I became her project. She was extra peppy—all positive thinking and up-and-at-'ems. When I couldn't decide to be happy and then do it, when my grief wasn't an easily conquerable goal . . . well, the yipping grated against my eardrums.

*Jonah*, she told me. *It seems like you're not even* trying *to be happy.*

*Happy?* I thought. I'm nowhere freaking *close* to happy. Happy is a distant continent. I was thrashing in the storm. Sarah didn't understand anything about my life. I hated being hustled out of pain I earned.

It's why I broke up with her.

It's why I won't hustle my mom out of pain she earned.

Sarah didn't cry when I ended it. She got huffy and mad. I guess I was probably the one project that talked back to her. Also the only one she couldn't finish, with honors.

My life still sucked. But at least it felt like mine again.

The sweat cools on my body as I head back toward the car. I've been impaled by my own thoughts this morning, and it's time to get back to distracting myself. When I can't actually cook to get my mind off everything, I make up recipes in my mind. Like arugula salad with grapefruit and avocado slices. And feta. With a champagne vinaigrette. Maybe some kind of nut—macadamia? I'm not sure yet. I can't always try them in reality because some of the ingredients I'd want to use are expensive. And not practical for a family of seven. But I do think I have some tip money at the restaurant from a wait shift I covered for Felix last week.

Money is complicated right now. My parents inherited our house from my grandparents, so at least that's paid off. Since Naomi, Silas, and I all work, we pool enough money to buy groceries and gas every week. Naomi takes care of finance stuff, so she talks to my mom about paying bills. There's money from life insurance. But it won't last forever. During the third month of our mom's departure from reality, Naomi downgraded our already-meager cell phone plan, got rid of the landline my dad insisted on keeping, and canceled our cable. Ironically, my mom has a degree in accounting. She did the restaurant's books and worked a little during tax season. Not this year, though.

When I pull into the restaurant parking lot, Felix's car is already there. It's weird that he'd get in at 8:00 a.m. and that he'd drive. He always walks from home. I use my dad's key—now mine—to the back door, and I'm surprised to see, not Felix, but his daughter Ellie. She's peeking around the prep counter. "Oh, hey, Jonah. I thought someone was breaking in."

"Ellie, hey. What are you doing here?"

"Freezer inventory. Just finished." She gestures to a piece of paper on the counter.

"I thought your dad was doing that later today."

"Yeah. But I lost a bet. Family game night thing. He and Lina smoked me and my mom. We bet freezer inventory, so I had to pay up."

As she steps around the counter, I can't help but notice she looks more like her mom than ever. She's almost as tall as me, all arms and legs and thin torso. And she's holding a frying pan in one hand.

"Making an omelet, too?"

She wrinkles her nose. "Grabbed it out of reflex. In case you were a burglar."

"A burglar with a key?"

"You never know." She spins the pan around once, like we're going to duel. It makes me laugh. "So what are you doing here?"

"Getting tip money out of the safe," I say. "I covered a wait shift for your dad last week."

"Ah." She smiles, up on her tiptoes to put the pan back. I've wondered before if Ellie does yoga or something. Everything about her is relaxed. Her movement, tone of voice. "Well, I'm glad to see you. How's your summer going?"

"It's . . . okay, thanks. How about you?"

She shrugs. "Pretty good. I got back from my grandma's a few days ago, and the rest of the summer is wide open. Working here a little. I heard you have a new girlfriend—good for you."

"Oh. Yeah." *Is* Vivi my girlfriend? It's only been two weeks, but it feels like a whole summer already. But I don't know what to call her, and she'd tease me if I tried to bring it up. Sometimes she treats me like a boyfriend, other times like a friend with benefits, sometimes like a science experiment. She pokes and prods at me, asks me strange questions.

"Are you guys coming to the bonfire next week? I'd love to meet her." Ellie slips into the office, setting down the inventory list.

The bonfire is an annual tradition for Verona Cove locals and the two tiny towns nearest us, right after the Fourth of July. "I think so. Silas drew the short straw, so he has to stay home with the littles. But I'll be there and probably Naomi, too."

Ellie looks back at me, frowning. "Is your mom out of town?"

Stupid, stupid, stupid. I let it slip that my mom can't watch three kids. "No. Yes. Well, kind of. Just for that night, she's driving down the coast to meet up with an old friend. Or something. I think."

"Oh. Okay." She slides out of the office and past me, smiling hesitantly. "Well, see you guys there, then."

I can't believe I lied to Ellie. When I was eleven, I split my knee open trying to keep up with Silas and Diego, Ellie's brother. Ellie, even though she was only ten at the time, dabbed ointment on the cut with a cotton swab and smoothed a Band-Aid over it. She's good to her core.

I step into the office, stooping down to the safe. I sift through to a little plastic bag with my name on it. As I'm squeezing out of the office, I shake my head, smiling. As usual, there are papers strewn all over the desk and even taped up on the wall. Felix, like my dad, takes the "it's not messy if I know where everything is" approach.

But my eye catches on something. A red stamp on an envelope, blaring *PAST DUE*. It's half-hidden behind another envelope, but I lift it up. There are a few more below it, all stamped in bright reds. Addressed to my dad. So much for the oatmeal and the running. I'm about to have a heart attack.

The sound of knocking at the door nearly does me in. I grip my chest in surprise, and it takes me a moment to recover. I slide the envelopes back under the papers.

I figure it's Ellie, back because she forgot something. Instead, I open the back door to Vivi. "Um . . . hey."

"I'm on my way to work, and I saw your car parked here." But she doesn't look happy to see me. She looks wounded. "Who was the girl I saw leave?"

"Oh. Just Ellie. Felix's daughter."

I swear I see her lip tremble. "You were here, alone, with her?"

Aw, crap. I am in a situation. "I wasn't *with* her. I stopped in to get my tip money, and she was doing freezer inventory."

She watches me still, judging every movement. "She's pretty."

I've never seen Vivi be anything but . . . joyful, and I can't tell if she's teasing me. She could actually be jealous or mad. I'm pretty sure I didn't do anything wrong, but there's no handbook. "I've known her my whole life, Viv."

She considers this. "Almost like she's a sister to you?"

No, not exactly. "Yeah."

"That was *not* convincing, Jonah." She crosses her arms, waiting for me to plead my case.

Okay. Switching tactical approach away from defense. I'll play flattery on the offense. It's easy because I mean it. "Viv?"

"What."

"You are the only girl I ever think about." It's true.

This makes her smile, almost shyly, which is not a typical Vivi adjective. The smile spreads—bright red and scheming.

Without giving me even a moment to prepare, she leaps onto me, locking her arms around my neck. She kisses me like someone with failing lungs, like her only source of oxygen is me.

If someone had asked me before I met Vivi, *Hey, Jonah, would you like a girlfriend who is all over you?*, the answer would have been yes. But, of all the quirks about life with Vivi, her ready-or-not approach to kissing me is the most disorienting. She goes from zero to pouncing in less than three seconds. I never see it coming. She'll be barely paying attention one second and then, in the next second, grab my face like she's been marooned on an island, and I'm the first guy she's seen in years.

I'm not complaining. But I can't do this here, not in my dad's kitchen. Not with those envelopes tormenting me. My mind can't shut off enough to kiss her back. I expect my dad to walk in any moment and ground me until the apocalypse. He won't, of course, and that thought makes everything worse. Really, the place where your dead dad feels most alive is probably the least sexy location ever.

"Viv," I say, setting her down on the prep table. She keeps her legs hooked around my waist. "I can't, okay? Not here. Where my dad . . . I just. Sorry." I wince preemptively. There's a good chance she'll storm off.

Instead, she releases her legs and wipes her lipstick smudges from my mouth. "Of course. Rain check. I just couldn't resist, you handsome devil."

We stay there together for a moment, eye-to-eye. She slides her fingers into my hair as if she can actually get ahold of my brain. Then she gives me that look, her blue eyes trying to cut right through me. She searches. "All right. What's going on in there?"

I shake my head, and she moves her hands down to my neck. The way they're wrapped, her thumbs could get an easy read on my pulse. "The restaurant . . . I don't think it's doing as well as I thought it was. I think there might be some money problems."

"Oh." Her lips twitch downward for a split second. Then she hops off the table. "Then you should fix it."

"Fix it?"

"Yeah. Make changes to improve business."

I hold my arms out at my sides because I can't quite speak the word: *What?!* I'm annoyed that she'd treat this like nothing. My dad's legacy, his life's work—failing. And I'm helpless. "I'm not an econ major, Viv. I don't know a damn thing about, like, finances."

"Jonah." Vivi squares her hands on my shoulders. "You know this restaurant better than you know most *people*. You know what it needs the way you know what Leah needs. Yeah?"

I can take care of Leah, sure, but I can't take care of everything. I can't take care of my mom. I have no idea what she needs. Nothing Vivi ever says is as simple as she makes it out to be.

"Okay, listen, I know what you're thinking." She pulls out a lipstick from her purse and reapplies it. "You don't want to make changes to something that was your dad's. Because then you'd be admitting that there are imperfections to his work here and, by extension, that he had imperfections, too. And I get that; I honestly do. But you're not *dismantling* his work if you're adding to it. You're helping a dream grow more, not cutting it down."

I hadn't even thought of any of that. Now I will. I can't keep up.

"Okay," she says, standing on her tiptoes to kiss my cheek. "I've gotta get to work, but you percolate some ideas like the little coffeepot of genius that you are. If I were you, I'd start with redoing the patio space, and I'd do it soon so you can throw me a birthday party there. Because that's what I want—officially. Okay? That is my formal birthday wish, and you should be glad because I *was* going to ask for a Vespa. Now I've decided all I want is a party on the Tony's patio, so make it happen. See you tonight, at which point I will be redeeming my make-out session rain check. Fair warning." She turns to wink at me, then disappears out the door.

Vivi has this way of leaving me shell-shocked. She never notices. Or maybe she does it on purpose—I have no idea.

In the quiet of my dad's old kitchen, I find that Vivi's

right. Somewhere in the folds of my brain, I've been storing ideas for the restaurant for years. Since way before my dad died. I'm not saying the ideas will work. But I do have them—menu changes and updates to the design of the space and different ways to draw tourists in.

I wander out to the patio space, which I've never really thought about. There's not much to it. The restaurant has this built-in nook made by the exterior—two perpendicular brick walls. Years ago, my dad poured cement for a floor and installed a low wrought-iron fence in the two open sides, making an L shape. But that's kind of it. There's an old grill out here, a rusty ladder, an extra propane tank, and a bunch of other crap.

From the street, you can see the patio if you're walking from uptown. That must have been how Vivi saw it. I don't know if outdoor dining would draw more customers. I don't know if it would be worth the work. But it'd be nice to put my backbone into something. Especially if I can make this old, broken space into something nice for Vivi's birthday.

So I sit on a stool by the prep table, with a piece of scrap paper from the office. I'm not sure how long I sit there, scribbling down ideas. Entrées that have never sold particularly well that could probably be replaced. Foods people ask for that we don't have—but we could.

I'm still writing when Felix comes in the back door. "Hey, Maní. I saw your car. I thought you were off today."

"I was just stopping in." Now or never, Daniels. No wussing out. I just hope Felix takes me seriously, man to man. "But I got to thinking about the patio. We could fix it up for almost no money. It might be a nice draw for customers."

"*Hmm*," Felix says. "We always did mean to but never got around to it."

"That'd be good for business, right? Outdoor space?"

He nods. "Could be."

"Business is okay, right? I mean, decent." The words flash in my head: *PAST DUE. PAST DUE*.

"Oh, sure." Felix waves me off, but I watch his eyes. I know his eyes like I know my dad's. Protecting me from something. "Ebb and flow, the restaurant biz. We're always fine."

I don't buy it for a second. "Well, I've got some other ideas while I'm at it."

"Let's hear them," he says, and slides onto the stool beside me. Then he rubs his brow, shaking his head even though he's smiling. "Hoo-boy, Maní. Sometimes it's like looking right at your dad."

I take this as a good sign.

## CHAPTER NINE
## *Vivi*

Tonight, sleep shows me images of my friends from home, Ruby and Amala. I'm in Amala's house, it's packed, music's thumping, and I'm late, I guess, but I find them in the kitchen. Ruby's wearing a plastic birthday crown with a plump pink jewel in the center. I hand over her present, which makes her shriek in delight, and we all take shots that taste like lime, syrupy sweet. Then I flash to the back porch holding smoke in my lungs, giggling upstairs as I slide his shirt over his head, feeling like a perfect vixen, but I scream back at my subconscious—*No, no, make this stop.*

I'm outside, and everyone knows what I did, though I can't remember how it happened. Amala sobs as a crowd gathers to watch the drama, and I'm across the lawn from them. The silly tiara looks so wrong on Ruby's head as she wraps an arm around Amala, trying to calm her. Amala's long hair swinging, her face contorts as she screams, "How could you *do* this to me, Vivi? Get out of my fucking life!" And I'm gone. I'm gone.

I gasp awake in my bed at Richard's house, palms and forehead damp.

A nightmare, a memory. A thing can be both.

I stare up at the ceiling. White, white, white. The emptiness of it aches.

∞

By the time the sun is winking midmorning, I'm on a ladder in the center of the room.

"What the *hell* is this?" My mom stands in the doorway with her arms crossed in a parental way that does *not* suit her.

"I found a fantastic inspiration image in a magazine. An accent wall, but the ceiling. Don't worry. I called Richard."

"You what? He left that number for emergencies."

I know, I know. But this was a Code Blue, bring-the-paddles emergency. I told him I couldn't sleep in this goddamn room. Too much blank space, like the walls are white noise, and it's screaming at my eyes. I could hear snippets of Mandarin in the background—serious voices, probably talking about stocks or bonds or, as I like to call them, soul-sucking tokens of a life lived for the wrong reasons. But Rich hurriedly said those five magic words, even if his tone was, frankly, a little rude: "Do whatever you want, Vivi."

So I did. When Thomas Hardware opened, I was right there, waiting on the bus bench with a to-go cup of coffee from Betty's. I chose rollers, painter's tape, a big container of Starry Night blue and a smaller one of Sterling. Then I found a ladder in Richard's garage and started in the center of the ceiling, rolling out long strokes, and now it looks like a navy-blue hole in an infinitely white universe—totally worth the crick in my neck, the numbness in my arm, and the feeling that my spine is made of creaky metal instead of flexible muscle and bone.

"Vivian," she says, prodding. "Are you kidding me?"

"I had an itch. Remember last winter, when you decided the bathroom *needed* sophisticated wallpaper *immediately*? Like that. Besides, Richard was glad for the free design advice and labor." I mean, he probably was. He *should* be!

My mom is narrowing her eyes at me. "Are you not sleeping well?"

"I'm sleeping fine. Are *you*?" The passive aggression beneath my question is, *Don't symptomize my sleeplessness as part of a greater problem, because you have artist's insomnia, too, and when you don't, it's usually because of an all-natural sedative called vino.*

"Not wonderfully, no." She sighs, resigning herself to my whims, as everyone eventually does. "Well, I'm walking to the farmers' market. Just wanted to make sure you were up for work."

"I'm leaving in a few minutes."

When she's gone, I climb down from the ladder and scrub off a few flecks of navy paint from the hardwood floors. I strewed newspapers all over the floor of the bedroom, but I didn't have time to line them up perfectly—too eager to begin my ceiling's "darkification." I unbutton the extra-large men's oxford I use as a painting smock to reveal a divine romper. Basically, it's like my vintage-style bathing suit—halter-necked and tight, only the shorts are a little longer and it's made of floral-patterned cotton. I slide my feet into sassy gold flats because I'm already an alchemist today, turning a blank-slate ceiling into a good night's sleep, aka gold. Then I throw on a fedora and a cardigan with elbow patches, giving myself a little chuckle as I pass by the mirror. You simply have to laugh at yourself when you look like a grandpa on the top layer and a 1940s woman vacationing on the French Riviera underneath. That is to say, fabulous.

I make my usual cliff-side stop. Today, I stand right on the edge, so close that one step forward would be like the final move in walking the plank. I rest a pill on the pad of my thumb and then flick it with my middle finger. *Thank you for your service, little pill, but you are no longer needed!* With that, I run toward town, skipping through the moss and grass, howling a victory cry—"AYE-YI-YI!"

The ocean echoes my sounds against its waters, I know it does, because even the ocean recognizes that I am a wild creature, a spirit child of a vast and star-drunk world. *HURRAH!*

They call these pills lithium, and I like the way the word feels against my mouth—soft, unassuming, even soothing. *Lith-ee-um*. When the doctor first prescribed lithium, I wondered how the drug companies named it, like if there's a committee that tried to decide on pretty, calming words. I wondered how they picked "lith" like *Lithuania, lithograph, monolith*. It means "stone" in Greek; I looked it up. And lithium *was* the weighty stone that pulled me back down when a wild, thrashing windstorm tore me away. But lithium isn't the brand name; it's a chemical element abbreviated *Li* on the periodic table, but I think it should be Line because it collected my highs and lows into a nice, flat line.

But I'm better now. I'm best, even! Besides, I still take my other pill because that one keeps the shadow creatures at bay. Last year, they curled their inky arms around me until my Technicolor world became crackling gray static. Until I felt nothing but blankness.

My phone buzzes in my bag, and I'm delighted to see that it's Jonah, who is one of several elixirs I use. When I kiss him, it's like a sedative, a warm feeling that rushes through my whole body and soothes my busy brain. His prudishness makes anything I do seem filled with intrigue, which is a bonus. He was scandalized that I'd perform a particular act on him in the outdoor shower after a beach trip last week. But I won him over to the idea. "Helloooo."

"Viv?" This is not his voice, subdued and casual. He's panicked. "Are you at work?"

"About to unlock the door. Why? What's wrong?"

"Can you—God, I hate to ask, I can't believe I'm asking. Can you get to Patterson's in the next few minutes?" I open my mouth, but he doesn't pause. "My mom went there this morning, and I thought it was a good sign, but Mr. Patterson just called and said she had some kind of breakdown in the baking aisle or something, I don't know. He said I should come get her because he doesn't want her to drive home, but she took the car, and I have the littles here, and Naomi's at her internship and Silas didn't pick up the phone at work, and I . . . I . . ."

It takes my mind a moment to catch up, but, when I get there, I shove my keys right back in my purse. "Jonah, listen to me. I'm going to Patterson's, and everything will be fine. Get one of the neighbors to hang out with the littles for, like, half an hour, then run over here, okay?"

"Okay."

I hurry down the street, thanking my half-hour-ago self for putting on flats instead of heels. Inside Patterson's, there's a man with a gray mustache pacing near the entrance. He's wearing a green polo shirt with some kind of vegetable logo, perhaps Mr. Patterson himself.

"Hi," I say, trying to sound calm and adultlike. "I'm a friend of Jonah Daniels. He'll be here shortly, but he sent me in the meantime."

"She's in the back room—door to your right." He shakes his head, bewildered and clearly questioning himself. "I don't even know what happened. Found her collapsed to her knees, holding a box of bread crumbs and having what I think was a panic attack. I wasn't sure what to do. I gave her an empty paper bag to breathe in like they do on TV."

I give him a nod with a look of severity that I hope says: *If you tell anyone about this incident, it would be very poor form, indeed, and I will start rumors about wormy produce and salmonella!*

The supermarket break room is where cheerfulness goes to die, so I'm not sure what he was thinking, sticking her in here. There's a brown plaid sofa that is outdated by half a century, a refrigerator, two vending machines, and a lot of notices posted on the cabinets. Jonah's mom sits upright in a plastic chair behind a round kitchen table, her hands folded in her lap. I'm glad to finally see her in person instead of just in pictures, even if she looks so sad. I know this feeling of being a ghost in your own life—no one sees you, no one *feels* you, so you stay still as if you could actually disappear at any moment.

"Hi." My voice sounds abrupt even though I'm striving for gentleness. "I'm Vivi."

She glances toward me, managing a weak smile that I know as Jonah's—the one when he is trying his best, but the sadness beneath will not be squelched. "Oh. Hello. Goodness."

She brushes her hands over her shirt like she's trying to tidy up. "My kids have told me so much about you. I feel like I know you."

"I feel like I know you, too, but I'm so glad to meet you in person." Sitting in the plastic chair closest to her, I look for the littles in her face. Grief has lined her eyes with an irritated pink, but she's lovely—fair hair and blue eyes like Leah and probably a little too thin. "Jonah's on his way, but I was just down the street, so I wanted to sit with you until he got here."

Mrs. Daniels's voice breaks as she covers her face with her hands. "This is so embarrassing."

"Eh. I've seen worse."

She gives a harsh laugh of self-deprecation, gesturing from her head to her toes as if summarizing her present situation. "I doubt that, but you're sweet to say so."

I hold my left wrist up to her and slide my sleeve down. The scar runs like a pale river, crooked and winding down my arm, and I feel, as I always do, the desire to erase it. This is perhaps the only time I've been grateful for proof of my former desperation.

Her eyes narrow, and she cocks her head—not in disgust, but in curiosity. I find myself relieved that she's not repulsed by something so ugly. I mean, I'm not sure if the scar itself is ugly—I've never thought about it—but it *represents* something scary and bottomless. She whispers again, hollowed out this time. "I didn't know."

"I'm better now. I have been for a while."

"Did you . . . did they make you take medicine?" She sounds like a child, afraid that the doctor will give her a shot, and I don't blame her. "I'm sorry—please forget I asked. That was unconscionably rude."

"I don't mind. Yes. They did. An antidepressant."

"And that helps?"

*Say the words, Viv. She won't tell Jonah; she needs to hear it, just spit it out. It's the right thing to do, do it, do it.* "It really does. The first kind they gave me was a nightmare." That first kind set me off, untethered me and sent me flying. It began the windstorm. "But this one . . . I feel like myself still, on it."

"I'm just so tired. I'm so, so tired all the time." A tear slips down her face, all the way down till it drops off her chin, and she doesn't brush its trail away.

And I remember being in that jungle, lost in the darkest, wildest part of it, where fearsome beasts and carnivorous plants lurk between every tree. All I could do was lie down on the wet leaves. Bugs crawled up my legs, and I couldn't care enough to brush them off.

"Oh man, do I know that feeling. But the medicine made me feel enough to get angry," I say. I don't add that the anger makes you powerful. I stood up and sickled myself the hell out of there, hack by hack, slicing through the vines. I screamed until my face turned purple because, by then, I was a fearsome beast, too. I had lived through the blackness and solitude and emerged roaring at everything in my way.

She stays quiet for a few beats. "I only feel angry at myself."

"Well, maybe that's a start." The room is silent except for the hum of the refrigerator as background noise, and I realize there's something important she needs to hear. "By the way, I think your kids are the definition of marvelousness, and I've been wanting to tell you that. Based on my own mother's experience, it seems hard enough to raise even one semi-normal child, and you made six truly magnificent ones."

"Yeah," she says, voice bitter. "Some mother I am."

"Hey." We both look up to find Jonah in the doorway. He's winded still, though I can tell his breathing is slower than it would have been after running here. I wonder how long he's been in the doorway.

His mom goes repentant immediately, as if his mere presence is accusing her of something. The tears form again in a blink. "I told Jim I could drive myself home, but he wanted me to sit here. I'm so sorry, kid; I don't know what happened—I was fine one minute, then my chest felt so tight, and I couldn't breathe. I just wanted to make cookies for you all, and—"

"Mom, hey. Hey." Jonah crouches down to her as I clear out of the way. "Don't apologize. You're fine. We're all fine. Let's go home, okay?"

"But . . . the cart . . ."

"I'll get cookie supplies later." He guides her up and out the door, his hand hovering by her lower back. In the parking lot, we walk on either side of her like bodyguards protecting a star from the paparazzi. Jonah opens the passenger door and shuts it after his mom slides in.

"I'm sorry for asking you to come here." He says this under his breath as we walk around the car, and the wind whips my cardigan enough that I pull it closer.

"Don't be. I told you, Jonah: I'm not intimidated by other people's pain."

He runs his fingers along his brow, pressing hard enough to leave red marks for a moment. "I think I need to tell Felix."

"I think you should ask your mom what she needs. Talk to her."

Jonah looks up at the sky like the answers will rain down on his face, clearing away the dusty pollen of grief. But it never rains in Verona Cove. "I think I should have told him a long time ago."

"Fine. Whatever, Jonah." I snap my fingers. Maybe he heard me, but he's not *listening* to me. "I've gotta go to work."

"Hey!" he calls. "What did I say?"

"Did you not even hear me? Stop acting like she has no agency! Holy Mother Earth, Jonah! Just . . . ask her questions."

His hands rise, a backing-off motion. "Okay . . . God."

As I storm off, I can hear his arms slap against his sides, and I'm sure he's tossed them up in frustration. Then I hear the car start, but I don't look up as they drive off, because he doesn't deserve it.

To the deepest, most cellular level of my being, I resent people who believe that depression is the same as weakness, that "sad" people must be coddled like helpless toddlers. So to think that Jonah—my own boyfriend, my friend, my lover, what*ever* he is—would believe that he knows what his mom needs better than she does? That her grief makes her unaskable, voiceless, unreliable? This is very hurtful.

My dark days made me strong. Or maybe I already was strong, and they made me prove it. Jonah Daniels has his own grief, but he doesn't understand what it feels like to waste away in a castle dungeon where you have been chained to crumbling walls. And, when the dragons close in, you only think: *Good. Let this be over.*

I'm so worked up that my hands are trembling a bit, so, clearly, I'm in no condition to work at a pottery shop. Imagine the shards, the precious handiwork mishandled by a shakingly indignant former sad girl.

Instead, I need to focus on me, on my joy, on my goals. I need a Vividay, which is like a holiday, only better. As long as I can think of a good excuse, my mom will let me borrow the car and then I can drive to San Jose. It's three hours south of here, but I'll tell her I'm in desperate need of decent shopping. Which is sort of true. San Jose is home to a Vespa store, and that's what I need right now. I can already feel it, my body pressed into the California wind at forty-five miles an hour and rising, and I'll wear a scarf around my hair like beautiful women in convertibles in old movies. I'll drive the one that goes the fastest, so fast that I outrun every dirty memory scattered like litter behind me. I'll drive it all the way back to Verona Cove, and I will speed past Jonah Daniels, as living proof that sad people can do anything. Living proof that we can ride again, better than before.

## CHAPTER TEN
# *Jonah*

I was lying on my bed when my phone rang. My eyes were closed, but I wasn't asleep or trying to be. After the grocery store disaster, I got my mom home and into her room. Then I sprawled facedown on my bed and tried to think of nothing. I wished my bed could come to life and transport me to another world. Like in kids' books.

I'm not sure how Whitney got my number, but she wanted to know if Vivi was with me.

"Not since this morning," I said, sitting up.

"She never showed up for work, and she isn't answering her phone. I'm a little worried."

I worried a lot after that call, until Whitney called back to say she heard from Vivi.

"She went on a day trip," Whitney told me. "She forgot she was supposed to work."

That's not true. She knew she was supposed to work. But somehow I pissed her off so much that I drove her out of town. It was a matter of time, if I'm being honest with myself.

Now I'm sitting on our driveway with Leah and a box of sidewalk chalk. She's drawing the ocean and a dolphin diving over it. I'm drawing a cluster of question marks in every color. In between them, random arrows spiking up at every angle. Next up: a self-portrait of me tearing out all my hair.

On some level, I'm mad at Felix for not sensing that there is a problem. He came by the house every day for the first month after my dad died, filling our refrigerator and talking with my mom in her room upstairs. Then he stopped. He replaced his visits with the almost-daily question: *How's your* mamí?

I couldn't verbalize the answer. I couldn't tell him she was asleep for most of the day in a bed covered with crumpled-up tissues. It felt too soon to be seriously worried, even though I was. And talking about it felt like I was betraying my mom. So I said, *She's all right*. Besides, I didn't want him to ask. I wanted him to stop by the house and see for himself. Then I wanted him to swoop in and fix it. Be the grown-up.

In a desperate moment nearly two months after my dad died, I invited Felix to family dinner. My plan was that I'd wait for him to come over that night. I hoped to work up the nerve to stand on our porch with him and admit my mom needed more help than we could give her.

"You know I'd love to have dinner with you all," he told me. "But your *mamí*, she asked me not to come by for a while."

I was transported to my childhood days in the kitchen, listing off every question that entered my mind. "She did? When? Why?"

"About a month ago." He sighed. "She needs time to figure out how to be alone, kid. I know that's hard to hear. But if I'm coming by the house, doing things your dad would have done, I'm taking that from her."

"She told you that?"

"She did." He laced his big, square hands together. "This is man-to-man talk, *sí*? Stays between you and me."

It didn't. I told Naomi and Silas, when we discussed what to do. As usual, we were in our separate corners or the ring: Naomi pushing for therapy and Silas arguing that we need to leave her the hell alone and me caught somewhere in between and bloodied.

A *vroom* noise pulls my attention to the street. It gets louder and louder until there's an ice-blue Vespa parked outside our house. Its rider is bare-legged, and when she pulls off the helmet, I'm surprised to see familiar white-blond curls.

Leah bounds toward Vivi, squealing out some very valid questions. Where *did* the Vespa come from? But

Vivi's striding toward us. We have bigger things to talk about.

"Why don't you go look?" I say to Leah as we meet Vivi halfway.

"Can I sit on it?"

"No," I say before Vivi can give her permission. "But you can put the helmet on."

"You can touch the blue plastic parts," Vivi says. "She's like a pony, loves to be petted."

Vivi takes me in, and I realize I'm dusted in chalk, sage green and ground-mustard yellow. She wipes a smudge off my forearm, thinking hard. Finally, she looks up at me.

"It was an emotional day," she says. I want to ask what, exactly, I did to make her so furious. But I don't want to bring it up when she seems . . . not mad.

"I know. And I'm sorry. I shouldn't have brought you into that situation." I rub at the dull headache that lives above my eyebrow. "That wasn't fair of me. It's not your problem, and—"

She places her fingertips over my mouth, halting my clunky apology. "Let's not talk about it anymore. Will you come over to my house and make me dinner? My mom's driving down to San Francisco for a gallery opening."

And just in case I was going to say no, she drops her hand and kisses me. I pull her in, hands behind her neck. This girl witnessed my mom having a meltdown. And me having a meltdown because I have no idea what I'm doing. And she still comes back.

"*Ew!*" Leah shrieks from across the lawn. "Vivi! That's my *brother*."

I look down at Vivi. Wipe a smudge of blue from her jaw. "Wow, lucky you. Covered in sidewalk chalk, getting heckled by a five-year-old."

She smiles, like she's in on a really good secret and says quietly, "I like it."

The damnedest thing is, she does.

# CHAPTER ELEVEN
## *Vivi*

"You told me you were taking my car to San Jose to go *shopping*, Vivian!" I thought my mom would be gone by the time I got back from Jonah's. But there she was, all dolled up for the gallery event, walking out to the car as I zoomed back from Jonah's on the Vespa. She marched me inside, face as crimson as her skirt.

"I was! For a Vespa! I *told* you I wanted one!" The very nice Vespa salesmen loaded it into my mom's car, and I drove it back to Verona Cove, and I had a neighbor help me get it out of the car, and now it's mine! Powder blue and quintessentially me—my mother cannot ruin this. "Why are you freaking out? I bought a helmet!"

It's a totally sensible purchase. I already have my motorcycle license because the guy I was dating when I turned sixteen had a bike. And it's a GT—fast enough for the highway! Now I won't have to borrow her car all the time.

"This was thousands of dollars, Vivian." I hate that she keeps saying my full name like it's a swearword. "From a credit card you stole from my wallet!"

"It's *my* card! And money Grandma left me! It's not stealing when it's mine!"

Her voice becomes hushed, scary. "I confiscated that card from you because you couldn't act responsibly with it. It was understood that purchases go through me first."

I am incandescent with rage, lighting up the kitchen with the redness of my face. "Stop treating me like a child! Do you even hear yourself? I'll be eighteen next year!"

Her eyes narrow, but I can still see her pupils trying to pierce into me. "You're not taking your pills, are you?"

"YES! I! AM!" I *am* taking them. Well, one of them. The other, I'm taking, too! To the cliff every day so I can watch them fall to their deaths.

"Let me see your purse."

"What? No! Why?" But then I realize: I have nothing to hide. "Fine. Here."

She extracts both prescription bottles and dumps the pills out on the table. She counts them and finds—I'm sure—the exact amount there'd be if I were swallowing them all daily.

I see her shoulders sag, in defeat or relief I'm not sure.

"You can't blame me for being worried. This is how it started last time. Next thing I know, you'll be getting another tattoo without permission!"

My eyes blur over with angry, hurt, everything-all-at-once tears. She knows I hate the stupid watercolor lotus inked on my side, that I'm getting it removed, that I recoil from it. "Don't talk to me about last time! I'm having a wonderful summer, and I'm better, and you're *ruining* it by not trusting me."

She has no idea. She was there, but she has no idea how scary it got—like my brain, my body, my whole *life* was on fast-forward and I couldn't push stop or even pause. How low it got after, living with what had happened. And then how numb. How much I missed feeling music in my bones.

I remember so much of it, and I would surrender my best vintage sewing patterns to forget. My mom doesn't know the worst of it because I've never told her, because saying it out loud would be reliving it, because I know she'd never look at me the same way again.

"I think I'll cancel tonight," she says quietly, but she's bluffing—she has to be. The gallery is showing one of her paintings.

"Well, do whatever you want, but I won't even be here," I say, as controlled and prim as I can muster. "I'm going over to Jonah's. He's making me dinner."

Okay, he's coming over here so we can be alone, but eh—details, schmetails.

Her posture relaxes even further, fists unclenched. "Well, that's sweet of him. He's quite the cook, isn't he?"

"He is." As far as my mom's concerned, Jonah can do no wrong. He's so normal, so stable—living proof that I'm doing fine. She saw him at the farmers' market one day with the littles and wouldn't shut up about how sweet and responsible he seems, how wonderful it is that I'm spending time with such a nice boy. She's right, of course, but he's not so nice that he won't come over when she's not home and make me dinner and spend the rest of the evening in my bedroom. I cover my mouth, as if I am thinking very hard. But I'm just hiding my smile.

"All right," she says, picking up her keys. "This conversation is not over, but we're tabling it for now. The Vespa's going back. I'm not happy, Viv."

Jonah shows up an hour later with a brown paper grocery bag. For some reason, this draws me to him even more, imagining he's my older, live-in boyfriend bringing home groceries to our big, modern beach house.

"This is good timing," he says. "I've been working on a few new recipes for the restaurant. You can try one tonight instead of waiting until your birthday party."

"I'm getting a birthday party?" I clap with delight, and I'm already imagining silly hats and fairy lights.

Jonah rolls his eyes. "You said what you wanted for your birthday was for me to fix up the patio, so that's what I'm doing."

I watch him unpack the groceries and lay them on the table, and there are plenty of things I don't recognize—something green and leafy that is not exactly normal lettuce, a vegetable that looks like a cross between a potato and a radish. We find pots and pans and spatulas together, roving through Richard's kitchen because my mom and I almost never use it, so I don't know where anything is. Jonah puts salmon in the oven, and he places the potato-radishes—which he called red potatoes—into a saucepan of boiling water.

My mom said she'd be home late. But, even after our fight, I won't be surprised if she has a few glasses of champagne and goes home with another tortured artist. I'll get a regret-filled text message by midnight, but it won't be so regretful that she actually changes her mind. I'm not judging her—I don't want it to sound like I am—because I understand; I do. My mom wants someone to love her, and I recognize that having a daughter who loves you is not enough and that she craves to be adored by a steady, interesting, kindhearted man. I'm not saying I think going home with randoms is the best way to figure it out, but it might be fun and it's certainly better than staying home and meeting no one.

I didn't figure that out on my own, about my mom. My aunt has always been chatty and judgmental about my mom after a glass or two of wine. Because she's not happy in her marriage and jealous that my mom isn't tied down to anyone. That part, I figured out on my own.

I sit on the counter, swinging my legs as I watch Jonah work. It's all so lovely, the easy rhythm as he slices peaches for a salad, the deftness of his hands in every movement between stove and island and sink. "This is really beautiful to watch, Jonah—I mean it. It's like watching you speak a different language, you know? It's like when you walk past two people speaking Spanish, and you don't understand the meaning of each word, but the sound of it is beautiful, and you can tell they understand each other. That's how you are with food."

He smiles, stirring at some kind of sauce. "It's not that complicated."

Well, only because he grew up speaking food.

"Hey, Jonah? What's a reduction? Like, it's on menus sometimes—a balsamic reduction or something."

"Oh. It's a technique for making a sauce. You heat ingredients in a pan until enough evaporates, reducing it. The remaining sauce is more flavorful. Sometimes thicker."

"*Hmm*. Good to know." From my seat on the counter, I'm eye level with him, which is new, so I grab him by the front of his shirt and tug him toward me. It's the kind of kissing we sink into so fast, my hands drawn immediately to that gorgeous hair, tugging him in farther. I feel that moment where rational thought swishes out of me, and it's like a lever that propels a train out of the station; I'm gone, there's no stopping me, we're riding this rail all the way to the end.

But he pulls his mouth away from mine, and I think he's going to say something sexy to me, but instead he says, "The salmon's going to burn."

It takes a moment for me to get my bearings because my mind is so fogged over, levitating above us. You'd think this would hurt my feelings, that my kissing talent isn't enough to distract him, like I can't transport him far enough away from the reality of cooking. But I don't *want* someone who makes it easy; I don't want someone who follows every slapdash plan that I create in my mind. Jonah Daniels can be such an enigma. There are smudges of my red lipstick across his mouth, making him more delicious than any of the food in this kitchen.

I watch him carefully as he lifts the salmon from the oven. "Jonah?"

"Yeah?"

"Do you want to be a chef?"

"I think so." He sets the pan down and lifts up the saucepan from the stove. When he drains the water into the sink, steam swarms the air. "I can't really imagine doing anything else."

"So you'll go to culinary school, do you think?"

"I hope so. Eventually." After he dumps what I now know to be red potatoes into a bowl, he adds a little milk and a cut of butter. I keep waiting for him to elaborate, but like I said, Jonah Daniels can be an enigma.

So I'll prod him. I know we're not in the most comfortable topical territory for Jonah, but it's good for him to talk about his feelings and plans. "Would you take over Tony's?"

Jonah frowns thoughtfully. He mashes the potatoes with a silver kitchen tool I don't recognize, and the muscles in his arms flex as he does so. I sit on my hands so they'll stop trying to reach over and unbutton his shirt. "No. I don't think so. At least not for a long time. I love the restaurant, and I love Verona Cove . . . but I want to live in a bigger city."

The scents carry across the air between us—faint garlic and melted butter and another earthy spice that I can't place.

"There's school for costume designing, right?" he asks. "Are those in big cities?

"New York and LA, mostly, I think. But I'm sure I can find an apprenticeship with some fabulous designer because I'm already a rather talented seamstress. Also, I want to go to Japan for at least a year. After that, I'll probably live in California for work." I consider this, opening my mind to the many possible visions I see of my life. "But maybe New York, doing TV or indie films. You know, people tend to think of costume design as, like, beautiful, accurately re-created gowns in period films. But there's such an art to costume-designing for modern realism, like in TV shows. You have to study the character and know what choices he or she would make, and you help create the idea of the portrayal, you and the writers and the actor or actress and the hair and makeup team."

"I can see you doing both," Jonah says, smiling. He's spooning the smashed red potatoes onto a bed of lettuce called arugula. I'm becoming very well-versed in vegetables tonight.

"You're right—I'd love to do a current-day TV show, but I'd have to have at least one big, sweeping statement movie. Because, you know, clothes can be the difference between a movie scene and an iconic moment in film."

"Oh yeah?" He looks amused by such a grandiose statement, but I'm right. I'm always right about costume design.

"Of course. Without the black scoop-back gown, the elbow gloves, and the statement necklace, Audrey Hepburn is just a random girl on a New York City street."

"And the tiara."

I blink at him a few times while I process this. "What?"

"She wears a little tiara, too, right? Holly Golightly?" He doesn't look up at me because he's carefully placing the salmon onto the mound of mashed potatoes.

I'm charmed. Oh Holy Mother Earth, am I ever charmed. "You've seen *Breakfast at Tiffany's*?"

"Sure. My mom made me watch all those old movies when I was little." Both plates are almost done now, and he's putting a little more glaze onto the salmon. This whole experience is mouthwatering, and I have to wonder how I got so lucky—a beautiful boy on this beautiful night, making me this beautiful meal.

"Hey, Jonah?"

"Yeah?"

"I don't really know how to break this to you," I say. I hop down from the counter and look up at him. "But I think you are maybe falling in love with me."

He hands me my plate, and his smile is the faintest bit smug. "Viv, I just made you wild-caught Alaskan salmon baked with mango chutney, on a bed of garlic red potatoes and arugula. While talking about an Audrey Hepburn movie. I think *you* are maybe falling in love with *me*."

I lift to my tiptoes so I can press my mouth against his. When I return to my heels, I smile right back. Even though there are no maybes at *all* in this situation and we both know it, I can be an enigma, too. "Maybe so, Jonah. Maybe so."

## CHAPTER TWELVE
## *Jonah*

The Verona Cove bonfire is always on the first Saturday after the Fourth of July. No one knows who started the tradition. I'm not even sure who brings the firewood or buys the keg. Or why the police let it happen. Silas has this theory that the cops let us get it out of our system this one night a year. Probably saves them trouble for the rest of the summer. The usual crowd is high school– and college-aged townies. It's an unspoken rule: no one under fifteen, and you age out after college. A few vacationers are invited, but mostly the ones who have stayed in Verona Cove every summer of their lives. From a calendar standpoint, they're one-fourth townie.

Naomi decided to walk from our house to the beach with me and Vivi, a surprise to both of us. Not that she's said anything on our walk. Vivi has skipped beside me the whole way, asking about who will be here (everyone) and whether there will be fireworks (yes, but just little ones). In Vivi's presence, it's impossible to deny that I'm weighed down. She's buoyant, feet barely tapping the sand she walks on. Her body seems subject to less gravity than the rest of us. Naomi has always been thin, and her bony shoulders hunch forward a bit. I always thought she had bad posture. I never considered that she's been as weighed down as I am, except for longer. Even before my dad died, Naomi worried like it was a hobby. About grades, about college, about money, about the other five of us, the environment and pollution. Seriously.

"Wow," Vivi says, "I mean, would you just look at these stars—they're unreal. I love this, being away from any city lights. It feels like if you walked off one of the cliff sides, you could step on each star like lily pads in water and jump from one to another to make your way through the whole solar system."

With that, she wraps one arm around me and jumps up to peck me on the cheek. I don't have to look to know Naomi is rolling her eyes. I smile anyway, even though Vivi tugging at me splinters the pain in my already-aching back.

My whole body is sore from working on the restaurant patio all week, in addition to watching the littles and working my usual shifts. On the first day, I hauled all the miscellaneous crap away. Half of it went into the shed out back and the other half went to the dump. I called Silas to bring the car and help me move an old, busted oven to the junkyard. Yesterday, I ripped up the weed infestation, but I left the ivy. Silas showed up, even though I didn't ask him to. We worked silently, me pulling at the deep-rooted weeds with all my force and Silas rerouting the electrical cords and testing which lights still work.

Today, I borrowed a power washer from Mr. Thomas, who owns the hardware store beside the restaurant. The patio is, at least, empty and clean. Everyone who uses the alleyway as a shortcut said how great it looks. Mrs. Kowalski said she wants a reservation for the first night the patio opens. I hadn't even thought that far ahead, but Silas and I thanked her anyway. Maybe it's lame, but it feels good to sweat for something I care about. The patio looks a little better each day, measurable progress in front of my eyes. I don't even mind the ache. I'm used to it.

The fire roars in the distance, and there are dark forms all around it. I can smell the smoke already, hear the laughing and chatter. Last year, I came with my friend Zach and a few other guys from the baseball team. I spent most of the night hanging with them and flirting with Sarah. That was when she was a cute Yorkie, not a yippy one. Since I didn't do baseball last spring, I don't even really see those guys anymore. But I can't let myself think about this—about how much can change in a year. It feels like someone driving the heel of their hand into my nose, in a street fight I didn't know I was in.

As we make our way into the masses, people call out greetings, mostly to Vivi. We pause for a moment as Naomi says hello to a group of old friends and Adam, the guy she dated in high school. When I look back for Vivi, she's a few yards away. She's chatting with Dane Farrow like she knows him. And she's already holding a beer.

Dane Farrow is a lowlife. That's the word my dad would have used. Kids at school go to Dane for drugs because his older brother deals. He does, too, by association—pot and Ritalin, I think. He leaves the harder stuff to his brother. I never really think about guys like Dane. I mean, what do I care what he does? Verona Cove is kind of a hippie town, so it's not like weed is a big deal here. But I don't love Vivi talking to him.

When Vivi makes her way back to me, I eye her. "How do you know Dane Farrow?"

"*Hmmmm*," she says, drawing it out. She's openly considering what to tell me. Like, how and to what degree she will lie. "We have a mutual friend."

"Named Mary Jane?"

Vivi giggles like it was a joke. "He knows Whitney. I met him at work. Oh, *relax*, Jonah; don't give me that face. What Dane sells is ditch weed; I'd never buy from him."

Would she buy from someone else? We've never talked about it. I've smoked before with friends but never bought weed. Furthest thing from my mind these days.

"Jonah, Naomi, hey!" Ellie's waving at us, walking over from a group of sophomores. "You came!"

She hugs Naomi and gives me a shy wave, saying, "I saw the patio, Jonah. It looks so great!"

I nod. "Thanks. It's getting there. Ellie, this is Vivi."

"His girlfriend," Vivi adds. We haven't had the definition conversation. I try not to react in surprise. Or relief.

"It's so good to meet you!" Ellie's tone is genuine as she sticks out her hand. Vivi shakes it daintily, as if Ellie is someone she'd rather not touch. "Leah talked about you nonstop last time I saw her."

Vivi gives her that painted-on smile again, but it's more than her lipstick. She looks like a doll with a permanent smile forced onto her face. "Huh. I haven't heard about you."

I frown because of course Vivi has heard of her. "Ellie is Felix's oldest daughter, remember?"

"Oh, yeah." Vivi fake-smiles still. "Right."

I feel like I'm a gazelle about to be mauled by two lions.

"C'mon, El," Naomi says, taking her hand. "Walk with me to the keg."

Without another word to Vivi, they're both gone. Maybe Naomi meant to save me, which I guess she did. But it still seemed like she was excluding Vivi on purpose.

"Sorry about Naomi." I sit down on the nearest log, and Vivi cuddles up beside me. These logs are another Verona Cove mystery, our Stonehenge. They're huge, like petrified wood or something. They curve around the bonfire pit, unused for 364 days a year. "It's not you. She's just like that. It takes her forever to like people, but she's known Ellie forever."

"Oh, give her a break, Jonah." She takes a long drink of her beer. "God, guys are so dense—like, honestly, I can't tell you how much your daily lives would improve if you figured out how to read body language."

I blink at her, sort of pissed. "What?"

She sighs, flicking her glance over to Adam. "When that guy talked to her, Naomi totally put on a face. I've never seen her look so friendly and pleasant, but it exhausted her. I don't know who he is, but I can tell his presence has this, like, major effect on her."

"He's her ex." Naomi never gave details about their breakup, and I never asked. She mentioned it once, very matter-of-fact, around the time she left for college last year. It's like when someone eats something bad and tells you they "got sick." You don't ask for details. You understand that the situation sucked, and that's all you need. "You think she's still hung up on him?"

"Maybe not hung up on. But definitely hurt." Vivi rolls her eyes at me. "Honestly, Jonah, I don't know how you can live in the same house as someone who is heartbroken without sensing it. I've known since the first night I met Naomi, obviously, because I can smell heartbreak on a person. It smells like incense, sweet but burning."

I want to tell her that I live with six heartbroken people, one of whom is catatonic. That kind of heartbreak smells like the aftermath of a car wreck, like hot metal. Oil. The chalky powder released by airbags.

"Anyway." She glances to see that Naomi's walking back over. "I'm going to go find Tasha real quick. Be nice to your sister."

I have no idea who Tasha is. Vivi flies off in a flash of blond and bare legs. I figured Naomi would nag me if I had a drink tonight, but she's holding two beer cans.

"Here," she says, taking Vivi's place on the log. "I got us decent ones instead of the piss they're calling keg beer."

She hands me a can and cracks open another for herself. "Cheers. To surviving this endless, fucking awful year."

Here's hoping. I knock my can against hers. It makes a thin, aluminum *clink*, and we both take long drinks.

"She's really something, isn't she?" My sister's dark eyes are watching Vivi, who is locked into conversation with some guy who is clearly not Tasha. She's laughing, occasionally pushing at his arm. I mean, she's openly flirting with him. But then she catches me looking and puckers her lips like kissing me from yards away. Her red lips stand out in the moonlight.

"Yeah." I chance a sidelong look at Naomi. "You'd like her if you got to know her."

The fire snaps in front of us, and a log splits within it. Naomi is quiet for what feels like a long time. Finally, she says, "I'm just trying to hold it together."

This isn't exactly an excuse for her perpetual bad mood. But I know what she means. "So is Vivi."

I don't know how I know this, but I do. I've never asked about the scar on her left wrist, jagged and intentional. She wears long sleeves almost all the time or, if she's in her bathing suit, an armful of bracelets. Isaac asked about the scar once, and Vivi told an elaborate story about getting attacked by a bear while camping near Mount Rainier. She's never told me the real story other than to say she isn't afraid of darkness. I believe her. Every once in a while, her temper flashes. It's like she's exhausted from beating down her demons.

I'm not sure how much time passes, sitting beside my sister. It feels like we're the only people who are still and sober. Everyone else creates a loud, smoky blur around us. Drinking with my sister doesn't feel weird like I thought it would. This past year made us the same age: old. Because we have real problems. Not that so-and-so broke up with me or I failed a biology test or will I get into Berkeley? Naomi and I are the grizzled adults drinking silently at the bar while the college kids grind on the dance floor.

When Vivi reappears, she has the guy she was flirting with in tow. Yay for me.

"Naomi, this is Ethan," she says, with mischief in her voice. "I was just telling him how you're doing an internship for your environmental engineering major."

Naomi doesn't smile, too suspicious of Vivi's motives. "Oh yeah?"

"I'm a junior at Stanford." Ethan talks fast, genuinely excited for some reason. His hands clasp against his chest like Naomi doesn't understand the pronoun *I*. And his eyes are locked onto my sister in a way that makes me want to punch him. "Majoring in environmental engineering."

This changes Naomi's expression. She softens, now looking at Ethan in wonderment. My sister is such a nerd for science, and no one in our house ever wants to hear about it. She gave up a long time ago. "I'm at Cal Poly!"

"What's your internship emphasis?" he asks. Vivi crosses her arms, triumphant.

"I've been compiling a lot of pollutant data—NPS and indicator bacteria mostly. But I get to transition to some groundwater-remediation-type stuff soon."

"That's so cool. I'm working at an environmental law agency this summer because I'm thinking about going to law school. We have a big Clean Water Act case right now."

"Please don't take this the wrong way, Captain Planet," Vivi says, touching Ethan's arm in her overly familiar way. "But this is more boring than watching glue dry."

Vivi's candor can be charming. It can also be rude as all hell. Naomi looks ready to throw her into the Pacific, but then Ethan chuckles. "She's right."

His eyes stay fixed on Naomi. "I'm actually kind of hungry. Do you want to walk to the diner? I think it's still open. I'd love to pick your brain about the environmental influences on Verona Cove."

"Sure." Naomi rises to her feet. I'm not used to seeing my sister's face so open and untroubled. "I'd love to."

They head off together toward town without even saying good-bye. I can hear him telling her that he grew up in landlocked Colorado, that Verona Cove's ocean life and varying terrain are fascinating to him. I stand, like I'm going to chase him down and warn him: if you hurt my sister, I will bludgeon you with a tree branch. Or drown you in unclean water. Or whatever you do to maim and insult an environmental engineer.

"Down, boy," Vivi says, patting my arm. "He's an Eagle Scout. Literally. We talked about it."

"I've never even seen that guy before! He could be . . . a murderer."

She rolls her eyes. "Violet Cunningham is his cousin. It's not like he's a drifter who hitchhiked into town with a rusty sickle."

Violet's a lifelong vacationer and well-liked enough to get a bonfire invite. But still.

"Besides," Vivi says, jabbing her elbow into mine. "Check that out."

Naomi and Ethan walk past her ex-boyfriend and his group of friends. She doesn't even glance over. And maybe, to Vivi, it seems like matchmaking. But it honestly took me this long to realize that maybe my sister just needs a friend. She comes home from her internship and looks after the littles. She goes upstairs to handle money stuff with my mom; she cleans up around the house and does laundry and grocery shops, same as the rest of us. I can't remember the last time I saw her with someone her own age.

"That's what I call killing two birds with one stone. Except I would never kill one bird, let alone two, so that's not really the right adage. But there's no adage for, like: gave one bird a cute boy named Ethan and made another bird named Adam jealous. Oh! Speaking of which. I'm getting a birthday dinner on the patio, right?"

The change in subject takes me a moment. "Right."

"Great, okay, so I've been promising Leah I'd help with her peacock costume, but she wants there to be an occasion, and my birthday party seems like a good one. So I want everyone to come to dinner, and I want everyone to dress up like their favorite animal because that will make everything *perfect* for me."

"Yeah, all right. Why not?" For the thousandth time in the weeks I've known Vivi, I wonder, *What the hell have I gotten myself into?*

"Hooray! Oh, and don't forget to invite Officer Hayashi."

Like I would forget a request like that. I still don't quite understand their connection. I know they eat breakfast together some mornings. And I know that, last week, as Officer Hayashi was leaving Tony's, he pointed at me and said, *You be good to that girl.* Then he patted the handcuffs on his belt all menacingly.

"Hey, Vivi!" someone calls from closer to the water. I've lived in this town my whole life, and Vivi has more friends.

"Be right back," she says, kissing my cheek. "Don't move, okay? We're talking more about my anthropomorphic birthday party. Isn't that a great word, *anthropomorphic*? I'm not sure if I said it right, but who the hell gets to decide how people use language anyway? I could make up my own language if I wanted to; there's no *council* that certifies these things, and . . ."

"Viv," I say. "Someone called for you."

"Oh, right!" She kisses me on the mouth this time, hands on either side of my chin, before running off.

I sit by myself without even looking around for someone else to talk to. I had weird motivations for coming here tonight. It wasn't to have fun. I guess I wanted to represent my family. Like, look, we're okay. Two of us are here. I even have a girlfriend. But all that feels stupid now. We're not okay, and there's no point in pretending. By the time I finish my beer, I'm ready to go home. I've made an appearance; I've said hi. I don't have a happy face, but even my I'm-okay face is tired.

Vivi startles me out of my introspection, back by my side and pulling at my hand the way Leah does. "C'mon, c'mon. It's time for skinny-dipping!"

It takes me a second. I've heard skinny-dipping happened at a bonfire a few years ago, when I was too young to attend. "What? No."

"Yeah! Oh, c'mon, it'll be fun." She taps my nose with the tip of her finger and glances intentionally downward. "Nothing I haven't seen before."

Is she serious? Or teasing me to get a reaction? I can never tell. "Viv, there's no way I'm getting naked in front of everyone I know."

"Oh my *God*, Jonah." She rolls her eyes, and I feel like the parent of a teenager on a sitcom. "It's dark! And you'll be in the water. No one will even see."

"Yes, they will." Most of the time, I feel drunk on Vivi. Light-headed and wanting more, more, more. But then there are moments where being with her feels like a cruel hangover. Or maybe it's just that I am cast in the role of Buzzkill. "And I don't want everyone here to see you naked either."

"Okay. I'll keep my underthings on, then. For you. Out of love." Before I can tell her that's not really what I meant, she's off and running, already peeling off her shirt. I want to yell at her to stop, please, that this is weird. But the words feel like gunky oatmeal in my mouth, stuck to my tongue. I don't want to be this deadweight, un-fun guy. It's just that

I've never seen Vivi wear a bra that isn't lacy and totally see-through, and I don't want other people . . . you know, seeing through it. I want to be the only one who sees the colorful flower tattoo on her side—the one that she hates.

There's a group of at least ten people at the edge of the water, stripping down. Even more run down to the shoreline when they realize what's happening. Seeing a big group of naked people is surreal. My instinct is to look away because staring seems wrong. The guys are stark naked, but most of the girls are keeping their underwear on. Vivi's right; it's hard to see in the darkness. As the group runs into the water, they're a nude blur.

Of course, everyone on the shore is encouraging them. I'm relieved that Naomi left. Because there's probably nothing weirder than your sister seeing your girlfriend almost naked. Resigned, I find my spot on one of the logs. They're well into the waves, and I sigh.

"Hey." A slim figure appears between me and the bonfire, and I look up to find Ellie smiling down at me.

"Hey."

"So, my dad tells me you're testing out some menu changes." She sits next to me on the log, adjusting her skirt beneath her. "He's really proud."

"Thanks." Proud—like a dad. I don't really know how to feel about that. Which reminds me.

"Hey." I drop my voice even though no one is really close. "Can I ask you a weird question?"

She nods.

"Do you know who owns the restaurant? Like half your dad, half my dad? And what now? Since my dad is—"

"Yeah, it's fifty-fifty. Your dad's half went to your mom." She smiles the tiniest bit. "I overheard. When your brother gets in as much trouble as Diego used to, you get really good at eavesdropping."

"So have you, um . . . heard your dad say anything? About how the restaurant is doing?"

She considers this, really mulling it over. Her brows drop and her lips pinch together. "No. But he's seemed stressed, and I've walked in on a few conversations where my mom and dad abruptly stopped talking. I figured it was about my brother's new girlfriend or something. Why?"

If Felix wanted Ellie to know, he would have told her. It's probably not fair to make her worry. But, based on the way she's looking at me, I think that ship has left the harbor. "Don't tell your dad I told you, okay? But I accidentally saw some papers that make it seem like we're a little . . . behind on payments."

"Huh." The fire reflects back in her dark eyes. "I didn't know. I had no idea."

"I don't want your dad to know that I know, but I'm trying to figure out what I can do."

She nods slowly. I understand how hard it is to process. I didn't think about money, let alone worry about it, for almost sixteen years of my life. Worrying about money makes you old. Eventually, she gives a wispy sigh. "Well, I want to help. I'll try to come up with some ideas, too."

"Without your dad knowing."

Ellie gives me a smile, like she understands that this is about protecting him. And, somehow, my dad, too. "Without my dad knowing."

The skinny-dippers are back near the bonfire now, pooling around the shore to get dressed. It's a miracle no one stole the clothes. A voluptuous blonde is turning cartwheels in her bra and panties—a thong, no less. Ah, yes. My girlfriend, bare-assed in front of everyone I know. I want to jump into the bonfire.

"So," I say, trying to sound like I think it's funny. "That's Vivi."

Ellie laughs, and I expect her to give me a look of judgment—I feel like I *deserve* to be judged—but her kind smile remains. "Good for her. I'd totally do it. Skinny-dipping, I mean. But Diego's stupid friends are here, and they'd probably tattle to my parents. Maybe next year."

I smile over at her. Maybe I'm being judgmental. Vivi's having fun—that's all. "I think she's had more than a few beers. Sorry she was kind of weird to you earlier."

Ellie waves my apology off. She looks all around us for a moment, at the people laughing, at our town. "Do you remember last summer, us talking about leaving Verona Cove?"

"Yeah." We were closing up, wiping down tables at the restaurant.

She's watching my face in the firelight. "Do you still feel that way? Even on nights like tonight?"

I nod. We'd both admitted that we want to leave after high school. That we love our families. We love the people and knowing a place so well. But, as Ellie put it, sometimes you can't breathe. "And I feel guiltier than ever, you know? How could I want to leave the place . . . my dad . . . ?"

"He'd want you to." She gathers her skirt to stand up. "We can always come back! See what's out there. It'll still be here. Well, I'll see you soon."

She's probably smart to leave before Vivi gets back. When I look around, I find Vivi posing for a picture with someone I don't even recognize. Wearing just her bra and underwear. That's it. I haven't seen how much she's had to drink, but clearly too much.

I walk up, unamused, but she's bubbling over as she buttons her shorts. "Hey! Ahh, that was such a rush—you seriously missed out, Jonah, I mean it."

Her charming ball of energy routine isn't going to work on me. I'm embarrassed and mad. "Great. We need to go home now."

"No! What? No way, it's just getting fun."

I drop my voice to a whisper. "Viv, you're drunk. And I think we need to leave. Before any more people have almost-nude pics of you."

"Excuse *me*." She snaps her fingers at her sides, over and over, and I keep expecting to smell the booze on her. Her eyes look bleary, like she's struggling to focus. "I'm not a child, and it's my body, and I can run wild if I damn well please, and screw you for judging me. What do you care what I do, anyway? You're so busy flirting with *Ellie*."

This stuns me. I stand mute. "That's not what it's like at *all*."

She makes a disgusted face. "Ellie. It sounds like a little kid's name."

"Short for Eliana." *Shit*, I think, seeing Vivi's eyes narrow. Should have kept my mouth shut.

"Well, isn't that *special*. What's her middle name? What's her favorite color? Do you just know *everything* about her?"

Now I'm just mad and swinging back. "Carmen, green, and you're being ridiculous. C'mon, we're leaving."

This was the wrong thing to say, too. I never say the right thing.

"No, no, *no*!" Her voice is so loud that my face goes hot. "I can't even look at you right now, with the way you're behaving, Jonah; truly, it's not okay."

"Feeling's mutual, Viv," I whisper. "But I'm not leaving you here by yourself, wasted."

"Damn right you're not. I'm leaving *you* here, non-wasted." Before I can get even a single word in, she takes off skipping toward the hill that leads back up toward town. I don't bother to call out to her. I don't bother to follow. So much for putting on a good show at the bonfire. People have totally noticed our conversation, staring as Vivi takes off.

I stalk toward home, my sister's words echoing in my head. I just want to survive this endless, fucking awful year.

∞

I'm not sure how long I've been asleep when I hear the latch on my bedroom door.

"It's okay, Leah," I murmur. "It was just a dream. You're okay. Everyone's okay."

But she doesn't say anything. I hear the door lock, and I sit up, suddenly wide awake. Vivi wafts in with the scent of campfire smoke and beer. She crawls up the bed, her body warm and suddenly next to mine. "Are you mad at me?"

"How did you get in here?" My room is on the top floor—just low-beam attic space with my bed and desk. She couldn't have gotten up using the roof.

She sighs as if my common sense is exhausting to her. "Silas let me in. He fell asleep on the couch. Are you? Mad?"

"I don't know." I really don't. And, right now, all I can think is that my mom or younger siblings will catch us in here. "I'm . . . confused."

"Okay. About what."

"I thought we had a good thing here. And then you strip down in front of every guy I go to school with? And you're mad that I don't like it? But then you freak out when I talk to another girl?"

*Sound needier, Jonah, seriously.* But I won't take it back. It's true.

"Jonah." Her whisper shivers in the air between us. "I'm trying to live to the fullest; I'm trying to feel everything. I prioritize experiences over anything or anyone, and maybe that isn't easy for you to accept, and I'm sorry, but that's who I am."

A non-apology. I didn't expect one anyway—not her style.

Vivi shifts across my twin bed, straddling herself over me. She looks right into my face. "Jonah, I think you're a wonderful person with a soul that reaches so far beyond your years. And maybe the humane thing to do would be to leave you alone because I'm not ever going to be some kind of dutiful, well-behaved girlfriend. But I don't *want* to leave you alone."

It is very, very hard to think with her on top of me. "Dutiful? I don't even *want* whatever you just said."

"Okay. Then how about you just let me be me, and I'll let you be you. We'll feel everything we feel and not apologize for it. If we get mad at each other, we'll have it out. And then we'll make up."

That's just it: Vivi *does* allow me to be myself. She never shoves me out of my sad moods. She never tries to talk me out of my frustrations. Vivi is all action—let's go to the beach, let's write a play, let's build an ice-cream sundae bar at the house and then play Candy Land while watching *Willy Wonka and the Chocolate Factory* with the littles.

She leans close to me, offering her lips for the taking. "Jonah. Make up with me."

I pull her in and kiss her. With teeth against her lips. Because I'm still mad. And because we fit together. And even when we don't, clashing only makes more sparks.

In the movies, the music always starts up right about now, slowly louder with a solid beat. When a girl sneaks into your bedroom, it's surprisingly quiet. But everything sounds loud for fear of being caught—mouths against skin, pieces of clothing dropping to the floor. Heavy breathing and the drone of the thought, *This is happening, this is happening.* And eventually the sound of your own voice asking, *Are you sure?* What you get in return is, apparently, a muffled giggle and the words, *Yes. God, you're so cute. It kills me.* You try not to think that it seems so casual for her. You try to convince yourself you feel the same. But you don't. Your feelings fill the room like an angry fire. Your feelings for her could blow the glass out of the windows.

∞

When I wake up in the morning, she's gone. The sheets are pulled back from her side, and there's a black Sharpie on the floor that I guess fell off my desk when I was fumbling around for a condom. It takes me until I'm getting dressed to notice, on the wood of my headboard where it meets the mattress, tiny letters: *Vivi was here.*

As if I'd forget.

## CHAPTER THIRTEEN
### *Vivi*

For two weeks after the bonfire, everything I paint is midnight and gold and maroon and ballet-slipper pink. Passionate and deep and metallic. I rip up an old dress—black with thin gold stripes—and sew it into a crop top and high-waisted shorts that look perfect on me. My mom decides I can keep the Vespa if I always wear my helmet and repay my account with money I make from my job. At the pottery shop, I glaze broken pieces from the kiln and make them into a mosaic for Whitney. I teach the littles how to swing dance using online videos and my own pizzazz. We have a picnic in the backyard, we decorate cookies in the shape of suns and palm trees and beach balls, we build a sand fortress at the beach.

I kiss Jonah Daniels four thousand times, every second his family isn't looking. We bicker about everything on planet earth and beyond. I think jellyfish are so beautiful! Translucent and dancing underwater in fringed skirts. Jonah wishes they would drop dead in the sea. I like boxed mac and cheese with that gooey yellow cheese sauce. Jonah's face turns pink with frustration, and he makes me homemade mac and cheese to prove his point. And of course I believe in extraterrestrial life! *I bet they've already been here*, I say, but Jonah shakes his head.

I drag him out to the beach late, late at night to see the sun rise. But we get all tangled up, tongues and skin and hands and gasps and yes, and, by the time I'm fully aware of the world again, it's gone from dark to glowing. I don't care that I missed the sunrise, because I'd much rather make one of my own.

∞

My birthday dress arrives, and I hang it on a nail in the wall because it is art. I order white butterfly wings online, and it takes me three tries to mix the perfect blue paint.

On the day of my birthday, I open my eyes to the sound of my mom's off-key voice singing me "Happy Birthday." I wasn't sleeping, but I was lying in bed, dreaming. She's holding an oversize strawberry cupcake in her hands, and the tall gold candle flickers as she walks toward me.

"Make a wish, chickadee," she says.

I sit up and blow it out and make my wish, and we relax against my pillows, devouring the cupcake and ignoring the crumbs that drop to my duvet cover. I open her glittery card, and a gift card for my favorite online art store falls out. There's also a scrap of paper which reads: *IOU, Save This Ticket.*

"It's not quite ready yet. I pick it up on Saturday." Her smile is very self-satisfied, so I'm intrigued. "Oh, and I almost forgot! This came for you, too."

She hands me a white envelope with my name in handwriting I know well enough to imitate. Return address: *Ruby Oshiro, Seattle, WA*, and I stop breathing.

"She called me last week for our new address," my mom is saying. I don't want to open this in front of her because I have no idea what it might say. "I was so glad to hear you guys are back to normal. She said you hadn't been in touch with her at all."

I told my mom that Ruby and Amala wouldn't speak to me after what happened in March. Which would have been true—I'm sure of it. So I didn't give them a chance. Amala didn't try, but Ruby called and texted and knocked on my front door. I never opened it.

"Chickie?" my mom asks quietly. "Ruby knows, right? About the bipolar disorder?"

My silence serves as an obvious answer, especially since I can't meet her eyes.

I feel my mom draw away from me. "Vivian! Ruby is your oldest friend. How could you not tell her? After everything that happened?"

"I don't have to tell her everything! And I don't have to tell you everything either!" Before she can protest, I cut her off. "You won't even tell me who my dad is. So I don't think I need to provide you with the status of all *my* relationships."

"That," she says darkly, "is entirely different. I am protecting you until you are old enough to deal with certain . . . realities."

"Maybe *I'm* protecting *you*." If she only knew. I mean, she knows a little—the tattoo, the outrageous money I spent on clothes and presents. She doesn't know exactly what happened at Ruby's sixteenth-birthday party last March. What I did.

"I know you've been asking to stay in Verona Cove. And I've told you that I'll consider it. And I will, if it is genuinely what is best for you." Her eyes narrow, the smugness of someone who is revealing the ace up her sleeve. "I will not consider staying here if you're just hiding."

She says this as if the two things are mutually exclusive.

"It's nothing to be ashamed of, Viv. You have an illness—"

"STOP. You are obsessed with this." Tears fill my eyes, and I feel my hands clench, bending the card. "It's my birthday—God, Mom!"

"I'm sorry," she whispers. "I shouldn't have . . . I just worry, and . . . well. Come downstairs if you want more breakfast. I got everything for German pancakes."

I open the envelope after she's gone and find a handmade card—of course. I've admired Ruby's cut-paper art for years, the intricacy and detail. She can slice a *National Geographic* photo of an oil spill into a tiny leather jacket, a cotton-blossom pattern into puffy clouds, trim strips of chevron and polka dots for a hot air balloon.

This card is more sentimental than Ruby's usual work, and the paper girl staring out her bedroom window is Ruby herself. Her jet bangs feathered on her forehead, her trademark fuchsia lips and black leggings. Floral for her comforter, birch for the window frame, stripes for her little boatneck shirt.

But her heart is pasted on the outside of her chest, as hot pink as her mouth. Beyond the window, instead of blue sky, is a square of paper from a map. A tiny red heart at the top of California.

My tears make it hard to see the inside. Oh, Roo. Break my actual beating heart, why don't you? In her calligraphy script: *Happy birthday, Viv. Miss you.* Nothing more, nothing less. No demands for an explanation, no accusations, no hint about if Amala hates me as viciously as I'm sure she must.

Fingers pinching the top of the card, I'm tempted to rip it to scrap paper. But Ruby would never create something to make me feel guilty. Only to feel loved. Still, the guilt pushes through my veins, roiling and acidic and spreading, spreading.

After last March, I knew I didn't deserve friends like that—I didn't deserve friends at all, when all I did was betray them.

But now, I allow myself one text. Line after line of her attempts to contact me, most of which I never even read, and I finally type three words that I've felt for months and months. *Miss you too.*

∞

I push these thoughts away at the Daniels residence because I'm busy turning a little girl into a plume-tailed bird.

"Spin," I tell Leah. She obeys. "Yep—you are the most magnificent child-peacock there ever was."

Jonah isn't home because he's already at the restaurant working on my party dinner, but Silas, Bekah, and Isaac all agree on Leah's magnificence, from her shiny blue leotard to the fanned-out feather tail to the way I rimmed her eyes in white and black face paint. She dances around, as giddy about my party as I am. The other three refuse to tell me their costume selections, on Jonah's order.

"All right," I announce. "I have to go home to get dressed."

Originally, I considered dressing up as a dolphin as an homage to my soul's former vessel, but you'd be surprised how difficult it is—even for someone as talented as me—to create a dolphin costume for an almost-seventeen-year-old human girl.

Besides, I want wings because, well, don't we all? Sometimes I bend my arms behind my back and feel the protruding shoulder blades—technically the scapula, but they feel like broken-off wings. Everyone thinks we evolved from apes, but I'm not totally convinced that we didn't once have wings, at least some of us.

For one night, I want my wings back. But not the wings of a mighty bird, beating powerfully enough to make noise against the air. I want to drift dreamily in the breeze, to let the wind direct me. I know, I know: butterflies are used in bad metaphors about metamorphosis, about bursting forth from a cocoon, born again and in flight. But I'm not dressing as a butterfly to prove that my caterpillar days are behind me—no. No symbolism. It is enough to choose things for their beauty.

My wings are wide and diaphanous—nylon stretched over thin, arced wire. I painted the inner parts with the eye-aching, perfect blue of a sunny day, but the edges are black as if dipped in ink. Between the two colors, I painted little rivers of veins like a leaf's surface.

The true showpiece is not my meticulous wings but my vintage dress. I paid a small fortune for it, but this beauty is worth every nickel. It's from the 1930s, a tight-fitting flapper dress slicked in glossy black beads. The hem ends in a fringe right about my knee, and the straps split into these fabulous V shapes across my bare shoulders.

Okay, fine, I'll admit I'm wearing a *very* padded strapless bra, but this dress deserves truly divine cleavage, you know?

I'm wearing black satin pointe shoes, which don't feel wonderful on my toes, but they look wonderful to my eyes and make me feel graceful, so there. I glued thick black lashes to my eyelids and lined them in a shimmering navy color. For once, I forgo the red lipstick for a cherry-blossom pink because that's how the makeup spirit moves me.

Jonah wanted to pick me up, but I begged him not to. If there's ever a night to zoom through town on my Vespa, it's the night when I'm the most glamorous butterfly to ever waft the earth. I drive slower than usual, so that my wings are pushed straight back, and I feel somewhere between a superhero and a pageant queen waving in a parade, my true self.

Jonah's waiting outside Tony's, done to the nines in a black tuxedo, complete with tails and a white bow tie and vest and oh my *stars*. My hands go shaky as I park the Vespa.

"Happy birthday," he says, before I even dismount. "Where's your helmet?"

Oh, please, like I was going to mat down the hair I spent forty-five minutes on just for a two-minute ride at twenty-five miles an hour. As usual, Jonah out-parents every actual parent in the world. "So what are you supposed to be? Just, like, fancy man?"

He smiles and stiffens his arms at his sides, toddling back and forth on each foot. "Penguin."

When I don't react at first—for sheer, gobsmacked delight—his shyly prideful smile fades to doubt. "No? I thought it would go with your dress, and . . ."

I stop him with a kiss because it's perfect and also because I've never kissed a boy in a tuxedo, and you know what? I could get used to it. I throw my arms around his neck and pull myself up to him a little, delighted by how anachronistic it feels, full-on making out in public while wearing vintage formalwear. Heavens to Betsy, forget this party, I'll take him home and have a party of our own. But he straightens up, collecting himself again, and I'm surprised to find my pink lipstick has left no mark on his mouth. I'll have to try harder next time.

"You look . . ." he begins, swallowing up my dress with his eyes. "Well. You know how you look."

"I do." With a curtsy, I accept his speechlessness as the compliment that it is.

He leads me to the side walkway, where there are lights and laughter twinkling from the patio. I'm holding my breath in excitement and all the extra air in my lungs makes my heartbeat more pronounced, thuddier against my rib cage.

Jonah opens the gate entrance, and my guests cry "HAPPY BIRTHDAY!" so loudly that it's like walking into a wall of sound, and the tears spring to my eyes, blurring everything into blobs of color and glowing light.

There are two picnic tables pushed together, lengthwise, with big pillar candles in lanterns down the center. The leaves are deep jade, crawling up the wooden trellises, and there are white fairy lights everywhere and Chinese lanterns that glow like planets suspended in the galaxy. And benches are filled with my mom and these beautiful people who barely know me and will not only show up but show up in costume. I can barely make them out, but I see the feathered pink flamingo costume that my mom was perfecting for herself this morning.

There should be a word for this feeling: *spectacuclarity* or *burstsomeness*. It's too much to dam inside my body, and I cover my face just moments before the tears spurt out. I don't even want to try to stop myself from feeling everything, from reacting the way I really feel, because I am only turning seventeen once, and I am honestly trying to live this life while I can. The emotion swells around me, into this huge, humid feeling that I must be doing something right.

"Viv," Jonah whispers. "Please tell me that's a happy cry."

I slide my hands down an inch, so my fingertips rest right below my eyes. Jonah's eyebrows are turned down, those dark eyes concerned and desperate to read me.

"This is literally the most wonderful thing that anyone has ever done for me," I choke out. Then I laugh, partially so everyone knows I'm okay and partially because I feel half-hysterical with love and gratitude. "This is already the best night of my life, and it just started!"

Jonah guides me to my seat at the head of the table, and I clear the tears from my eyes to take in all my guests. Isaac is an owl, with a yellow construction-paper triangle taped to the noseband of his glasses. The bottom of Silas's nose is painted black, and he's wearing a sweatband around his head that is mounted with two long black socks—droopy puppy ears covering his own. Bekah is in what looks to be a store-bought bumblebee costume, perhaps a relic of Halloween past. Whitney's dress is covered in glued-on white cotton balls, and little black sheep's ears stick up from her curly, wild hair. My mom, the flamingo. Leah, my peacock, my tiniest friend. And, between them, Officer Hayashi.

"What animal are you?" I tease, since he's just in a nondescript blue sweater. But it looks like he's combed his white hair, and I could die from the sweetness of him sitting between Leah and my mom.

"Grumpy old bear," he says, and I laugh and laugh, interrupted only by someone touching my arm gently.

"Sorry I'm late," Naomi says, although her tone is unremorseful. She didn't wear a costume either, but I like her dress, which is brown with white polka dots. After she takes her place by Silas, she reaches into her purse and pulls out a headband with two pert little ears on either side. She's a deer—of course she is—with her long limbs and speckled dress. The tears want to start again, but the food is coming, and I choose to focus on that.

Ellie emerges in a white shirt and black vest, our waitress for the evening, and I'm having such a nice time that I don't even care that her skin glows like amber in the candlelight. She serves us the food Jonah has made, all family-style in big bowls or on platters—beautiful green salad glossed in champagne vinaigrette, and coconut tilapia, breaded and fried and slathered in some sort of spicy pineapple relish that my mind can't explain but my taste buds can relish, savor, memorize.

My eyes well up as I open my presents—a book from Isaac and silvery-pink nail polish from Bekah and a hand-drawn portrait of me from Leah and a mug Whitney made herself.

"Here. Give that to her." Hayashi has Leah pass me a little plant still in its plastic container from the nursery. "It's a—"

"I know." A Japanese maple seedling. If I can't go to Japan yet, he gave a little piece to me, and it's almost impossible for me to swallow.

"Well, I know how you like trees," he says gruffly. "Maybe if you grow your own, you won't be tempted to deface arboreal public property."

"*What?*" my mom asks, and my jaw drops open. He's seen my tree in Irving Park?

"Oh, nothing," Hayashi tells my mom. "Silly joke."

My eyes are still flooded when Jonah brings the cake out. It's black cherry and chocolate, two layers, with sparklers instead of candles. I watch them sizzle, and I wish for nothing. How could I dare? How could I *dare*, when I have all this?

∞

Jonah and I leave only after I have hugged everyone in attendance at least twice, even Naomi, who stiffens at my embrace, and then we take off on my Vespa with Jonah driving, even though he's technically not supposed to. He makes us stop at home to pick up the helmets. One more surprise, or so he says, and I close my eyes with my arms latched around his waist, wings thrashing violently at my back.

He's driving farther and farther toward the coastline, not stopping until we're in front of a building that looks like a small-town church with a steeple. But, no. It's a lighthouse. The light isn't on, but I can see its shape—a tower with a circular walkway and black iron handrails. A glass planet trapped inside a birdcage.

"Come on," Jonah says, pulling me by the hand after we climb off the Vespa.

"Are we going in? Can you get us in?"

"Yeah. My dad knows the caretaker. Knew him, I mean."

From his pocket, Jonah produces a key on an old lanyard and opens the front door. The piping along the edges of the house reminds me of gingerbread, like you could shingle the roof in licorice and cover the windows with giant peppermints. Inside, the room is dusty and piney and filled with racks of postcards and model ships. Jonah watches me as I survey the trinkets, running my hands along shelf after shelf filled with maritime books. "My dad's friend starting volunteering at the gift shop when he retired. The lighthouse obviously doesn't get used for boats anymore, but the Verona Cove Historical Society restored the building and light a few years before I was born. There are actually lots of lighthouse tourists."

"Enchanting." My voice is a whisper as to not disturb the delightfully spooky atmosphere. "Can we go up?"

"Where do you *think* I'm taking you—the basement?" He smiles, lopsided and pleased with himself. "You sure you don't want my jacket?"

I fluff my hair. "Oh, Jonah, as *if* I'd cover up this dress."

He leads me up a spiral staircase, and I can tell even from the back of his head that he's smiling because he knows I'm totally taken with this, all of it. My heart beats four times as fast as our footsteps up the stairs, *th-thump, th-thump*, at the quietness and anticipation. The wind whips straight into my ears as we enter the lighthouse's deck, but the air off the Pacific is warm, and I gasp at the view. For a moment, I nearly lose my depth perception, trying to reconcile the new heights with the stars and the sea, and I understand why the guardrail rises all the way to my waist.

"Wow." The word is a hush against the night. For all the joy that tonight's dinner gave me, all the fullness and humanity and communing, this is something else entirely. I'm at the bow of the terrestrial Earth, steering straight toward the cosmos. I'm watched over by the dove-gray moon, his gentle head bowed, and I have to wonder if this is *yūgen*, profound beauty in the natural world—so subtle that it calls up a feeling of wonder without naming it. The word has no English counterpart and neither does this feeling, so I stand witness to the universe without any thought but enjoying my front-row seat.

"Close your eyes," Jonah says, and I do it immediately—I close my eyes, and the first thing I hear is music coming from what sounds like a crackly old radio. And then I feel light flash against my eyelids, a sun exploding right in front of me. I open my eyes toward the sea to find that I'm backlit. The light on and ablaze, too bright to look back at.

Jonah appears beside me, his hands on the rail. "The town paid an insane amount of money for it to be a working lighthouse. They only turn it on for special occasions."

"They let you light it for my birthday?" I can't believe this; I honestly cannot. How silly I was at the beginning of the summer, believing Jonah needed me to make him happy.

His mouth slips into a smile. "Let's just say I'd rather beg forgiveness than ask permission."

We stand together for what feels like a long time, the radio playing melodies over the white noise of sloshing waves.

"My dad used to take me here," Jonah says finally. "He's the one who brought that radio up here, to listen to baseball games. I was obsessed with baseball and boats as a kid. We don't really have boats in Verona Cove, but we pretended."

"Of course you love boats." I adjust the straps of my wings. "You used to be a sea captain."

He smiles at me, shaking his head in that *Oh, Viv* kind of way that lets me know he's so terribly fond of me and the things he perceives as eccentricities.

"I haven't been back here since." This feels like an admission, like he's confessing to a weakness or flaw. "But I wanted you to see it."

I know what he means to say: I wanted you to see me. And I do see him—illuminated with his downturned eyes and the mouth that must be pried into a smile, that gorgeous hair dancing in this wind. I also know he can't talk about his dad so easily, like each word tries to float up his windpipe, but they get stuck to the back of his throat. For once, I keep my damn mouth shut because I want to leave room for him.

"Have you ever heard that saying 'Ships are safe in harbor, but that's not what ships are for'?"

I nod, although I'm not sure where or how I've heard. Maybe it's one of those phrases that somehow exists in the collective subconscious of all people—and especially those of us who are drawn to the sea, who hear a siren call to the water.

"My dad had that quote engraved on the underside of this watch that his dad gave him. He said it's the reason he spent all his money opening the restaurant, why he married my mom and had us kids so young." He sighs, looking down at the ocean below us. "He said the measure of the man is in those decisions. Do you keep yourself and your family safe in harbor, always? Or do you move forward and brave the storms?"

At this, I reach for his arm, placing my hand over the sleeve of his tuxedo jacket. "He sounds like such a good dad."

"He was." Jonah's stare stays out over the water. "I keep wondering if it'll ever hurt less. This . . . this hole in our lives."

"Oh, I imagine it'll hurt less eventually. I think there will always be a hole, though. But lace is one of the most beautiful fabrics, you know. All those holes and gaps, but it's still complete somehow—still lovely."

This makes him smile, at least. "I wouldn't have thought about it like that. Sorry. I'm being a downer. I was lucky to have him for as long as I did. I know that."

This makes me tilt my head away from him, frowning as I consider what he means. "Jonah, you don't have to justify missing him just because I don't have a dad. They're totally different things."

He locks eyes with me, daring a question. "Do you ever miss your dad?"

"Is it possible to miss someone you never met?" I ask. But I do—miss my dad, I mean. Or, at least, I wonder what I might be missing by not knowing him. Every once in a while, when my mood starts to whirlpool, I feel angry at him or my mom or I feel sorry for myself. "Yes, I suppose it is possible. Because I miss *your* dad sometimes, even though I never met him. I feel like I know him a little, like if I collect fragments of the six of you and tape them together, there he is: a mosaic of your pieces."

This gets a smile, if a sad one. "Do you know anything about your dad?"

"He was a musician, I think. I've figured some of it out, even though my mom refuses to talk about him. I badgered her so much when I was little, just for one detail, that she finally told me she met him when she was at a concert." In my mind, I can see my mom, only nineteen, and this blur of a man I've never seen or met. I imagine him with longish hair and a stubbly, rock-star beard, maybe tight pants and tattoos. "I don't really blame him for not being around, you know. He's a creative soul, a free-spirited musician, and I think that's partially where I get my wild streak from. That's just who he is, wherever he is, and I like that I come from artistic stock anyway."

I cock my hip, posing with one hand in my hair. "I actually feel bad for the guy. He doesn't even know what he's missing."

Jonah looks at me so admiringly, and my heart bounces like a pinball from my stomach to my throat to either side of my rib cage. I know I am something special—I know that I am because I am trying to be, and it is nice to be seen, the way I see him.

I face the ocean, and he wraps both of his arms around me, chin on my shoulder. I have this feeling that if we fell forward into the water, hanging on to Jonah would buoy me, drag me back up to the surface.

Some of the guys I've been with, they've tried to pin me down. They wanted to box me into the details, the wheres and whens and hows of our togetherness, and it always pinched my nerves that they needed to map out a plan for *feelings*. Other guys, they seemed totally content to let me prance in and out of their lives, relieved that they didn't have to agree to future plans, no concert tickets for a show later that summer, no prom tickets months in advance.

Jonah doesn't do either thing. We are together for now, above the choppy black water and the flicking white waves, and it is enough.

And the next horrible thought is how badly I want to tell Ruby and Amala about him. I try to push away the idea of them. In my mind, we're always in Amala's bedroom, dyeing the tips of Ruby's hair some fantastic color and howling over stupid jokes. We went to art museums and the most hip coffee shops and record stores and concerts. Why do I go back to the simplest moments, in pajamas?

"Viv?" Jonah asks. "You okay?"

"Yeah," I say, almost hesitating. "Did you have a group of friends? Before your dad?"

He nods against my shoulder. "Good guys. They're not gone or anything. I'm just really busy. And . . . you know. They don't know how to talk to me about everything."

Before I can say anything, he jumps back in. "You never talk about friends back home. You must have a thousand, based on the hundred you have in Verona Cove."

I lift one shoulder, glad he can't see my face. "We had a bit of a falling-out before I left. Water under the bridge. I'm here now."

So why do I wish I wish I wish I could take a picture of me and Jonah and send it to Ruby and Amala and say this is falling in love with someone GOOD and it is so good.

We stand there pressed together for a while until it is no longer my birthday. I think about boats, how they're powerful but so delicate compared to the fickle sea. I think about lighthouses, about safe mooring and how easy it is to crash. I think about love and what I deserve and how I'm trying to accept everything the universe is giving me.

Then the radio changes to something upbeat and folksy.

Jonah's voice is near my ear. I can hear his smile. "I like this song."

At first, we stay standing together, but then the chorus plays, and it's free and alive. So the serious-eyed boy in the penguin suit takes the butterfly-winged girl by the hands and spins her. We sway our hips and stamp our feet like the drunken revelry of turning sour grapes into wine. Our bodies block the beam from the lighthouse as we wave our arms and, even though we can't see it, we're casting shadows onto the sky.

This is where I am, somewhere between the night's total darkness and the light's utter brilliance, and I grin as I dance and the night wind kicks up Jonah's hair. The glow of my birthday candles and the fairy lights would have been more than enough. But Jonah Daniels? He lit up my whole world.

Even the constellations can see us now: we are seventeen and shattered and still dancing. We have messy, throbbing hearts, and we are stronger than anyone could ever know.

## CHAPTER FOURTEEN
## *Jonah*

I woke up to the sound of rain. In my exhausted state, I thought the sound was the roof caving in or my window AC unit dying of emphysema. Verona Cove doesn't get rain in the summer. It just doesn't.

Sure enough, the sky beyond my third-story window is a mechanical gray. It's not a summer shower. My clock reads 10:00 a.m., which is not possible.

I pass Leah's room on my way to the kitchen. She's still curled in a ball like a sleepy kitten. I never realized it's the sunshine that wakes her up so early every morning. Downstairs, Bekah and Isaac are playing a board game I haven't seen in years. They're quiet. Not fighting.

Today is confusing.

I shower and make us egg sandwiches for breakfast instead of oatmeal because, hey—the world is backward anyway. It's raining, my siblings are mellow, and we're eating high-cholesterol food. Leah makes a face at her egg sandwich after one bite, so I bring it up to my mom. She's sitting on her bed with a pile of papers fanned out around her. But she's dressed in something other than pajamas. And her hair looks different. Shiny. Brushed?

"Hey, pal," she says, looking up. Her face is alert. It's hard to explain why the change is so immediately noticeable. When someone is so sad for so long, they lack the energy to move even the tiniest facial muscle. Like they're too sad to even fully lift their eyelids. This morning, there's a twitch of movement in my mom's cheeks. Her forehead isn't drooping.

"Hey. I brought you a breakfast sandwich. It's slightly used. By Leah. But still warm."

"Thanks." A real smile.

Seriously. Whose life did I wake up to?

I squint at the papers around her. I can't resist asking. "What are you doing?"

She tucks a wisp of hair behind her ear. "Well, Naomi has been taking care of a lot of household stuff for me."

All my muscles cramp. Money talk makes me feel sweatier than a marathon runner.

"She's been doing a wonderful job, but she needed some help with it this month. So I'm rebalancing to make sure we're all set." Maybe she senses my hypertension. "Which we are."

"Do you know why I majored in accounting?" she asks, scribbling something down on the pad of paper in her hands.

I do know this, actually. It's easy to forget how well I know my mom. Her grief seems like a disguise but, underneath it, I know her. "Because you love math."

"I really do," she agrees. "And I love math because there's always a right answer. It's not interpretive; it's not subjective. There is a correct destination, even if you have to hack through confusing parts to get there. That's not always true in life."

I'm glad she's staring down at her numbers and figures. She doesn't see my jaw drop just enough to part my lips. My mom is seemingly functional and even—God—musing about life? I feel insane for reading into this. It's a mirage, like when she tried to go to the grocery store. It looked like a good sign. It ended in public sobbing.

"You're right," I say dumbly. "Well, let me know if you need anything."

I'm still shaking my head, stupefied, when my phone beeps. I expect Vivi. Come to think of it, I'm surprised she hasn't shown up yet. At our front door, wearing a raincoat and boots and imploring us to dance outside with her. I assume she picked up a shift at the pottery shop. Still, it's a rare morning that I don't wake up to a series of dirty and imaginative text messages. She doesn't sleep much.

But it's Felix. *Slammed. Come in?*

The restaurant is almost never slammed during lunch, especially on summer weekdays. Most vacationers don't even realize we're open for lunch. But the morning beachgoers have to drive by Tony's on their way back into town. They're probably ducking in for lunch and hoping to wait out the storm.

Verona Cove's tourist brochure calls the weather here "perfect." It's never sticky hot in the summer, and almost never freezing in the winter. But today I feel the cold front. I hurry through the rain with an old golf umbrella I found in the hallway closet. By the time I reach Main Street, the backs of my jeans are splattered.

The Tony's sandwich board is out on the street. Someone wedged an umbrella handle in the space at the top where the two sides meet. From a distance, it looks like a very short, very squat person huddled under an umbrella. But the open umbrella protects careful chalk writing. I can read the bright white letters even through the rain. RAINY DAY SPECIAL: Hot Soups and Homemade Bread.

We've never offered homemade bread, and we only ever have one soup of the day. I pinch the skin on my forearm, hard, because this feels like a dream. One of those weird ones where it's your life but the details are all messed up.

Inside, the kitchen is especially steamy, and the smell is overpowering and savory. More than that. Fragrant and yeasty and baked. Felix is chopping vegetables like a madman. Gabe is manning a stovetop full of deep soup pots.

"Jonah!" Ellie calls. "Hey!"

She's at the prep station near the ovens, rubbing the tops of four loaves of bread dough with shiny olive oil. Her dark hair is tied back loosely beneath a too-big baseball cap that I recognize as Felix's. She's wearing a floral apron that she must have brought from home.

"Hey. You wanna catch me up here?"

Her hands move so fast it looks like she has four or six arms—a frantic cartoon character. Yet her voice is controlled, all business. "We're doing six soups: classic tomato, minestrone, chicken noodle, hot and sour, tortilla, and a special Thai coconut that I thought was risky, but my dad nailed it—customers are obsessed. We also have four breads to choose from: French bread, corn bread, Asiago, and garlic rosemary."

Ellie pauses, taking a breath. Her hands sprinkle loose herbs onto the bread loaves, which she then pats down expertly. "A bowl of soup and your choice of bread as a side for five dollars. Or, for three dollars extra, you can get a grilled cheese with your soup. Add more than one type of cheese for fifty cents each. The available cheeses are—"

"I know them." I created the dairy organizational system in the fridge last year. I can recite the cheese alphabetically or by flavor, mild to sharp. I'll have to put that on my college applications. *Jonah Daniels: cheese arranger.* I may have quit all my school activities to take care of my siblings, but, hey, I can keep a kitchen staff from mixing up provolone with mozzarella slices. Full-scholarship material.

"Oh, right." She laughs at herself as she washes flecks of rosemary off her hands. "I'm sales-pitching you like you're a customer. We need another person on the floor, so I'm going to take orders if you can handle the bread for me. Unless you want to wait tables."

"No. Cooking, good." My mind is already whipped up in the rush of the kitchen; my hands are on autopilot, tying my apron behind my back. The kitchen is best when we're on the brink of chaos. Being understaffed is a total adrenaline rush. It doesn't happen enough.

After Ellie explains the bread schedule and leaves, I stand there for a moment. It's a lot to take in. Felix laughs at me as he slides a mound of vegetables from his cutting board to a huge pot. "She's a girl with a plan."

Okay, game time. I transfer the now perfectly crusted Asiago bread into the warming oven and move to the corn-bread batter. "How'd you come up with this?"

Another snort of laughter from Felix. "C'mon, Maní, you think I came up with this? It was all that kid of mine. She woke up early and smelled the rain like a basset hound. Next thing you know, she's down here with her *abuela*'s bread recipes, talking me into her plan. All right, quick run to Patterson's for more carrots and celery and . . . what else did we say?"

"Coconut milk!" Gabe calls from the stove. When Felix is out the back door, Jack, one of the prep cooks, looks up from plating the soups with the grilled cheeses. "How old is Ellie?"

"Sixteen. *No,* Jack."

"Yes, Jack!" he says. "I'm only eighteen. What? I think I've got a shot. She's a cool girl."

"Dude, she would eat you alive."

"What!"

"Ellie takes zero shit." I put the corn bread in the oven.

"And you are full of it."

He and Gabe live to joke around in the kitchen, and I have to admit they're funny. But, as if to prove my point, the kitchen door swings open. Ellie sticks her head in. "Hurry it up, you clowns."

The restaurant stays packed through the lunch hour. Bread in the oven, bread out, season the chicken broth, on and on. My mind numbs in that way I've only ever found in the kitchen. And with Vivi. Despite the frantic pace, I sneak a moment to peer out the kitchen door. It's a swinging door with a Plexiglas circle window out to the dining room. When I was little, it made me think of a submarine. There are families at every table. Lifting spoonfuls of soup to their mouths, slathering butter on their bread. Heads leaning back in loud laughter. The restaurant is busy, but the world feels slow. No one is hurrying because there's nothing to hurry to. They're together. I miss my dad so much that my stomach almost heaves. I have to keep moving, keep working.

By 4:00 p.m., they've cleared out, and the dinner-prep shift has started to overlap with our finely honed routine.

"Go home, both of you," Felix tells Ellie and me. "You worked a good day."

"Okay," Ellie replies, leaning over to kiss her dad on the cheek. She turns to me. "Are you walking home? I have something to show you."

"Yeah, uh. Okay." I glance back at Felix to see if he looks in the know. He looks amused.

"You're a dick," Jack says, pointing at me.

Outside, Ellie's waiting. The rain has stopped. The air still smells like wet dirt and ozone. As we walk out the door, she hands me a folded sheet of paper, which is covered in the blue ink of her neat handwriting.

"Some notes. Well . . . observations, I guess." She points to the first line. "I spent some time thinking about trends in my interactions with customers as their waitress. Because, you know, they ask me about certain dishes or tell me which ones they're trying to decide between."

I start at the top. *Overview. Types of Customers: Townie Regulars, "Something Light and Healthy" Vacationers, and People Who Just Want the Most Possible Amount of Food.*

My eyes jump to the bottom of the page. *Conclusions:*, it says, like this is a paper for school, *Create an official kids' menu with a few simple offerings, expand our salad menu so customers can add grilled chicken or shrimp, designate meals on the menu that are vegetarian and gluten-free, and also create a few more options that are vegetarian and gluten-free . . .*

There are more. "Uhh . . . wow."

Ellie clears her throat. "After today, I also think we should consider a sandwich-and-soup combo for the lunch hour."

"Yeah, great." My word bank has depleted after the dizzying lunch shift. This *is* great. And unexpected. I know Ellie said she wanted to help, but I had no idea she cared this much. "Great."

"I hope you don't think I'm stepping on your toes! After we talked at the bonfire, I realized I have some insight about our customers and what they seem to want."

"No!" I say. "This is great. I mean, wow. It's so organized and . . . clear."

Ellie looks momentarily embarrassed, though her easy smile makes me think I imagined it. "What can I say? I was inspired."

"I'm glad. It's great."

Say *great* again, self. Seriously.

"One last thing. I think, for vacationers, it's unclear what kind of restaurant Tony's is. I know it's a big change, but I was thinking . . . what if we called it Tony's Bistro?"

"Huh." I consider this. "Yeah. That sums it up. Casual but nice. You think your dad would go for it?"

She nods. "I really do."

I fold the paper and slide it into my back pocket. We pass the pottery shop, and I glance in to look for Vivi. Only Whitney is in there, and she waves to Ellie and me.

I check my phone for texts, but there's nothing to find. It's not like her.

"So," Ellie says. "How's your mom? I've only seen her at church once or twice since I got home from camp."

"Oh, you know . . . fine."

Most people nod solemnly, relieved to have the awkward social obligation of asking out of the way. Ellie is quiet, so I glance over at her. She's narrowing her eyes. I can hardly see past her heavy eyelashes.

"Jonah." She slows her pace considerably, and I do, too. "How is your mom really?"

We both stop. We're standing on the sidewalk outside the park. I cross my arms. I open my mouth to say *fine* again, more convincingly this time. But saying it again seems like even more of a lie. Ellie's dark eyes study me, waiting, and I finally confess. "Not good. At all."

I start walking again, making a getaway from those four words. I broke the barrier between our family and the outside world. Exposed us. Ellie catches up, right beside me.

"Like *how* not good?" Her whole face is soft. Being pitied makes me feel pitiful.

"Like barely gets out of bed, okay?" My voice sounds mean even though I would never intentionally snap at her. "Sorry. It's bad. It's . . . I don't know."

I expect her to ask why the hell I haven't gotten my mom some help. I expect her to judge the entire way

I've handled this situation as harshly as I judge myself for it.

Instead, she whispers, "I *knew* it."

She whispers this to herself, like how you say *dammit* under your breath after you drop something.

"I'm so sorry, Jonah," Ellie says. "Maybe it's none of my business. I've just . . . had this feeling about it."

"God, don't apologize." I try to laugh, but it sounds bitter. Because I am. "We've been trying to give my mom some time—Naomi and Silas and me. But they go off to school at the end of August, and I can't take care of the three kids on my own. Silas is talking about putting college off for a year. I don't want him to, but I don't know what else to do."

We walk a few slow steps, and I'm conflicted. As relieved as I am to let all this out, I feel like I'm doing something behind my family's back.

"Hey, you two!" Mrs. Albrecht calls from across the street as Edgar pauses to sniff at the fire hydrant. Ellie and I both wave, but my face burns. It's embarrassing the way that someone walking in on you in the bathroom is embarrassing. Caught in a private moment.

By the time we're out of earshot, Ellie and I are standing at the corner where we have to go different directions.

"You do realize that, after everything with Diego, we know a lot about depression—medication, therapy, listening to one another, and talking." Her eyebrows are scrunched together, but I can't tell if she's confused or hurt. Or both. "Why haven't you told my dad?"

"Because . . . because it's only been seven months. Because, in a weird way, it feels like her business, not mine. I don't want to embarrass her. There are a lot of reasons, I guess."

She nods slowly. "Fair enough. What can I do?"

"Nothing." Just like that, I snap shut. It's an instinct, after seven months. "I mean, thanks, but we're fine."

Now is the time to go our separate ways. But neither of us moves. Ellie's looking up at me, waiting. She's smoking me out with silence. If I go much longer without saying anything, it will become painfully awkward instead of just a little awkward. It'd be easy enough to stammer *Okay, see you later* and walk away, but my mouth and legs won't cooperate.

"Actually," I say, before I even mean to, "I keep chickening out of talking to your dad. I know my mom stopped doing the books for the restaurant after everything happened, but if your dad asked for her help again, I think she'd like that. Do you think you could suggest that?"

Ellie nods like it's totally normal to ask your friend to ask her dad if he can ask your mom for accounting help. "Of course. I'll bring it up with him subtly. Maybe that'll sort of open the door between my dad and your mom. And, Jonah, please tell me if I can babysit or pick up some groceries or I don't know what. Anything. I'd really like to help, if I can. And if you ever need to talk, really . . ."

"Thanks. We're actually doing pretty well most days. It's after Naomi and Silas leave that freaks me out. But Vivi keeps saying she might actually persuade her mom to stay in Verona Cove longer, so she might be around to help, too."

Ellie smiles. "That would be great."

"And thanks for coming up with ideas for the restaurant." We're inching apart now.

"It was fun. Think them over when you have a chance. I already showed them to my dad. We can talk about it on Thursday if you want. See ya!"

She's a few steps away when I call out, "What's happening Thursday?"

"Nothing. It's just our next overlapping shift."

I turn back as we walk away, and she does the same, waving at me. Maybe I should feel guilty for outing my mom without even running it by Naomi or Silas, but I don't. I feel like we've added another person to our team. Or maybe just realized that there was someone else there all along.

# CHAPTER FIFTEEN
## *Vivi*

Here is why I ransacked my mother's room: I had to know. I've been thinking about it ever since the night of my birthday when Jonah and I talked about our dads at the lighthouse. Jonah's dad was always in his life, so that loss is a staggering subtraction. I wonder now—could my dad be a meaningful addition to my world?

So many years, I told myself, *I don't need to know about my dad*. But I think that might be some sort of myth that I created about myself: I am no man's orphan, not a silly girl who is having an identity crisis, nothing like that. Except what if I *am*, you know? Like, what if I let myself be that girl for a minute?

So I did. I gave myself a tiny open window to really feel what I feel, and a gust of curious wind poured in. I studied my own face in the mirror yesterday, searching for clues of him on my very flesh. I have my mom's button nose and full lips, but she has dark eyes, and I have blue. So these are his eyes, which I guess I've always known—his genes are right inside my eye sockets, and I don't even know what his first name is. My natural hair color is darkest blond, and so is my mom's. But my eyebrows. My eyebrows are full, and my mom's are sparse; she fills them in with eyebrow pencil anytime she leaves the house. My mom has long, slender fingers, and my hands are teeny. I have his eyes, his eyebrows, his hands, what else? When I emerged from the bathroom, it had been over an hour.

If my mom had married someone, maybe I would have forgotten about my biological dad completely. There was only one person I ever wanted for the role of stepdad. When I was little, there was this man named Adesh, and my mom loved him in a way that made her a different person after he left, and I loved him, too, because he was handsome and so unbelievably kind. If he had ever yelled, I think I would have burst out laughing because his accent made everything sound beautiful. But he would never yell—no, never; he was too busy singing and introducing me to new music and making my favorite meal called *makki paneer pakora*. He moved back to India to take care of his aging parents, and I remember overhearing a conversation in which my mom said, *Let me just come with you.* He wouldn't let her uproot her life and me, is what he said. *What is meant to be will find a way*, is what he said. They wrote letters back and forth for so long, real letters, and she keeps all his words bundled at the back of her underwear drawer.

I snooped and read all the letters years ago because I missed him, too, and my mom got too sad when I tried to ask about it. In the last one, he tells her he's engaged to a lady named Saanvi and that he will always love my mom in a special compartment of his heart. After I read that last letter, I felt guilty. I don't regret discovering the letters, but I feel like I crossed a border that was not my own, that I wandered into private territory. But Adesh's leaving was a sad tale in my storybook, too, and I deserved to know the end. In the winter, my mom still wears a beautiful scarf he sent her from Mumbai. She wraps it around her neck slowly like she's savoring the fabric's lushness, and I know she's wishing it still smelled like him, like sweet spices and warm air and the days when love wasn't lost.

Anyway, that's what made me think to look in the underwear drawer. I mean, that's where she hid her most secret things in Seattle; if there's anything worth finding in this house, it would be there, right?

Patience is *not* my virtue, but I knew I had to bide my time to be careful. I waited until this morning, when I knew she'd be gone, when she left very early to drive three hours to San Francisco and pick up some supplies at a specialty art shop.

Sure enough, I find Adesh's letters in her underwear drawer. I uncover a stash of photos, too, labeled on the back in my mom's scratchy cursive. *Me and Mom*: a faded picture of my mom as a little girl, standing with her own mother, who died very young. *Carrie & Adesh*: a picture of my mom and Adesh, nose-to-nose and smiling with their eyes closed like they're high out of their minds on love. *My Viv*: A picture of me when I was four or five, wearing pink sunglasses and holding an ice-cream cone out to the camera. These pictures are the most precious to my mother. But there are none of my father, none of my mother at age nineteen or pregnant with me.

I give up; I accept the temporary fate that finding out more about my father was not meant to be. The sky is barely light, and I press my hands against the glass walls in the living room, the ones that remind you that the only thing separating you from nature is an inch of building material. Whether framed by wood and plaster and insulation or simple glass, a house is part of a larger ecosystem. It is so foolish to think we exist unconnectedly from nature. Foolish, I say.

Don't even ask me how my wild brain works, which points connect to the other points, but the interconnectedness makes me think of bureaucracy—I don't know. And for some reason, a new thought beats against my temples: Where are our important documents? Our Social Security cards and birth certificates? At home, she keeps them in a safe that I have never guessed the combination to. She's not the kind of mom who would bring filing cabinets or plastic bins with labels here to Verona Cove. But she's also not the kind of mom who would not have them in an emergency. They've got to be here.

Crazed by this lead, I riffle through her other drawers. Nothing, nothing, nothing. I pillage the joint, clothes flying like I'm the tornado. Finally, in a back corner of Richard's closet, where the rest of my mom's clothes are hung, I find an unmarked manila envelope. Our birth certificates, our Social Security cards, a life-insurance policy in my mom's name. And a long envelope. The return address is a lawyer's office in Washington.

I nearly rip the birth certificate trying to read it. Vivian Irene Alexander because I'm named after my mom's two grandmothers, and I've always liked that my initials spell a word. Born in Olympia, Washington, on July 23, right on the horoscope borderline of sensitive Cancer and fiery Leo. I self-identify as Leo, though, *ROAR!* Mother: Carrie Rose Alexander.

Father: James Bukowski.

Inhale, a gasp; exhale a gust. Chest rising and falling, pant, pant.

I'm quivering like the warning tremors before an earthquake, tears flooding my eyes faster than I can finish reading it.

. . . *Am I still breathing?*

Hands trembling, I slide a single sheet of paper out of another envelope. The document surrenders full legal custody to my mother, like my father can't show up later and have some kind of claim on me. It's notarized from the year of my birth. My father signed at the bottom, one quick swipe of ink, like he was getting it over with.

My father's name is James Bukowski. Of Berkeley, California. My whole face goes tingly with this new information; my blood buzzes inside my veins, a hum against nerve endings. He has a name, it is James, his last name is one I never would have guessed, a last name that could have been my own had things gone differently. Does he go by Jim or Jimmy, does he live in Berkeley still, why, why, *why* would my mother do this to me? Why would she keep me from him? Was he a dangerous man? Was she protecting me from him?

I think, on some level, I believed I would never in my life know anything about him, and now I'm questioning whether I really ever wanted to. No, I did. I do. I don't know. I know nothing.

As much as I loved my previous human life as a ballerina in the 1920s, I am so colossally grateful for the Internet, and I search and search, fingers typing in a frenzy of clacks. The thought often terrifies me, actually—how much personal information you can find online. But today that is working in my favor, I have to say.

There is a man in Berkeley, California, whose name is James Bukowski. All I can tell is that he works for Berkeley College, and I guess maybe my dad could be a professor of music? Like he segued his rock career into teaching—that could happen, right?

I have to know. Even if it's not him, I have to know.

My thoughts give way to my most secret feelings, the hopes I've always had that I never let myself fully imagine. How my dad probably has an old record player and the coolest collection of vinyl and we'll listen to it and dance around his living room. How he doesn't know anything about fancy cooking but he calls scrambled eggs his "specialty" and can make a mean veggie burger in the summer, filling the whole backyard with that grill-smoke smell. How he has a collection of vintage hats—bowlers and fedoras and newsboy caps—and he'll let me borrow them. He probably has tattoos. *What kinds?* I wonder. Maybe we'll get one together, something to symbolize our free-spiritedness, how we are connected but independent and we get each other.

So I saddle up Cherie—that's my Vespa, *obviously*—and I put my helmet on because my hair will look like a flailing mess if I drive bare-headed on the highway. In my favorite T-strap pumps and a white-collared blouse, I'm a vision, especially since I'm wearing the most beautiful skirt. It falls all the way to my calves—the kind of skirt that can twirl and twirl because the bottom of the hem makes a big circle. I sewed it myself with vintage fabric, which has a white background but is covered in red and peach and blue flowers. I have to press my legs tight to the Vespa to keep my skirt from flying all over the place, but even if it does, it's like, who cares, you know? I have much bigger concerns floating all around me like the clouds in the sky down the coastline and we're drifting, drifting.

I didn't pack anything really because I won't need anything once I get there. Either it's not my dad, and I turn around and come home or it *is* my dad, and he'll have everything else I'll need. So I just take my cell phone and my lipstick and my emergency credit card and ID, which were already in my favorite little purse. I have the address of this Berkeley James Bukowski tucked on a scrap of paper. At least, this house has a mortgage out with his name on it, so it's probably him. Still, I drive and drive until I find it, and I park my Vespa near the end of the driveway. I have arrived.

The house is so homey, so suburban. Brick and square and fancier than I expected. But no matter. This is it, my moment, and I could finally be meeting my dad. I know it's probably not him, but if it is, he'll be so thrilled. All these years he's had to legally stay away from me because of that stupid custody agreement, but I found him, and now he can know me. Now we can fill those gaps in our souls—him from never knowing a child, me from never knowing a father. The front porch makes me feel small, like I'm peddling cookies or holiday gift wrap. But my knuckles find the door, and it's only a moment before someone answers.

"Hi," I say. My voice sounds like a little girl's. "Are you James Bukowski?"

"Yes. Can I help you?" This can't be my father. He's older than my dad would be, older than my mother. He's wearing a tie and a pressed shirt rolled up at the sleeves. His hair is starting to gray at the temples; he has a beard trimmed short to his face. But he has blue eyes, full eyebrows, like mine, exactly like mine. No.

"Are you . . . ?" I begin. "The musician James Bukowski?"

"No. I'm a professor." He's confused, perhaps imagining that I'm a groupie and stalker. "Of economics. Why?"

So it's not him. I think I'm relieved; am I relieved? "Okay. Okay, thanks anyway. Never mind."

I turn to walk away, and he's still standing with the door half-open. But something spins me back around like a windup ballerina in a music box. "I'm Vivi. That doesn't mean anything to you, does it?"

I'm sure it doesn't, but his expression changes—it drops to the concrete porch below us and shatters. His eyes turn from confused to angry in a single flash, which I can't comprehend. I'm finally here, his daughter—I finally found him so he can know me. He steps out onto the porch, pulling the door closed behind him. But not before I see them. The pictures in the entryway of kids. His real kids.

"You can't be here."

I stand paralyzed, a lawn ornament frozen in horror. His face pools with blood, red and pulsing. "You cannot be here."

Oh my God, it *is* him. Oh my God, this man is my dad, and he hates me, and his family doesn't know about me. I want to say no, YOU can't be here. This can't be happening. You can't be this ridiculous person, this boring non-rock-star *professor*, with a life that is all neatly formed. He's not a wild musician with a drifter's heart. He's a regular man. *He's a regular, responsible old man?!*

"Carrie promised me this wouldn't happen," he said, like he can rationalize my presence away. "I've sent the check every month. Is that what this is about?"

My body makes a sob noise, the air forced from my stomach and out my mouth as if someone punched me in the gut. I'm not crying or maybe I am; I really have no idea what is happening except this angry man who has my eyes, and I can't believe how poisonously I hate him.

"I'm sorry," I whisper, but then hearing my own voice is proof. I am here. I am someone with an opinion and rights and, actually, I'm *not* sorry. At all. A deep breath fills my stomach and I think I'm yelling. "I'm a real *person*. I am not a promise someone made about me! And *you*—you know what? You're *pathetic*. You may not want me, but now I don't want you either!"

"Lower your voice this instant," he hisses at me, and now I'm sure that I'm crying, I'm sobbing, making these gross, primal noises like a grief-stricken cow braying on his front porch.

Lower my voice? He doesn't get to tell me what to do! Like a dad. I gather enough breath to retort. Oh, I will, oh yes, because my lungs are swirling like a windstorm, circling up the words like floating leaves, and I will carry them together with violent force. "LOWER *YOUR* FUCKING VOICE! YOU ARE THE BIGGEST DISAPPOINTMENT OF MY LIFE. So just KEEP your REAL FAMILY because I really don't CARE. I'm just SO RELIEVED to know I was never missing anything. But you were, JAMES BUKOWSKI. Because I'm pretty FUCKING GREAT, and I'm SORRY FOR YOU that you don't know it. Have a GREAT LIFE. I will NEVER think about you AGAIN."

My legs carry me in long strides, but I curse myself for wearing heels, even low ones. I didn't think I'd need a getaway plan, didn't think I'd be running for my life from a man who is everything I don't want to be. I'm sobbing so much that snot is warm beneath my nose.

"Jim, what the hell is going on?" I hear the shaky voice of the woman behind me as I run down his driveway toward my Vespa, and I glance back in time to see the door close. Good. GOOD. I'm glad his wife knows. If he didn't have the balls to tell her he's had a daughter for seventeen years, I'm glad she knows now. Maybe I was the angel of death for his marriage, and I wouldn't even be sorry, I swear to God I wouldn't be. DO YOU HEAR ME? I AM NOT SORRY FOR MY CREATION OR MY BIRTH OR MY LIFE.

# CHAPTER SIXTEEN
## *Jonah*

When Vivi calls, I can barely make out the words. It's sobbing and it's a chant, half my name, half *pleases. Jonah, Jonah, can you come get me? Please, Jonah. I can't—I just. Please come get me.*

"Vivi." My voice sounds the way it does after a long run. "Viv, are you okay?"

"Yes. I don't know. Jonah, please just come get me."

"Okay, I'm coming. Where are you?"

"Cloverdale?" Sniffling. "I think."

That's over an hour away. "Did you call your mom?"

"NO. Not my mom, Jonah, please, just you."

"Okay," I said. "Okay. Go somewhere safe, okay? I need you to find an intersection you're close to and text it to me. I'm leaving now."

Fortunately, Naomi's home from work early, and I drive, and drive, southbound, and I don't know what to expect. The sun starts to drop and so does my stomach. Once I get close to where I think Vivi is, I scan every street for pale hair and skin, for a shock of red lips. I call, but the phone goes to voice mail.

I finally spot the Vespa and the little ball of person next to it. She's sitting on the sidewalk in front of a dumpy apartment complex. Her legs are tucked up and hidden by her skirt, which is ripped at the bottom. Her black-streaked face is pressed against her knees. I bail out of the car like in an action movie, barely sliding it into park before my feet hit the ground. I don't bother to shut the door behind me.

"Viv! Vivi, hey," I call to her. "Hey."

She scrambles to her bare feet and runs to me. Her white shirt is untucked and dirty. Before I can process that, she's in my arms, face buried against my shoulder. Her tears soak through my shirt, warm and wet on my skin.

"Why didn't you go somewhere safe like I told you?" I ask. She cries and cries. Wrong question. "Where's your helmet?"

"I think it's . . . on . . . his . . . lawn. I got pulled . . . over . . . for not wearing it."

Wait, what? "Viv, what are you doing down here?"

"I hate him," she wails. "I *hate him*."

"Who?"

"My . . . dad."

I feel her breathing, the way her heaving chest pushes against my own chest and against my arms. Oh my God. She found her dad? Here in Berkeley?

"It's okay," I tell her, and she sobs into my shoulder. It's clearly not true. I just want it to be.

"I wish I'd never met him, I wish I'd never met him," she mumbles into my neck. "I wish I'd never met him. I wish he was *dead*."

Holy shit—she did find him. I hold her there, on the sidewalk, while she cries. Finally, I put her in the car. An older man stops to ask if he can help. He's carrying a gallon of milk home from the convenience store around the corner, and he sets it on the sidewalk before I can reply. We heave the Vespa into the back of the van. Vivi's reclined on her side in the front seat, hugging her arms to her chest. She's motionless enough to be asleep, but her eyes are open. Staring into nothing.

"Is she okay?" the man asks after we've shut the trunk. "Do you guys want to come in and regroup for a few minutes? My wife and I live down the street if you need a cup of coffee."

"That's okay." God, do I appreciate the offer. It's nice to have someone older than me try to help. "Thanks, though. She's just had a really long, really bad day."

He chuckles, clapping me on the shoulder like we're old frat bros. "Hang in there. Any time we have car trouble, my wife has an emotional breakdown about it. She'll feel better tomorrow."

"I hope so," I tell him. Inside, Vivi's rocking herself a little. Her hand is curled near her mouth like she wants to suck her thumb. "Thanks again."

I start the car without knowing what to say. *Are you okay?* She clearly is not. *Do you want to talk about it?* She clearly does not.

I wonder how many people felt this way toward my family—unsure of what to say. Sometimes I think everyone should be handed a manual for this stuff when they turn fourteen. That seems like a good age. Starting high school. Staring at the business end of your childhood, when you have to start growing up. So maybe the school should distribute a book called *The Field Guide for Broken People*. Between Vivi and me alone, we could write a bunch of chapters. Dead Dad. No Dad. Despondent Mom. Flaky Mom. But each broken person is different, and there is no right way for everyone. Just a lot of wrong ways.

Viv shifts beside me. I can't believe this is the same girl who went streaking down the beach. Who sneaked into my house in the middle of the night. Who made my little sister talk and dance and laugh again. I want to pull over to the side of the road and pull her into my arms. I want to find her in this sadness the way she did for me. For us. Another glance at her, and I have the overpowering urge to make comfort food for her. This is a legacy my dad left me. The hardwired impulse to feed people. I wish I could make the food myself, but there's no time for that.

"Viv, have you eaten today?"

I take my eyes off the road to look for an answer on her face. She shakes her head once. Her expression doesn't change. She looks thinner than she did the day we met. I don't know why I didn't notice before today.

I stop at a drugstore off the highway and buy her a pair of two-dollar flip-flops. I don't ask where her shoes went. I also buy these things that Naomi has in our bathroom closet—makeup remover wipes. When I get back in the car, I slide the flip-flops on her dirty feet. She doesn't move. I clean her face off. She stares ahead like I'm not there. Like I'm not touching her.

At a twenty-four-hour diner across the street, she looks out the window and I order for both of us. It's dark enough outside that our reflections stare back in the windows. But she's looking beyond herself. Into the recent past, into the future, I don't know. When her pancakes come, she eats one bite. She cringes as if she's been made to swallow soggy cardboard.

"Hey," I say, reaching for her hand. "I know you're not hungry, but it will make me feel better if I bring you home fed. Okay? Please?"

With a wrinkle of her nose, she slurps some of the whipped cream off her hot chocolate. I ordered it in place of coffee because I want her to sleep on the way home.

"It's good," she says quietly. But her hand doesn't move to her utensils.

I use my fork to split a sausage link in half, and I run it through a puddle of maple syrup. "Don't make me do it, Viv. I'll do it."

She furrows her eyebrows at me, grumpy.

"*Vvvvveeewwwww.*" I make my best airplane noise. Loudly. I steer the fork toward her mouth. A truck driver in a nearby booth turns to look at us. I try to make my voice sound like a pilot's, whatever that means. "Sausage supplier asking permission to land. Over."

She presses down a smile. "Are you kidding right now?"

"Nope! SausageFork to tower, this is an emergency. We request emergency landing." I try to make the crackling noises of a radio transmission. Then malfunction noises. "*Neeeeeer, neeeer, ahhh, ahhh.*"

Viv laughs, opening her mouth for just long enough for me to wedge the food in. The piece of sausage pushes her cheek out. "God, okay. I'll eat it."

She eats all her sausage and drains her hot chocolate all the way down to its powdery dregs. Then, out of nowhere, she starts laughing. It's giggly and a little crazed and, because it's Vivi, musical.

She gets out a few words in bursts. "I threw my shoes at his front door. I can't believe I did that."

"You threw your shoes?"

"Yeah. I did. Everything else is a huge blur; I barely remember it, it's like I blacked out. But I'm sure about that part because . . . hello, my shoes are gone." She dabs at her mouth with a paper napkin. She squints like she's trying very hard to remember something from years ago instead of only a few hours. "I was storming away from his house, and he had closed the door behind me so he could tell lies to his wife in private or whatever. My shoes were slowing me down, and I was still so *mad*. So I pulled them off and ran back to the house and threw one square at his front door—*SMACK!*—and then the other right behind it, and I think the heel dented it. God, it felt so good. I remember that. It felt so, so good. Then I rode off on my Vespa in a blaze of glory. For a second, anyway. Then I felt so sad that it felt like my rib cage was collapsing in on itself."

I know this feeling. I also know that emotions come from the brain. So why do people feel real aches in their chests? Why does it feel like we carry every feeling in our cores?

I pay for our meal, and we head back to the open road. There are very few cars on the highway, and Vivi plays the radio low. She talks nonstop, working through her feelings in a gush. I try not to add anything. If she's talking, I'm not getting in the way of it.

She understands that her mom was trying to protect her. But she's mad. She doesn't know how she feels about her dad paying child support all this time. Or how he hid it from his wife. Is she glad that he cares enough to do that? Or does he only pay so her mom won't tell his wife? She just doesn't know. What she does know is that she's not sorry if she ruined his marriage. Vivi understands secrets. But not ones like this. Not when you fail to tell your wife that you have an extramarital daughter.

"God, he's such a rat; I can't believe it, Jonah. I really can't believe it." She's shaking her head. She's still upset, but it's a relief to see her animated. "You know, some people act like every kid is entitled to two responsible, loving parents. I don't feel like that's a given. We're born alone, and we die alone. If you get an adult who's genuinely there for you, that's pretty lucky. So I'm not bitter about having grown up with a single mom—I'm really not. She's enough and I'm proud of everything she does for us, even when I'm so mad at her that I want to set her canvases on fire. So it's not that. It's that I've lived my whole seventeen years so far thinking I had this rocker dad who wasn't cut out for fatherhood, and it took me a while, but I understood that he didn't *try* to create me and couldn't handle responsibility or whatever. Instead, my father is this guy who is, like, a responsible and stable citizen, who has a family, who has lived on the same coast as me my entire life. How hard would it have been for him to know me? He's already a dad, so why not be a dad for me, you know? God, now I have to come to grips with the fact that he sucks as a person, and that's half of where I came from."

There's a pause, a spot for a reply. A thought pops into my mind so quickly that it doesn't feel like it's my own. After all these weeks with Vivi, I sometimes feel as though Vivi has changed the chemistry of my brain. Like she rearranged neurons.

"I'm not convinced that he's your real dad." In my peripheral vision, I see her face turn to mine. Her interest piqued. "Modern science would disagree, but they don't know you. I think maybe your mom is your mom but your dad is the Man in the Moon. I'm just saying. I wouldn't put it past you to be half-Lunar."

There is a quiet that settles between us.

"Jonah Daniels." She says my full name, as she often does, only this time in a whisper. She's shaking her head. "I don't deserve you."

She's quiet again, but this time she grabs for my hand, gripping onto me for the miles and miles toward home. I steer one-handed.

# CHAPTER SEVENTEEN
## *Vivi*

Time all but stops inside my room. My phone died yesterday, and I haven't bothered to recharge it. I haven't left except to use the bathroom nearest to my room. But at least I showered, so nobody mind the sad blonde drawing all-black ensembles and sewing black netting onto a headband like I'm attending a funeral for the dad of my daydreams, the one who possibly lived on a houseboat with tapestries hung on the walls.

Today I'm sketching my own expressionless face, reflected back by my full-length mirror—wide-set eyes and unremarkable nose. I define my jaw, shading and erasing, my hair, my shoulders and the sweater that is slipping off on one side. The details have to be perfect. The shape of my lips, the yarn of my sweater. It takes minutes or hours or days.

When it looks like me, blank but sullen, I clip my self-portrait to the easel. Swipe two curves of runny black paint under my eyes, dripping down my cheeks. I blend purple and black and white, painting blooms of bruises on my shoulders. Like smudgy violets. I paint my lips ruby. *Ruby*—the word bites at me, and I push it away while I use too much paint, and it drips like blood from my mouth.

Then I cross out my eyes unceremoniously with black pencil.

Maybe I'll glue things to it later.

Most mothers would, I assume, be terrified of this little portrait. Mine checks on me and, last time, put her hand on my shoulder, saying, "I'm so proud of you for using creative expression to handle these emotions."

I know that.

Here is what also I know: my father is not a musician. My father was a graduate student, nearly finished with his PhD when he met my mother at a concert in Berkeley. He was almost ten years older than her, and she thought he was cerebral but in a very cool way. He had hair to his ears and a scruffy beard. He was out with the other econ almost-doctorates to celebrate one of their birthdays.

He wasn't wearing a wedding ring that night. He should have been.

I have two half siblings. My half brother was two years old the night my mom got pregnant with me. He's in college now. My half sister is three years younger than me. They don't know I exist, except maybe now they do. They don't feel like siblings because we don't have anything in common except for half of our genetics. It sounds like a lot. But it isn't.

He has paid child support my whole life. Some of it is in a fund I can use for college. Some of it, my mom used for groceries or to make rent when I was little, before the last few years when her painting took off. Once or twice, she used it to buy me a new coat or pay a babysitter while she was working an extra shift. She explained this like she felt guilty, but that's ridiculous to me. I don't even know how I feel about having his money. Part of me thinks he owes me that, at least—that he should make at least some nominal sacrifice for being such an incredible asshat to my mom and to me. Another part thinks I don't want to take anything that is his. *Ever.*

I claw my fingers down the portrait, and my nails dig up thin lines of paint.

Because it's too late. There are already things of his that are mine—my goddamn eyes, which I want to scrape out of my head after meeting him. Maybe every time in my life that I've been hideously selfish . . . maybe that wasn't the teenage self-centeredness that my mom mutters about. Maybe that's him shining through. Maybe I'm also genetically predisposed to be an abandoner, a narcissist, a liar.

"I am *not* sorry about you and never have been a single day in my life; do you hear me?" my mother asked, that fierceness in her voice imploring me to nod. I did hear her, and I do know this, that I am her world, as she has told me throughout my whole life. She cleared her throat. "But I am so very sorry you didn't wind up with the dad you deserve."

I keep thinking that I'm a different Vivi than I was just days ago, and I don't know how to be the new version. I just know I can't go back to the endless possibilities. I have an answer. And I wish it was a different one.

I'm not saying I *hate* Jim Bukowski because, you know, I try really hard not to have hatred in my life. It's just . . . you know that Sunday-night feeling, where the dread of reality sinks in, that you've mismanaged your time and now the anxiety of homework and the wasteland of early mornings and school stretches ahead of you? Well, I hope he has that feeling every minute of every day of his entire life. That's all.

When the doorbell rings, I slump down to answer it because my mom went out for a while. It's Officer Hayashi, in full uniform, looking stern—all business—as if I summoned him here. "You haven't been at breakfast."

I stare back at him.

"Do you need anyone arrested on your behalf?"

*Hmm*, now there's an idea. "Well, if you happen to be in Berkeley, you're welcome to arrest my father. The official charge is being a shitweasel slash never wanting to know me and hating that I'm alive."

"Sounds like a moron." His eyebrows lower in this protective way that makes me think he might actually growl. And I guess I expect him to say that he's sorry or that he thinks I'd be a great daughter to have. Instead, he straightens. "But that's life. Gotta deal with what you got."

Oh, is *that* all I have to do? If only someone had told me sooner! That I just have to *deal* with what I've *got*. *Snap!* I think I just did it. I narrow my eyes at him. "Do you even have kids?"

He ignores me, turning to go. "You need to eat and get some fresh air. Won't do you any good locking yourself in your house."

He's gone before I think of a comeback, so I slam the door and make myself oily black coffee. I push the French press down harder than necessary.

"Oh good, you've emerged," my mom says, keys jangling as she comes through the front door. I think it's the third day after my misadventure to Berkeley. "Did you even remember I was going to pick up your birthday present this morning?"

I glance up from my coffee. She's still standing in the entryway, and I can't see what she's holding over the kitchen ledge. When she leans down, I hear the scrambling of feet.

A wriggly white pouf of a dog, no bigger than a loaf of bread, bursts into the kitchen, and her tiny claws are clicking all over the kitchen floor. It's love at first sight, and I gasp.

"Wait, really?" I scoop up the dog, and she's so warm and squirmy, complete with two little pink bows on her ears. "She's mine?"

I've wanted a dog since before I understood words and certainly since before I could speak. People say they don't remember their earliest years, but I swear I remember being in a stroller and pointing at passing dogs, trying desperately to communicate that I want *that thing* to be *mine*.

"She's yours. Her owner moved into a retirement community, and she had no one to take care of her. Her name is Sylvia."

"Sylvia," I whisper. She *is* a Sylvia, saucy but innocent, elderly with her white hair but young in spirit. She wastes no time licking my neck. Yes, a stuffed animal come to life to keep me company in my hollowness.

"Viv," my mom says, smile fading a bit. "Sylvia is your dog now, so she's your responsibility. You're all she's got. If for some reason you're not around, I will not take care of her. I won't feed her or walk her, okay? Do you understand?"

I narrow my eyes at my mother—clever woman.

Sometimes I think my mom doesn't really know what to do with me. She got a whirling dervish of a daughter, and the best she can do is brace herself for the violent winds. I know what she's telling me with this dog: don't run away or end up in the hospital again. Now someone else's life depends on me keeping it together. This little, innocent girl-dog, who is working her pink tongue around the back of my ears.

"Okay," I say. I know it's a trick or at least a trick wrapped in a present, but you know what? I will *take* it. "I understand."

Upstairs, Sylvia roams around my bed, inspecting my stuffed animals at first and then lying down amid them. I place my head on the pillow right next to her, and it's nice to have the company of someone who won't try to talk to me or tell me what to do. She dozes off eventually, and her breath is so hot that she's like a fluffy miniature dragon on my bed. When she hears a knock at the front door, she startles awake with a little bark. I'm *not* talking to Hayashi again.

I hear my mom's footsteps, then my door creak open.

"Viv," my mom says. "Jonah's at the door."

I give her this look like *So?* because I'm being horrible, and I don't even care that I'm being horrible. I want to retreat into myself, and no one else is invited except for Sylvia.

"Viv," my mom repeats. "Come on."

She means: come on, don't be rude, Jonah drove to Cloverdale for you, he loves you, he isn't the enemy just because everyone else in the world is the enemy. I don't feel like putting makeup on, and I don't care if Jonah sees me bare-branched. Normally, I care a lot, but I don't have the energy to be his Vivi today, not by a long shot. So let him see that my eyelashes are golden brown and not thick black, that my cheeks are actually fair and not flushed rose. I pick my cotton-ball doggie up so she's resting on my arm. She seems right at home.

When I appear in the doorway, I can tell Jonah's taken aback by my nude face because he's never seen it. He's not repulsed, I don't think—just surprised.

I open the door a little more so he can see Sylvia.

"This is Sylvia. Sylvia, meet Jonah."

"Hey," he says. His grin makes him look younger, like Isaac. He holds his finger out for Sylvia's inspection, and she sniffs at him. "She's so cute."

"She's my birthday present from my mom."

His smile drops away. "How are you?"

This feels weirdly formal, the tables turned—Jonah showing up at my house unannounced instead of me showing up at his. Only Jonah seems to hesitate, like maybe my sadness is too much to surmount. I can't be his wings, the person who lifts him up from the sad days. I'm hopelessly earthbound, and I'm in no position to save anyone else.

"C'mon," he says. He holds his hand out to me, palm up. I like a lot of things about Jonah Daniels, and some of those things are very shallow pleasures—his hair, his strong arms, those molten brown eyes. But I really love his hands, which are easy to underappreciate as a feature. Plenty of people have stubby fingers or knobby knuckles or shredded cuticles. You don't really notice a pair of hands until two really good ones are holding yours. Jonah's hands are square and tanned and smooth—really great boy hands.

I don't want to leave my house, but this is Jonah's allure: he is so handsome and so *good*, good enough to show up even knowing I might knock him backward with my shrewishness. And I can't help but put my hand in his.

∞

We let Sylvia romp through the mossy grass on the bluff overhanging the ocean. Behind us, flowering trees shed petals like tears. It's my favorite spot in all of Verona Cove—the usual scene of my pill disposal—and perhaps the quietest place in this quiet town. But the bluff is noisy if you listen because it's filled with the sounds of the natural earth. The sky is clear blue, the wind cool as it shushes low through the grass.

"Are you sure she's okay off a leash?" Jonah asks, ever the conscientious grown-up.

"I'm sure."

We sit near the edge but not too near, and about a foot apart from each other because I don't feel like being touched by anyone or anything except the clouds. Jonah tells me about what the littles have been up to; he tells me about the restaurant changes under way, new wall paint and recipes.

"It rained for a few hours earlier this week," he says, when I haven't responded to any of his other soliloquys. "The day you were in Berkeley."

I know this already because I could smell it on the earth. Jonah has been trying so hard today, like he's approaching me from every different angle, searching for an entryway. When all I do is think about what he says instead of saying something in return, he tries another path, another topic. My soul, it is a labyrinth, and Jonah, he will find a way in. I have to admire this kind of fortitude, so I throw the poor guy a bone.

"You know," I tell him, "in Botswana, the word for rain is the same as the word for currency: *pula*. It rains so rarely that the value of it is immense."

"Oh yeah?"

"Yeah. And everybody knows about rain dances, but some cultures did other things to bring on rain for their crops, too. They knew which tribesmen were born during rainstorms, and during droughts they would send those men to wander in the wilderness. Like human good luck charms, searching for rain."

"You know a lot about rain."

"I know *everything* about rain."

"Because you grew up in Seattle?" Jonah guesses, but I frown. "I can't imagine the rain all the time."

"Seattle isn't even in the top ten rainiest cities. And—I'm telling you—the sunny days, they're unrivaled. And even when it *is* gray, it's still beautiful and it's still home, and I love it." I look over at him. "I would think you would understand that."

He meets my eyes, and I hope he gets what I mean.

"Yeah, Viv. I do."

I know I'm being horrible—snippy and unyielding. Sometimes I can identify facts in my mind, but I can't feel them. What I mean is, I know that I am not malnourished and I don't have aggressive cancer. I sleep in a safe, warm bed at night, and I can eat ice-cream cones whenever I want. Even right this minute, I smell the salty ocean and wet sand in the breeze, which ruffles my hair. Cognitively, I recognize my good fortune. But I don't *feel* lucky. I want to start my whole life again—like I want to float my soul back up to the cosmos and come down as a different girl, in a different life. Certainly with a different father.

"People have been asking about you," he says. "Two months in, and you've got a whole town wrapped around your finger."

I snort, thinking of my morning visitor. And the curiosity breaks my usual policy about meeting people's ghosts for myself. Because Officer Hayashi wears a wedding band, but heartache rises off his skin like heat. "What's Hayashi's deal? He's married, right?"

"Uh. Was. His wife and daughter died in a car accident when I was . . . seven? Eight? His daughter was in college at the time."

My hand moves to cover my face, and I can barely whisper out the words. "Oh, good God. He lost his family?"

"His son is fine. He's grown. Has kids, I think. He lives in Portland."

Maybe I should be thinking that Hayashi had all the right in the world to tell me to deal with what I've got. But all I can think is that the world seems so pointlessly sad sometimes—so harrowingly, impossibly, uselessly sad.

I stare down at the ocean, which pools farther offshore but weaves in closer, between the craggy cliffs. To land squarely in the water, you'd need a huge running start and the wind direction working in your favor. A standing hop would plunge you straight into the rocks, but I can think of worse ways to go. It would feel like flying, like soaring, the wind barely resisting you, and you'd die on impact, or so they say. Still, God, the landing. I shudder to think.

"If you were going to kill yourself, how would you do it?"

Jonah is silent for a few moments, and I don't turn to see his expression because I don't care—if he's shocked, if he's judging me, if he's offended, I don't care. "Jesus, Viv. I have no idea. I've never thought about it."

Ugh, of course he hasn't, noble Jonah and his duty to his family.

"I'm just being hypothetical, Jonah." Honestly, the sensitivity. Get over it, you know? I don't appreciate how often people hide their scars and doubts. Really, it's not fair to people who are struggling, to go on believing that everyone else just has it totally together and never has one bad thought in their lives. Like, I know you people sometimes lie awake at night torturing yourselves over the atrocities in this world and mortality and meaning. I know you're not just daydreaming about riding a pink pony to your job as a cupcake taster. "Do you believe in heaven?"

I always think I don't believe in God because I don't go to church and I don't care what people do as long as it doesn't hurt anyone. But if that's true, then why do I mumble to a higher being sometimes? *Please help me*, I ask sometimes. Or I get angry at some unknowable form in the sky for my lot in life. *This isn't fair*, I complain. *You are not being fair to me at all.* Sometimes I believe in reincarnation and sometimes I believe in the heaven that they tell little kids about, like golden streets and choirs in the clouds and being happy forever. Sometimes I believe in nothing at all because life can be such a wormhole of despair that I have to think we're on our own.

"I *want* to," Jonah says after a while.

"That's not the same thing."

"Yeah." He sighs as if this thought has crossed his mind excruciatingly often. "I know."

*That's it for Jonah*, I think. I've sucked the energy

right out of him—sapped his remaining ability to put up a cheerful front. If you want to push someone away, I strongly recommend rambling about death and theology. That oughta do it.

I watch the waves swell and break down the coastline, swell and break. My chest threatens to crack on the left side.

The heart is such a strange little beast—a lump of thick muscle with pipes sticking out. Sometimes I think my heart is made of rubber, and the world stretches it and twists so that it writhes in my chest and aches. This is why I have spent most of my time on this planet here but hurting. Sometimes I think a heart of porcelain would be easier. Let it drop out of my rib cage and break on the floor, no heartbeat, the end. Instead, I get a bouncy heart that bleeds when the world claws at it but keeps beating through the pain.

Near us, Sylvia sniffs the wildflowers. I scoot over to where Jonah's sitting and position myself on his lap. I climb right in like a little kid, and he puts his arms around me, and I press my face into his warm neck. No matter what heaven you believe in, your time on this earth will end. What I'm saying is that you should listen—really listen—to the slosh of the waves and the distant call of Pacific birds. You should feel a boy's pulse against your cheek; you should fill your lungs with ocean air. While you can, I mean. You should do these things while you still can.

"Hey, Jonah," I whisper. "Can you sneak over and sleep in my room tonight?"

He thinks for a moment. "Yeah. Just tell Sylvia not to sound the alarm."

∞

That night, I let him in after my mom has closed her bedroom door, and we lie beneath tangled-up sheets. Sylvia's fluffy body rises and falls at the end of the bed, where she is curled up like a powdered-sugar doughnut. Jonah and I are restless as we drift off—on a bumpy road to a peaceful destination. We curl together like heat rising from a teacup—swirls and arcs moving over each other, under each other, fluid and never still.

My head is against his shoulder, so I feel it when his breathing slows, and his lips barely part like a sleeping child.

"Jonah," I whisper, just to check.

"It's okay," he says, eyes closed. He's not even awake. "It's okay."

He says these words even in his sleep, like he has said them so often that it's his mouth's default sentiment. All this pain in his life, all this care he doles out to everyone else. And yet he still cracks his broken heart open even wider—wide enough to fit me, too. I wonder how much this must hurt him, the toll it must take to give more of himself to me when he already has so little left to give.

In slumber, his arm stays wrapped around me, encasing me for safekeeping. He would protect me even in his unconscious state, as we lie beneath my ceiling's half-painted sky.

This thought is enough to swell my heart—to swell, and to break.

## CHAPTER EIGHTEEN
# *Jonah*

I return home from the lunch shift to find Felix sitting at the kitchen table with my mom. They're chatting over coffee in the easy way of old friends. My mom is wearing jeans and a button-down.

So apparently I've walked through a portal to the past. Like, almost eight months ago when I had a mom who showered and walked among the living.

Two months ago, I would have thought, *This is a good step*. But she's psyched me out too many times. I know she's putting on a show for Felix. It's a show she can't bother to perform for us, not even for one day.

"Hey, pal," she says, sensing me in the doorway.

"Hey." A single syllable from me could disturb the balance. That's what it feels like, anyway. There's this movie Leah loves. In it, the sorceress makes herself look like a princess. Except when she looks in the mirror, her true self reflects back. If I held up one of the stainless steel pots near my mom, she'd reflect back in pajamas with swollen eyes.

"I took my daughter's good advice, Maní," Felix says, gesturing at the papers laid out across the table. "Called your mama this morning for help with the books."

"Is everything okay?" I ask. Even though I know he wouldn't tell me anyway.

"It will be," my mom says. "We're going to head down to the restaurant and go through some papers there. Can you stay with the littles? Silas and Naomi should be home from work in an hour or two to take over for you."

I narrow my eyes. I resent her telling me this like I don't know. She's not the captain around here, but she's grabbing the wheel for Felix's benefit. "Sure."

Felix gathers up the papers, and my mom pecks me on the cheek as they pass me. I steel my body to resist jerking away. I don't want her to pretend to get better. I want her to actually get better.

Some days I wish I could fall asleep and wake up in two or three years. Maybe I'll be in culinary school. Maybe I won't have to push our broken-down family along the road. Maybe, years from now, we'll be fixed enough to move forward.

I nod off on the couch until Bekah complains about being hungry. I make chicken sandwiches and force everyone to eat side salads, too. Then Leah and I go to her room to play horses. Plastic horses have many personal accessories—brushes and flowers for their manes and ribbons for their tails. We've barely unpacked everything when I hear Bekah and Isaac bickering.

Then I hear something shatter. Shit.

"Stay here," I tell Leah.

Downstairs, Isaac and Bekah are still fighting. They're pulling the remote control between them, both flushed from anger and exertion. I'm relieved to see it wasn't the TV they broke. It was a picture frame, facedown on the side table near their tug-of-war.

They see me and exclaim "He did it!" and "It's her fault!" at the exact same time. I look between them, and Bekah says, "I was here first, and he knows I always watch this show!"

"That show is stupid, and there's a show on about dinosaurs, and I told her about it last week!" Isaac makes another grab for the remote.

"Stop." I hold my hand out. "Give me the remote. No one is watching anything because you guys are acting like five-year-olds."

"But!" they both say.

"Now." I rip the remote from Bekah's hand and slide it into my back pocket. "You *broke* something, and it wasn't enough to stop you? Do you understand how ridiculous that is?"

I lift the picture up gently, and no glass pieces fall out. It's just cracked in the center from hitting the edge of the table, splintering off into several arcs of fragmented glass.

It's my parents' wedding picture. Glass is shattered over their smiling faces. And I'll never see my dad smile at my mom like that again. I'll probably never see my mom smile like that again, at anyone, ever. The best years of their lives are gone, and sometimes it feels like mine are, too. Like life will never be that good again. I didn't even appreciate it at the time.

"The dinosaur show is *educational*," Isaac begins, making his case, as if I'll change my mind.

"Come on, Jonah! It's bad enough that you guys made us get rid of cable!" Bekah shrieks, turning on me.

The broken picture has knocked the wind out of me. Hit me right where it hurt—in my own broken places. Part of me wants to sob. But instead, I yell, anger roiling up from inside me.

"God*damn* it. Are you two fucking *kidding* me?" My voice echoes against everything. I'm pushing air from my stomach. "You're making this so much harder than it already is. Do you understand that I'm seventeen? I'm not a grown-up! And you're down here . . . fighting like idiots and breaking Mom and Dad's wedding picture. Look what you did!"

I hold the picture up, and Bekah's eyes brim with tears. This should stop me, but it doesn't. "You've *got* to stop being such assholes. Just *stop*. You are not the only people in this family, and the rest of us think about each other constantly. You only think about yourselves."

They're side by side, lips quivering and eyes wide. Tears streaming.

"Jonah," Silas says, appearing in the doorway. He's holding his work apron in one hand. "That's enough."

"I'm sorry," I reply automatically to him, and I turn back. Isaac wipes at his cheek. I'm the shittiest brother of all time. "I'm sorry. I shouldn't have yelled. I shouldn't have . . . I'm sorry."

I'm off and running. Fleeing. The neighbors' houses blur in my peripheral vision. Months of weight stacked on my shoulders finally broke me. My brothers and sisters—how much longer can we keep this up? My mom—what to do, whether to let her grief run its course or tattle to Felix. My dad—how it still sometimes doesn't feel real that he's gone. How it makes me question everything. On top of everything else, the restaurant—his one legacy, his life's work—may or may not be struggling.

And me. What the hell am I doing with my life? If I have the same fate as my dad, I'll be dead before my forty-second birthday. That used to sound old. Now it's a little more than my current age doubled. And I've spent the past eight months just trying to get through each day. I have one more year of high school left, then what? My grades are decent but not spectacular. I have no particular skills to get a scholarship. I should be spending this year like everyone else—trying to figure it out.

I have basically two achievements in life: my perfect hollandaise sauce and the fact that I've helped take care of my family since January.

And I screamed at them. I called them assholes.

Maybe I shouldn't be here, on Vivi's front stoop. She's been so low. But I need her right now.

I knock on the front door. On the outside, the house looks more like an office building. A big square with sharp edges. I knock again. No answer. So I start around the side of the house, to below her bedroom window. She's usually blasting music in her room and can't hear the door anyway. Her light is on, and her window is open.

"Vivi!" Nothing. "Viv!"

It takes me a few tries, but I launch some twigs until one sails through the window. If she's not actually home, that will be confusing to come home to—twigs in the middle of your floor. But she pops her head out.

"Heyo, darling," she calls down. She's wearing huge earrings and a red wig with very straight edges. "Let yourself in—it's open!"

In her room, Vivi is the center of a cyclone. A cyclone of art supplies, color and texture smeared around her. There's a long strip of fabric half-fed through the sewing machine. A propped-up canvas with a few long drips of sea blue and curry yellow. Scraps of magazines splayed out on the floor. The TV is playing an old black-and-white film, but it's on mute.

I'm relieved to see her feeling better. It's like all her creativity was pent up, and now it has exploded everywhere.

"Hey," I say, staying in the doorway for a moment. She waves with one hand but doesn't look up from her spot in the middle of the floor. She's wearing some kind of robe with droopy sleeves, like a wizard's costume, and she's taking a pair of shears to an open magazine. "I knocked a bunch."

"Sorry, lovey-o, I guess I didn't hear. My thoughts are so loud and jumbly that I can't hear much else at all. They're like wriggly puppies, all diving over each other to get my attention, ha."

Sylvia herself is not diving at all but dozing on the bed. Vivi climbs to her feet. I expect her to put her arms around my neck, but she moves toward the canvas. I sit on the edge of her bed, which is covered in mangled blankets, scraps of fabric, and various buttons and jewels. With anyone else, I'd wait to be asked why I'm here. But it's Vivi. I don't need a reason. Nobody needs a reason in Vivi's world, least of all Vivi herself.

Tilting her head, she smashes the paintbrush at the top of the canvas and watches as a glob of neon orange drips beside the blue and yellow. Then she smears the line, the brush making swipes against the canvas.

I don't know how to bring up the reason I came here—the things I said to my family. Instead, another question pops into my mind. "Can I ask you something?"

"Always, darling, you know that. I'm a fountain of truth, splashing past each concrete tier until I hit the bottom and spout right back to the top." She laughs to herself.

"Do you ever think of us, like, long term?"

"Well, sure," she says. *Swipe. Swipe. Swipe.* She doesn't look back at me. "I've imagined us living together in a tiny apartment in a big city, like drinking coffee in bed and you kiss me on your way out the door to your job as a sous chef at some fancy restaurant, and I own a vintage shop where I alter the clothes to be more stylish and then sell them. And I keep some, let's be honest. And, like, maybe I find out I'm pregnant, and at first we're like . . . oh shit, because we're so young, you know? But then we decide to go for it, and we have this baby boy who comes with us everywhere, and we just make it work, you know, like this little urban family."

So she sees us together for a long time. It sounds like a nice life. Like a real possibility. She served it out just like that, something that could be my two- or three-year plan. A busy city to distract me, a job that keeps me interested, and a Viv to come home to.

She's not done. "But you have to understand, darling, I imagine *everything*. I've imagined us moving to

India, and I fall in love with the country, but you think it's too hot and crowded, so you come back to the States. *I* stay and marry, and I spend my days wearing beautiful saris and perusing open-air markets for the most colorful fruits and lushest fabrics. I've imagined you go off to a really scenic college on the East Coast, with lots of oak trees and green lawns, and I visit you on campus but wind up having an affair with one of your professors, primarily on the desk in his office. I've imagined that you trash your life here and move to Jackson Hole to a remote cabin and, like, live off the land, and I pine for you my whole life but I know you're a mountain man, and that's not the life for me. Still, when it's a snowy winter and there's a fire roaring, I imagine you in a flannel shirt making forest delicacies in your rustic kitchen, and I wish I could transport myself to you just for the night."

I mean, what do I say to *that?* I can barely keep up. I leave India or I go to a traditional college where Vivi cheats on me with an older man or I retreat to life in a log cabin?

"Not Japan for us, then?"

"Oh, darling, when I dream of Japan, I am *always* on my own. But don't fret—maybe I can visit you in Jackson Hole! Over Christmas, that would be the best! That's the one thing about Verona Cove that I can't quite imagine, Christmas without a little dusting of snow. OH! We should have Christmas in July! Wouldn't that be a gas, let's do that right now! There's got to be a holiday shop year-round, right?"

She turns to me, the painting all but forgotten. The costume, the *darling*, the *be a gas* lingo. It's like watching old movies has caused her to develop a new facet of her personality.

"It's August first," I say.

"*Is* it?" She turns to me. "Well, I'll be damned. Summer slipping through our fingertips, *quelle tragique* . . . alas. Next thing you know it'll be back to school, and . . ."

Vivi takes a deep inhale. I take my moment to get a few words in. "I yelled at Bekah and Isaac."

"I'm still thinking I might convince my mom to let me finish senior year here, which would be so fabulous, really . . ." She's prattling on. I slide my palm around one of her arms. The touch makes her meet my eyes.

"Viv. Did you hear me? I screamed at my little brother and sister."

I can barely see her blue eyes, blinking beneath the overpowering eye makeup. "Welllll . . . did they deserve it? Because sometimes you have to scream to be heard and sometimes you have to open your lungs and let the words fly because they're inside you and have to get out, know what I mean? And—"

"No," I say, defeated. I release her arm from my grasp. "No, they didn't deserve it. They're little kids! But I'm so tired of them fighting. I called them assholes."

"Hey!" Vivi says. "Do you think the hardware store is still open?"

"What?"

"The hardware store. I have some stuff I need for projects, and I just want it now so I can keep working, and..."

She's had a bad week. I get that. I'm relieved to see her up and about, but why the hell isn't she hearing me? Maybe she needs it spelled out for her.

"Viv. I screwed up. Bad. I don't know what to do."

She tilts her head back, staring up at the ceiling. "My ceiling is driving me mad, being half-painted, so I should do that tonight, but I hate, hate, I mightily *loathe* doing the edges."

All right, that's it. I'm pissed. The one time I need to unleash, and she can't even *pretend* to pay attention. "You know what, Viv? Fuck it. I don't even know why I came here."

"Such *language*, Jonah Daniels," she says, though she seems unfazed. "You ain't the only sucker with problems, honey child."

"You're acting crazy, all right? Are you drunk?"

"HEY." She whirls on me, eyes blazing. Her fingers are snapping at her sides, over and over. Is she *stoned*? No. Too hyper. "I'm in the midst of a stroke of creative genius, and you cannot go flinging despicable words at me. I'm not *drunk* except on art and music and *life*."

She's lost me. I'm spooked, to be honest. I thought *I* was coming loose at the seams, but apparently Vivi is too. If she can't turn off her Vivi-ness for a few minutes to help me when I really need it, then I'm done. "Forget it, Viv. I'm glad you're having a great night. *I* am having a *shitty* night, but who cares about me, right?"

"UGH, *Jonah*, stop treating me like I am the antagonist in the play of self-pity that you are writing. I am not your bad guy, and I am not your princess. I am me, and I am my own. You cannot REDUCE me! So just STOP. KILLING. MY. CREATIVE. ENERGY." The snap of her fingers, frantic now. "You can't kill it! I'm having a breakthrough!"

Here's what I learned from the past five minutes: you can't out-crazy Vivi Alexander. On the grouchy to blissful spectrum, she spends zero time in the middle. She wallops me with the change in her moods like a one-two punch. Thrilled! Pissed! And right now, with her glare burning into my skin, she *hates* me. The feeling is mutual, and I slam the door behind me.

∞

I'm at Felix's house minutes later, buzzed on adrenaline. It was just instinct, coming here, and I have no plan. I have only the aftershocks of a meltdown.

The moment I turn to go, I hear Ellie's voice. "Jonah?"

She's standing at the side of the house holding a garden hose, half-lit by the setting sun. I want to take off running.

"I'm almost done," she calls. "Wait one sec, okay?"

So I stay standing on the sidewalk like the jackass that I am. I watch Ellie spray the red dahlias and the gloriosa daisies with water. My mom used to garden. Watering the plants was one of my chores, too. Our yard is bare this year.

Ellie shuts off the water and coils the hose back up. There are a lot of reasons why I like Ellie—why I've always liked Ellie, even when it wasn't cool to be friends with girls. She's so nice that she could probably feed a deer out of the palm of her hand like one of the princesses in Leah's movies. But, in junior high, I saw her punch Patrick Lowenstein in the stomach after he called her older brother a pussy. It wasn't because she was sticking up for Diego. I know that because she yelled, "GIRL PARTS DO NOT MEAN THE SAME THING AS 'WIMPY'!" right before her fist doubled Patrick over. I thought that was so damn cool.

"Hey," she says, walking toward me. "I thought that was you. Do you want to come in? My mom could probably heat up din—"

"No," I say. "No thanks."

She stops in front of me. Her eyes shift across my face, left to right, reading me like a book page. Something is wrong—a lot of things, actually—and she sees it all over me.

"C'mon," she says. I follow her to the front porch. It feels rude not to say hi to everyone while I'm here, but politeness is not happening for me tonight. Clearly.

Ellie pats the spot next to her on the porch swing, and I sit. She pulls her legs up, bare feet on the edge of the seat.

I square my feet on the concrete, propping my elbows on my knees. I can't even look at her right now, so I press my hands into my face. "I screamed at Isaac and Bekah. I called them assholes. I made them cry. And then . . . Vivi . . . wasn't even listening . . . God, I just . . ."

I want her to yell at me. Or, hey—she goes to church. Maybe she can give me a set number of Hail Marys to recite. This is my confession, and I want absolution.

Instead, Ellie rubs her hand across my back. For the first five seconds, her touch makes my muscles tenser than they already are. My chest heaves like I'm crying, even though I'm not, and I relax.

"Jonah, you're such a good brother. We all snap sometimes. It's nothing to be ashamed of."

"It is, though. I feel—"

"Guilty. I know. But they know how much you love them. I know you try to hide how stressed you are from the littles, but maybe they needed to see it, you know?"

My mom used to rub my back when I was little. And that's the thing. Obviously I'm tired of *being* a stand-in parent. But I also miss *having* a parent. Sometimes I want to be the kid, embarrassing as that is. I know I'm seventeen. I shouldn't need someone to rub my back and tell me it'll be okay. That I'm not screwing up everything as badly as it feels like I am.

I still can't quite get words out, so Ellie keeps talking, swiping the palm of her hand over my shoulder blades.

"You know, last year, I was studying for a huge math test, and Lina kept bugging me to play Legos with her. She kept interrupting: 'Has it been an hour? Is it time yet?' I was so exhausted and stressed. Finally, I told her to shut up and go away."

At this, I glance over for a moment, less afraid to meet her eyes.

"She cried," Ellie says. "And then *I* cried, because I felt so guilty."

"Really?" Ellie, one of the nicest people I know, made her little sister cry, too?

"Really."

"Ugh. I just don't know how I'm going to face them."

She shrugs. "You'll go home and apologize. Try your best to explain why you reacted that way. They'll bounce back—I promise."

All I can think is, *What if they remember this forever? What if I've spent so much time trying to make life okay for them and all they remember is me yelling that they're assholes?* "I hope so."

"I think it's time to talk to your mom." Her hand stops in the center of my back. "Tell her you can't handle this anymore. Jonah, I've known her my whole life. If she knew what this is doing to you and Naomi and Silas, it would crush her. She needs to get some help from an adult. A therapist or group."

When I turn to look at her fully, she pulls her hand away. "Yeah. I know. That's part of the reason I snapped tonight. Your dad was over at my house, and my mom was pretending to be fine. He had no idea. It pissed me off—that she can't pretend for us, but she can pretend for someone else. So I can't pretend anymore either. I can't pretend like it's okay anymore."

I didn't realize how true that was until I said it.

"I'm going to tell my mom she needs to talk to someone. Soon. If she doesn't . . . I'm going to tell your parents what's going on." I swallow hard, and my Adam's apple feels stuck. I hate the idea of giving my own mother an ultimatum. "I think . . . I think that's what my dad would want me to do."

Finally, I lean back on the porch swing, picking my legs up just a bit. The swing creaks as we rock back and forth.

When Ellie finally speaks, her voice is quiet. "I think so, too."

"Thanks." I mean, I don't know what else to say. "I'm sorry I came over here and unleashed on you."

Now that I've calmed down, I can't believe that I raged over here like the Hulk or something, juiced up on anger.

She was just going about her chores, and I staggered onto the lawn like a mental patient who flew the coop.

"I'm glad you did. Really, Jonah." I look over at her, and I can tell that she's hesitating. "If the situation were reversed—if I lost my dad, I mean—I think I'd lean on you guys a lot. Because our families *know* each other. And not in the way people at school know us. Like we know each other's childhoods and quirks and, like . . . embarrassing moments and stuff."

I'm living one of those embarrassing moments now. No matter how nice Ellie is about it, this situation is not cool.

We stand up, and she hit-pats the side of my arm because I think a hug would seem weird. I say "seeya" like a loser, like this was a totally casual hangout, and I start my walk home.

It comes out in a rush once I get home. I sit Bekah and Isaac down on the couch and say I'm sorry I lost my temper. That I worry about them and about Mom, and I miss Dad all the time. It felt like too much, and I snapped.

"You never talk about missing Dad," Bekah whispers.

"Bek, of course I miss him. All the time. Every time you see me in the kitchen, with his pots and pans, I'm missing him."

All this time, I thought talking about how painfully I miss my dad would put more weight on them. But they both look relieved, exchanging glances with each other.

"When you're sad, you should say it," Issac tells me. "We all should, okay?"

"Okay," I say. "Okay."

∞

My phone wakes me up in the middle of the night, vibrating over and over. Five missed calls and seven texts, all Vivi. *Wake up!! Helloooo, Jonah, c'mon. Come downstairs. Back door. I'm down here. Are you ignoring me on purpose? Jonah, seriously!!!!*

*Hold on*, I type back, to buy myself some time. If I go down there, it might be a yelling match. Or she might just want to apologize. If I don't go down there, she'll probably either wake up my family or sneak in here anyway. Or both. I move slowly down the stairs, holding my breath and cringing at every tiny creak. I step out into the darkness of our backyard, making sure the door is unlocked.

"*Finally*," Vivi says, too loudly. She's wearing a costume. A fedora and a khaki trench coat, unbuttoned to expose a clingy nightgown. "Honestly, Jonah, I was almost to the point of moving on to someone else—I mean, way to make a girl work for it."

"I'm still mad at you." It sounds childish, but I don't give a shit. She basically ignored me the one time in eight months that I've actually asked someone to pay attention.

"Good," she says. "I mean, not *good*, but fine, whatever, I don't care. I'm mad at you, too."

"For what?"

"For being mad at me." She moves so close that one of her feet is placed between my legs. Half her body is up against mine. Her hat brushes against my chin. She presses her lips against the base of my throat, warm and full. I know from experience that she left a red lip print behind.

"Viv, don't. It's not going to work," I lie. Her perfume drugs me. It fills my nostrils and my lungs. I feel it enter my bloodstream, rushing through me.

"Okay," she whispers, near my ear. She slides her hand behind my neck.

I struggle to keep my arms at my sides. "Not working."

"Jonah . . ."

Her hands find my wrists, pulling them toward her. She slides my palms under her nightgown on either side of her silhouette, then up her bare hips. She's not wearing anything underneath. Even when my brain is pissed at her, the rest of my body responds. My brain is mush now. She knows she's got me.

Her mouth is on mine, and I kiss her back almost angrily. I feel her lips form a smile. My thoughts burst in and out, disjointed as she slides her hands across my stomach. Like she can't get into my head, so she gets into my pants. I don't want to feel like she's doing this to keep me from being mad at her.

"Viv, I don't want to be apologized to. Like this." The words are hard to get out.

"Ha," she says. "This is *not* an apology. Why would I apologize when I'm mad at *you*? But I don't feel like fighting right now, Jonah. I'd rather take it out on you. Like. This."

I move her onto the lawn until we're behind the shed, hidden. She presses against me, hands in my hair. I try to pull back for half a second. There's always this moment where we pause and look at each other with quick smiles. But tonight Vivi won't slow down. And I think that's why something feels off.

But then I don't feel anything but Vivi.

# CHAPTER NINETEEN
## *Vivi*

On the way home from Jonah's house last night, I passed a white mailbox with metal numbers attached: sixty-six. *No way*, I thought, staring down at the numbers I'd written down in my bedroom hours before. I was cutting out various and sundry fashion photos from magazines because I was going to do *something* with them, I actually don't remember, but my eyes landed on page sixty-six.

Sixty-six is a nice number—not a mirror image or anything, but it's round and curly and full. But, more important, my name in capital letters makes a Roman numeral: VIVI. Okay, technically, that's not the actual Roman numeral for sixty-six, but I think we can agree it is *very* close. It seemed like the magazine page was calling out to me—why, of all pages, did my eyes land on this one? So I scribbled it down on my hand and did some important work around my room. Eventually I went to see Jonah because I was craving someone's mouth on mine the way you crave cold lemonade on a summer day, like it's the only thing that sounds good in the world, like you'll *ache* until you get it.

I'm onto something; I can feel it in my very bones. My senses tickled my arms and the back of my neck. It's kind of like how elephants can sense an oncoming earthquake because of their hearing or vibrations or something. Only I sensed *numbers*. I stared between the digits on the mailbox and the ones in permanent marker on my hand. The universe, it was trying to communicate with me. What are the odds of me writing down a random number on my hand for the first time ever and then coming across that exact number? It must not have been a random number at all, but what did it mean?! The red flag was up on the mailbox, so I opened it and looked inside to find one envelope—pink, with a girl's name and a Virginia address on it. I squeezed my eyes shut and spun the envelope around in my hand, and when I popped my eyes open, they landed on 1011, the street address written on the envelope. One-oh-one-one, I chanted to myself until I found a pen in my purse and wrote it below the 66 on my hand.

So I'm wandering through town, waiting for my arms to get goose bumps, waiting to see the next instance of 1011 that I'm sure wants me to find it. There are ghosts dancing down Main Street in the darkness of night. Everything is so quiet, oh beautiful Verona Cove, with streetlights like glowing planets, and I can almost see the town's history—from way back when women were only allowed to wear dresses. The town swallows me up, and I hunt in every direction—the outskirts of town and the sleeping neighborhoods and the beach, because you never know. I'm everywhere, for seconds, for hours, for eternities, on the prowl. I see everything there is to see.

The sun is up when I find myself back in the center of town. *Hmm.* No clues. Maybe I got the last one wrong. There has to be a 1011 somewhere. I walk the length of Betty's Diner, reading the white letters on the window. They list the hours for every day of the week, and oh my God, OH MY GOD.

Thursday: 5:00 AM–10:00 PM
Friday: 5:00 AM–11:00 PM

Sandwiched right there—1011—vertically, in the middle. I knew it; I *knew* the numbers would lead me forward, and I skip through the diner doors with the knowledge that the universe sees me and has something spectacular planned.

"Morning, baby doll," Betty says as I slide myself into a booth. "You look like a gumshoe. Better button up, though."

I glance down at my own lap, and my nightgown is visible between the open flaps of my trench coat—which, you know, I couldn't care less about, but I fasten the coat just because Betty is my friend, and I have too much on my mind to disagree at the moment. I guess I'm still wearing the fedora I wore over to Jonah's house last night because

I was trying to sneak over there and the number *sixty-six* was beating around my head.

"Officer Hayashi asked about you."

"Why?" My eyes dart to her as panic floods me. "I didn't do anything wrong."

"Well, of course not. He just expected you for breakfast like usual, I think," Betty says. "You okay, honey?"

"Of course! I'm really top-notch, like sashaying around town on a mission, and I'm not a hundred percent sure where it's leading me, but it's going to be good, Betty, you'll see."

"So what'll it be this morning? Pancakes? Veggie omelet?"

I tried to work my way down the menu at the beginning of the summer, but then I couldn't anymore because I had to go where my feelings took me. Now I have no idea what to do. None of the meals are $10.11. The pancakes cost $4.99 and the veggie omelet is $5.49 unless I add extra veggies and then it's . . . more, my mind is working too fast to add, I need to write it down.

"Need a minute?" Betty prompts me. I had forgotten she was standing there; God, this is impossible. How am I supposed to know? My breathing is loud in my nose.

Sixty-six brought me from the magazine to the mailbox, and then 1011 brought me here, but now what? I'm drowning in all the options because everything is too much. Nothing adds up . . . but I need a new number anyway, like I originally got 1011 from the mailbox. But what's next? Fate! I'll leave it up to fate.

"Betty, can you decide for me? I mean, surprise me, you know? I like everything so it'll be swell no matter what, okay?" I exhale deeply. *Whew.* This is the right plan. I'll get my next number from my bill, once it comes. 'Tis meant to be!

"All right, sugar. Wheel of fortune it is."

I sip the coffee that I do not need because it's something to do while I think, while I doodle all over my napkin, and I rearrange all the condiments and sweetener packets. Betty brings me a stack of waffles, and I'm not really hungry, but I eat them just so she'll bring me my bill sooner. When she does, I scan over the numbers. My total is $7.60. Seven-sixty. My next clue. Here I come, world!

∞

I don't know how long I've been searching exactly, but it's night again, and I am empty-handed, magic-numbers-wise. So I stop at home to look around my house for 760.

My mom is in the kitchen with a local painter friend, drinking wine and looking kind of dressed up.

"Hey," she says. "I was just starting to wonder where you've been."

"Oh, you know, just playing around with the kids and Jonah," I say, hurrying past. *Jonah.* The magic word—one quick mention and whatever I'm doing is wholesome and innocent and inherently good.

She laughs and rolls her eyes at her friend. Once I'm halfway up the stairs, I hear her say stuff like how I'm almost never home, always with my cute boyfriend, ya know, teenagers in the summertime, gotta love it.

There's some dirt on my trench coat, though I have no idea how it got there, so I pull a new outfit from my closet—a colorful skirt that sits low on my hip but flows all the way to my ankles. It covers a lot of skin, so I choose a black tube top that shows some of my stomach. I toss the fedora onto the bed and pile bracelets up my arms. I'm a jangly, brightly hued vision. A vision! Sylvia dances around my room in hyper approval.

My laptop catches my eye, and I figure, you know, why not? I search *760*.

Oh Holy Mother of the Infinite Stars. It's one of the area codes for San Diego.

That's it!

And in the very same moment, I start to wonder what this number trail is leading me toward. It could be anything. It could be something the rest of the world doesn't even realize exists. It could be the secret to *time travel*. Maybe the universe has chosen to reveal this secret only to me, and if I just keep following the numbers, I'll be the first human to achieve it. Oh, where will I travel to first? Maybe the universe will give me a number sign for that, too! Back to the 1920s, to my ballet days, into suffrage and jazz? I dearly hope so. I'm delighted to be the chosen one, and I'll do the universe proud, too. All my life has been building to this. My hands tremble with the knowledge that I'm heading toward something so remarkable.

Maybe I'll find it in San Diego, maybe San Diego will just give me numbers to lead me farther, but no matter: I'll follow the clues anywhere.

My Vespa keys jangle in my hand, and I call to my mom that I'll be back later, and she barely looks up, laughing to her friend about who knows what.

I walk smack into Jonah on my front porch.

"Hey," I say, breezing past him. I'm a girl on a mission.

"Hey." He trots beside me until he's in my peripheral vision. "Is everything okay?"

"Everything is *magnificent*, lover, but I've gotta bolt. Got a date with history."

He keeps following alongside me. "I don't know what that means."

"Neither do I, really, but I'll find out, won't I?"

I feel him grasp my arm. His eyes trace down my whole body. "What are you wearing?"

"Um, clothes, what does it look like?"

He frowns—what a buzzkill, honestly—and whispers, "Viv, that bra thing is, like, completely see-through."

"It's a *tube top*, and I don't care. Nothin' you haven't seen before!" Then I laugh and pull my tube top down for a second just because I can. Jonah looks horrified and tugs it back up, glancing around to see if the neighbors have noticed my bare breasts in the one split second I set them free. Prude. "Relax, my love, everything is wonderful, and there's nothing to worry about."

Jonah frowns, and at this point, he's seriously cramping my style and pissing me off. "Are we okay?"

Ugh. "Of course. Why wouldn't we be? I mean, *I'm* fabulous; I don't know how you are."

He circles his arms around my waist, and the heat of his bare skin feels good on my stomach—soothing. "I haven't heard from you all day. You didn't answer my texts. I don't know. We fought and then . . . you came over last night, and . . . I don't know."

My mind can barely make out his words because I'm looking at his lips and my body is like a *hmmmmmmmm* sound from the tips of my ears to my toes. I pull him into me, closer, and I kiss him with all the ferocity that I feel. It's like heat blooming all over my body, and I can't think of any reason not to get naked with him right here in front of God and any of the neighbors because I really don't care. Sex is a natural thing, you know, like, big freaking deal.

He wrenches back from me and says, "Hey. Can we just talk?"

Jesus. Like, honestly. Way to slam the brakes on what could have been a lovely naked roller-coaster ride, but WHATEVER.

"Can't. On a mission. Gotta fly because there are big things in store for me."

"Where are you going?"

"It's a surprise." I mount my Vespa, my noble steed.

"Can I go with you?"

Nope! Wait. He could be useful for directions. I don't have a plan for that, and it would be easy enough to drive south and wait to see signs for San Diego—or more numbers before I even get there; who knows?! But he might as well come, I guess.

"Okay. Sure. Climb aboard, second matey."

His face disappears under the extra helmet, and he hands me my new helmet.

"Um, no. I cannot be caged inside that thing; I can't breathe."

"It's literally illegal for you to not wear it. You got *pulled over* for not wearing it."

He is dragging down this entire adventure already, and I think about breezing off and just plain old leaving him here. But I'm in a freaking hurry, so I smash the stupid helmet onto my head and rev the engine like a purring cat—no, a jaguar!—ready to *prrrowwwl*.

We whizz through Verona Cove and I relish the Vespa's rhythm beneath me, the way a rider feels the horse's steady heartbeat beneath him, and they are one. That's a lost dream of mine, to be a jockey in a tall velvet cap and high leather boots, and I would have been a fantastic jockey, too, because I love horses; I love their proud features, their spirit, their loyalty, even the names of their coloring—bay, palomino, pinto—and I always thought equestrians looked attached to their horses, both being operated by the same control system, like trunk and branch, except you can't tell which is which because they move together. The Vespa and I breathe in sync and it gallops beneath me and I grip the reins tighter, tighter.

The road transitions into Highway 1, or maybe it's not even called that—like, I only think it's called that because it's the number one highway in the world, if you ask me. On the left side we pass trees and trees and little houses, and the right side drops off into the ocean.

"Viv, pull over! Pull over!" Jonah is screaming, blah-blah-blah, overreacting, holding on way too tight to my waist, blah-blah. "I swear to God, Vivi!"

I don't really hear him until he digs his fingernails into my ribs, and I feel that, yipping.

When I finally veer off to the side of the road, I feel him leap from the bike. He whirls back at me, pulling his helmet off his head. "WHAT is your PROBLEM?"

I push the plastic screen on my helmet up. "*Shhhhhhh*, stop yelling, I can't hear my own thoughts, Jonah!"

"You're speeding like you're on coke! And did you not see the stop sign back there?"

"Oh, Jonah. Stop signs are just red octagons that people assign power to."

"Let me drive. Give me your keys." He's standing in the grass, a bend in the road, and he has become a bend in *my* road. I just can't have him keeping me from my destiny. "I'm driving you home because you're obviously drunk or high or both."

"I am NOT, and you will do NO SUCH THING."

"Viv, you're scaring the hell out of me right now, okay? Blah-blah-blah-blah-blah-blah." That's what I hear anyway, so I toddle my head back and forth, la-la-don't-care-not-listening. I tune in only for the end of his red-in-the-face rampage of blah-blah glory. ". . . then I'd rather walk home."

"THEN WALK HOME FOR ALL I CARE, BYE!" I call, and I wish I wasn't already on the scooter so I could traipse away from him, so I could *flounce* without a care in the world. Gotta go! Got a whole big world to see, and a whole big world that needs to see me, too, and I can't be held back by a boy who is naysaying my journey, no matter how beautiful he is, because I'm going to thrash down the coast, scouring through between sea and sky, and I CANNOT BE HELD BACK.

The engine growls, and I stand up on the bike as it lurches forward and the wind grabs my skirt, and I yell "AYE-YI-YI!" because I am made of moondust and twinkle lights, because I'm impervious to the shortsighted mortality of my peers, to their finite days on this planet that they spend being closed-off and insecure and inert. No, no, no, I am more than this world, as wide as the trees all around me. Huzzah!

My grip loosens and my legs compress for a moment, like springs of a coil pressed down. When they release, the tension pushes me up, and I've done it. I'm airborne and weightless and soaring and free.

# CHAPTER TWENTY
# *Jonah*

What just happened, it happened so fast, what, what, what, NO!

It happened.

My legs and arms go cold, shaky, cramped. I try to run forward, but I stumble. My knees hit the ground, the heels of my hands burn from skidding against ground. I struggle up again.

Someone is screaming. Someone is screaming "HELP SOMEONE HELP."

I think it's me.

It happened. Just now. I saw it. Was she actually drunk? I could've stopped her.

Vivi went flying from the Vespa. It hit a tree. Was she on it when it hit? I don't know. Oh God, the thud of her body, the crash of the metal. How she crumpled. I see blood—from her shoulder—and, oh God, bone. My legs fold beneath me again, and I'm retching onto the grass. I try to move toward her even as I heave and heave. When I'm done, I try to pick myself up again.

Someone catches my arm, then my other arm. Two arms pull me back. A woman in a long nightdress. She holds me to her, trying to keep me from getting to Vivi. Her body is big and soft, and I feel like I'm being held against pastry dough. Comforting. A man is running from their little house toward Vivi, a phone to his ear. He's wearing a gray T-shirt and flannel pants.

I think the woman asked me something. But I can't make words come out. Her mouth looks like she's shushing me, lips pursed but exposing front teeth. Am I making noise? I can't hear anything except the deafening ring in my ears.

It happened. Make it go back. Make time go back one minute. I won't let it happen.

There's some sort of hot film over my eyes; I can hardly see anything. I think neighbors have gathered around us. I think another woman is running toward Vivi. Purposefully. Please let her be a doctor. Let her be more than a doctor. What would Viv want her to be? A "miracle-ist."

I can't breathe. The blood, the bone. Inhaling feels like trying to blow up two balloons with holes in them. So much effort, but empty. Thin air.

How long has it been like this? I think I'm dreaming. This can't be real. In the distance, red lights pulse, sharp color in the dead of night. They're here for her. They'll take care of her. I need to beg them, but I can't. My legs snap like old ropes and then the world is black. My head.

I hear voices. And then I don't. And then I do again.

The last thing I remember is the sound of beating wings.

# CHAPTER TWENTY-ONE
*Vivi*

## CHAPTER TWENTY-TWO
# *Jonah*

A deep voice. "Has he vomited?"

"Several times but dry heaving at this point." A woman's voice. They sound fogged over. Far away. I think I'm outside, but the ground is not cold. A smell wafts through the cool air. It's like smoke and oil and heartache. I know where I am. *Vivi.*

My eyes snap open. I try to jolt up, but I'm held down by strong hands.

"Lay still," a voice says. "Try not to move. Relax."

"I'm okay," I say. At least, I think I am. I'm on a stretcher, looking out the open back doors of an ambulance. But I can't see Vivi—only flashing lights, people milling around. "I'm okay. Is Vivi okay?"

"She's being helicoptered to the hospital." That means she's alive. Thank God. Oh, thank God. They wouldn't bother with a helicopter if there was no chance she'll be okay. Right? The person speaking is a paramedic. He has black hair in curls that fall to his ears. "Her driver's license had a Seattle address and phone number. Do you have a home number for her?"

"Yes. My phone . . . it's in my pocket. Her mom's number . . . is under 'Carrie.'"

"Stay still," the paramedic says, reaching into my pocket. I couldn't move if I wanted to. My legs and arms are restrained. *Am I okay?*

He calls out to someone, who rushes over, and the paramedic reads off the number. Then the doors are closed behind us. We lurch forward.

"No, I want to go with her! I don't need an ambulance. I . . ."

"It's precautionary. Look here." He shines a flashlight straight into my eyes. "We need to keep watch for a possible concussion, so we'll keep you at the ER for observation. Not for long."

"I'm really fine. Just not good with . . . blood." Or bone. Oh God, the memory of Vivi's arm and shoulder makes me woozy again.

I lean to the side just as my stomach lurches again. The paramedic has a bag in front of me, though all I do is heave. I wipe my mouth anyway.

"Deep breaths. I think we're gonna need to get you some fluids," he says. He holds up my cell phone. "I'm going to call your parents now and let them know what's happening."

"No. Don't bother. They're . . ." They're what? One is dead and the other one is barely able to make toast, let alone handle a crisis? "Um . . . out of town."

He asks me questions like if my head hurts, if I know who the president of the United States is, if I know what day it is. I answer them. I ask him questions about Vivi and what is happening. He dodges them. When I roll my eyes in frustration, he breaks his flashlight out again and directs the beam at my pupils. I'm not sure if it's a medical precaution or punishment.

"Wait," I say, when the ambulance stops. "I can't go in there."

With such a short drive time, we can only be at one hospital. This is the building where my dad was pronounced dead. I consider asking the paramedic to call my mom after all. Don't they need consent or something? She could say no. She wouldn't, though. She'd just freak out.

"Hey," the paramedic says. He grasps my arm. "You're fine. Everything's going to be okay."

The ambulance driver opens the back doors and climbs in to help slide the stretcher out.

I want to thrash. I want to break loose like an outtake from *One Flew Over the Cuckoo's Nest*. They can't take me in against my will. But the truth is, I'm so worn down.

I've got no fight left. In fact, once I lie back in surrender, something occurs to me: it's kind of nice to have someone else wheeling *me* forward for once.

∞

I didn't even feel the needle go into my arm. I was in the bed, but I wasn't really there. A nurse tucked a warm blanket around me. *The IV fluids will make you cold*, she said. I felt nothing.

"Hey, Jonah."

I look up to see Mrs. Fischer, my friend Zach's mom. She's in pink scrubs. I should have figured someone I know would be working here. It's a small town.

"Hey, Mrs. Fischer." My throat hurts from screaming for help. I unbundle myself from the blanket and sit up straighter, trying to look less like an invalid.

"I spoke with the doctor and looked over your chart. How are you feeling?" She stands at the bedside.

"Okay." I can't bring myself to meet her eyes. "Did they call my mom?"

Mrs. Fischer looks sad, maybe even guessing why I wouldn't want my mom to know. "You're a minor. It's protocol."

I nod. I'm not mad or anything. I just feel so bad for my mom. I didn't want to trouble her with this. I really am fine. I wanted to go home, where she could see with her own eyes that I'm fine. Now she has to know that her kid is in the place where her husband died.

I look up, pleading. "Do you know anything about Vivi? The girl they flew in? My friend?"

I hear Vivi's voice in my head. *My friend? Is that what I am, Jonah, you darling goof?* No, Viv. At least that's not all you are. Please be okay. Be okay.

"They got her to St. Elizabeth West for surgery."

"So it's really bad?"

She pauses, considering, either because it's really bad news or because there's nurse-patient confidentiality that I'm hoping she'll bend for me. The pause feels like the space between the edge of a cliff and the ground below. "Well, it's not good, but it could be a lot worse. One of our paramedics helped at the scene. He said her head and spine were okay."

Then she says words like *severe, road rash, irrigation, compound fracture, ligament.* I lose track until she says, "Thank God she had the good sense to wear her helmet."

And that's when I press my face into my hands, shaking my head over and over, wondering how I got here.

∞

They release me not long after. I figure I'll call Silas once I get to the lobby. Mrs. Fischer said there's no point in waiting around to hear about Vivi. She'll be in surgery for hours and then sedated so her body can start to heal.

It feels weird, after everyone else being in control of my body tonight, to walk down the hall independently, on my way out of the hospital. This night has been made up of a million slow minutes, so slow that it seems strange that I'm still wearing the same clothes. I still can't believe that it happened. I feel light-headed, which I'd never confess to the nurses.

I stop dead.

My mom is standing at the end of the hall, at the nurse's station. She's wearing pajama pants and a too-big sweater. But she's talking intently. Standing up straight. Gesturing with her hands. I want to call out to her, but I can only stare. I'm remembering years ago, when Isaac got stung by a bee and puffed up like a croissant. She must have been terrified, but I remember her saying firmly, "It will be fine," and we all believed her. She was the mom, and she was in control. That's how she looks now, even in her grieving uniform. Like *my* mom. She is the parent—*I do still have one parent.*

I'm almost close enough to touch her when I say, "Mom?"

"Oh, thank God. Jonah." Tears blink to her eyes. She pulls me into a grasping, desperate hug. I can feel her shake against me. It's been so long since she's stood up straight in my presence. Even with her upright posture, she seems small to me. Have I gotten taller these past eight months? Or did she shrink? Maybe both. When she backs away, her lower lip is shaking. She places her hands on either side of my face. "You *never* do that to me again. Are you okay? They told me you were, but . . . I didn't know . . ."

"I'm fine. Vivi wrecked her scooter. I wasn't on it with her, but I saw it happen. They made me come here because I passed out. I could see . . . I guess it's called a compound fracture. I got sick a few times, so they gave me fluids. But I don't even have a concussion."

"Thank goodness. Is Vivi all right?"

"She's in surgery. At a bigger hospital. I don't know, Mom. I don't know anything." I'm crying before I even realize that it's coming over me. In my mind, Vivi's unconscious on an operating table, under bright lights—pale skin and bloodred lips, unsmiling. Are the doctors stitching her up or cutting her open? My stomach groans.

"Oh, pal," my mom says, pulling me into a hug. How many people have stood in this place? Clutching onto someone to keep from collapsing. My mom runs her hand over my back, telling me over and over that it will be okay. It makes me cry harder.

I know I'm only going to make it worse. But now is the time, if there ever was one. My voice cracks as I choke out the words. "I miss you, Mom."

I can feel her start to cry, too, and we stand here, quiet except for the sniffling noises.

Finally, she whispers, "I miss me, too, pal."

Over my mom's shoulder, I see the red neon sign through tear-blurred eyes: EXIT. It's what I want. This is the place where my father died, and all I want is to start moving away from the darkness it left in our lives.

"Let's go home, okay?" I point my mom toward the exit, and I guide us out.

It's what I've been trying to do all along.

## CHAPTER TWENTY-THREE
### *Vivi*

Everything is dark and rattled. My brain is an empty cavern, dank and full of nothing but echoes. I scream inside my head, and it goes from the back of my skull to the front, then bounces side to side until I'm exhausted from hearing it over and over, and I sleep.

My eyes are gummy. I want to rub at them, but my body is too heavy to move. *Hmm.* IV in my arm and a monitor clamped to my index finger. Left arm casted and in a sling. I want to examine the rest of myself, but it's too much.

I should hurt. But I don't. I feel *smeary*.

My mom is asleep in a hospital chair, limbs bent in an uncomfortable-looking way. There are flowers lined up by the window. I want to crawl to the windowsill and sleep there. Or arrange the plants around me. The muted colors of the medical equipment, the unpainted walls, the beeping, I can't. I can't.

What have I done?

I feel my eyelids sag, shades dropping against my will. But it's not against my will. Sleep, sleep, let me wake up in a different life or not at all.

∞

I am bleak, and the sky is incongruously blue. If the weather walked into my hospital room, I'd slap her face and demand, *How dare you?*

I don't know what day of the week it is. Maybe Saturday. Maybe it is someone's wedding day and every person there is remarking: *We couldn't have asked for better weather!* and *How about this gorgeous day, eh?* How nice for them.

But I feel betrayed. The universe usually understands me better. I need drippy rain; I need hurricane wind to rattle the windowpanes. I need gray skies and white snow, mucked over and melty from car exhaust.

Outside, it's hot, hazy, eye-shielding summer. Inside me, it is parched earth and desolation, and nothing will ever rebloom.

Sleep now. Gone. My short-circuiting brain and me.

∞

My mom is looking right into my eyes. It's dark in the room now.

"Hey, chickie," she says, squeezing my hand.

"Hey."

A tear drops down her cheek. "I'm so happy to see you. We're so lucky you're okay."

"How long have I been here?" My voice sounds like a scratched-up record.

"A little more than forty-eight hours. You had surgery, and you've been heavily sedated since then. The doctors eased up on that a few hours ago to see how you do."

I press my palm against my face. I'm not sure why that's my first instinct—I had a helmet on, right? There's a splintering pain in my shoulder. A sling cradles the cast on my arm. "What did I have surgery on?"

"Your humerus. You also have two broken ribs and a lot of wounds up your left side, and they had to be irrigated. You're on a lot of pain medicine, but it might still hurt."

"It does," I whisper. I look down at my hospital gown and wonder what my skin looks like under there, mottled and forming scabs. I tug at the hospital sheet to see my legs. I want to know that they're okay. The side of my left leg is covered in gauzy bandages. Only a few little spots are uncovered, little pellets of wounds like someone shot me with a gun full of gravel. "God."

Craning my head down, I can see more gauze peeking out, over my collarbone. "And here?"

"Stitches, baby. Probably from a piece of rock on the road that you landed on. I'm sorry." She tightens her grip on my hand. "I'm so sorry. Do you remember what happened?"

I remember everything that happened, but not as if it was me in those memories. I remember everything like it's a movie—something I watched as an outsider. I remember what I did and what I thought, but the logic behind it all? I could never even begin to explain, so I just nod.

"Are you mad at me?" I whisper to my mom.

"No, baby. No, of course I'm not mad at you."

"But I lied to you. I lied to your face. I stopped taking my pills." The dull ache in my shoulder and the fuzzed-over feeling in my brain . . . I deserve them. I lied to my own mother, who tries so hard to trust me.

"It's okay, chickie. It's all right."

"Am I . . ." I glance at the IV. "Am I on medicine?"

"Painkillers and a few things to hopefully make you . . . steadier."

That explains why I can be still—like, I have to be still. Even in pain, even sluggish, it's a bit of a relief.

"Mom." My voice creaks, but the tears won't come out. The medicine in my veins has dried them up. Still, my breathing sounds like sobbing as I get out the words, a desperate whisper. "What . . . if this . . . ruins . . . my life?"

"*No,*" she whispers back. Her tone is fierce, eyes unblinking. "This is going to ruin a few days. It might make some weeks harder. A few hard weeks in a great, big life. You can do that. We can do that. Look at Uncle Mitch. He has really tough days, but his life is so great that we're jealous of it!"

My little sob noise almost becomes a laugh. My uncle has severe anxiety. And a sweet little apartment in San Francisco and my cousin Pip and these great friends whose laughs sound like a big, cacophonous symphony together. My mom and I lived with Mitch for a short while when I was little. I used to fight to stay awake so I could hear the group of adults laughing around the kitchen table. Mitch has his work at the museum; he has Golden Gate Park runs and wonderful food. He has medication and therapy. He's had some hard weeks in a great, big life.

"How much longer do I have to be in here?"

She presses down on her lips, so I know this isn't going to be good news. "Not too much longer. They want to keep you under observation."

"Oh my God." My eyes flick all over the place. "Could I *die*?"

"No, no, no," she says, shushing me. "It's just . . . it wasn't clear if you crashed your scooter or if you . . . jumped off, trying to . . . hurt yourself."

Now it's my turn to flood my eyes with tears. I can barely get the words out. "I wasn't. Mom, I swear."

"I believe you, baby. It's just that you have a . . . history."

That scar is now covered by a cast, the scar that runs down my left wrist like a scarlet *S*. But I was not trying to kill myself—I really hadn't thought that far ahead—and I don't know how many goddamn times I have to explain this. I didn't want to die. I was just trying to feel something. It turns out feeling a cold blade slice into your flesh and then warm blood slopping onto the floor is actually infinitely worse than feeling nothing.

I clear my throat. "I know it doesn't make sense, but I jumped off the Vespa thinking that I wouldn't get hurt. I wasn't even really thinking about it. I thought . . . I was thinking about flying."

My mom nods, processing this. Her eyes are lined in tiredness. She looks older and younger at the same time.

"As long as you're doing okay tomorrow, the doctors need to move you to another hospital in Santa Rosa. It's partially an insurance thing, you know, because—"

"It's a psychiatric hospital. Right?"

"It has a psychiatry department, yes. But mostly you'll be there to recuperate physically. They want you to have access to the psychiatric staff while you do. It's only for a few days." Her tears start in earnest again. "Viv, I would do anything for you—you know that, right? You're my whole world, and I know I am not a . . . conventional mother, but I . . ."

"A conventional mother?" I give a weak laugh. "What does that mean?"

She looks embarrassed, something my mother has never been in her life—at least, not in front of me. "You know. I don't bake chocolate chip cookies from scratch or care how late you stay up. I don't keep tabs on you at all times or think you need lectures every day to make good choices."

We look at each other for a few moments before I know what I want to say.

"Do you remember when I was little, when it was our turn to bring cookies to school? You bought sugar-cookie dough and let me put anything in them that I wanted." My mind drifts back to pink sprinkles and mini marshmallows and those silver sugar balls that seem too pretty to be edible. I was always so proud that I made the cookies, that they weren't like anyone else's.

My mom frowns. "I remember."

"Mom, I *loved* that." More tears stream down my mom's cheeks, and I'm unbearably sad that she feels this way. "I'm so sorry. I'm so sorry that you have to deal with—"

"You *never* apologize to me about this, chickie." She's gripping my hands so hard now, like she can press these words right into my skin. "*I'm* so sorry. You're so strong, and we're going to figure it out. We just have to work better together. That's what Dr. Douglas says."

"You've been talking to Dr. Douglas recently?" She's my therapist from Seattle, the one they made me see after the "suicide attempt." At the time, I resented every moment spent in that chair. Now—I can't explain it—I want her here. Because she already knows the worst of it, knows every hideous weed in my garden.

"Yes." My mom doesn't elaborate.

"Can she come here? Or can we go there?"

"Yes, we can figure that out," she says. There's yet another look on her face that I've never seen before. She looks steeled. Sure of herself. "I obviously can't help you on my own. I should have known you weren't taking your pills. I'm your mother. I should know how to help you better. I have to learn more, and I need to talk to her, too."

I'm feeling so tired again, like the air above me is pushing me down so that the bed will swallow me whole. "Will we go back to Seattle?"

"We'll talk about it, baby. When you're feeling better, okay?"

That means yes. Good. For some reason, going back feels like the right thing. We stare at each other, and I don't know how much time passes before I whisper, "Okay."

But it doesn't feel okay. I feel like I went to sleep, and my whole world changed. My summer nosedived right into the ground. I'm too tired to keep up with all this new information. I'm too tired for anything.

## CHAPTER TWENTY-FOUR
# *Jonah*

I've seen Vivi twice since her accident, but she hasn't seen me yet. She was drugged and out of it both times I was there. This morning she was transferred to a different hospital, in Santa Rosa. A hospital with a psychiatric ward. Which makes a bit more sense now than it did right after her accident.

I'm leaving for Santa Rosa soon, and I keep checking the time. Vivi's mom thought I should wait till the afternoon to visit. So Vivi has some time to get situated in the new place. I'd rather keep myself busy in the meantime.

There's a ring of sweat around my T-shirt collar as I power wash the hell out of the patio's concrete floor. It's not a pretty task. Let's just say birds flying overhead have created graffiti in a few spots. The spray is so powerful that it feels as if it could do damage. Instead, it blasts them clean. It's useful stress relief, as it turns out. I actually wish I had more stuff to power wash.

Vivi's mom has been at the hospital most of the time. She did leave to give me Vivi's house keys so I can take care of Sylvia. We sat on the front stoop because she didn't seem to want to come in.

"Viv has bipolar disorder," her mom said. "She said I could tell you."

I failed to move or speak for at least a minute. She gave me this sad, gentle look during the uncomfortably long silence. It was a lot to take in. I mean, I thought "bipolar" meant, like, really moody. Which I guess Vivi is. I just . . . I didn't know where to start.

"I only knew about her arm," I said eventually. "I mean, the scar. Is that even the same thing?"

"Part of it." Carrie turned to look at me, watching my reaction. "I thought it was depression last year—we all did. We got her on meds after that. And it *was* depression, but that's just not all it was."

"So they didn't work?"

"They worked for the depression. She was happy again, sewing and painting. I caught her drinking, smoking pot, taking my credit card, sneaking out. But I thought it was teenager stuff. Acting up. A sign that she was definitely okay. I had no idea they were symptoms until it got really bad. Then we got her help. And different medicine. There's a lot I didn't know." She turned her gaze to the ground. "There's a lot I still don't know."

Her mom was clearly torn between wanting to be honest with me and wanting to protect Vivi's privacy. I told her that it's okay, that Vivi can tell me more when she's ready. Really, I needed some time to Google it.

Now I've read a lot. Irritability, sexual behavior, disjointed thought and speech patterns. Bipolar I, bipolar II, mixed, rapid cycling, cyclothymic. They seem pretty clearly defined, in separate boxes with definitions. But I honestly can't even guess which one Vivi has.

I sat in front of the computer, head in my hands. She's been different the past week. Should I have known? Did I take advantage of her, without knowing it? I absolutely didn't mean to. Will she feel different about me now? I know it's not about me, but I'm the only person I'm in charge of. And I just don't know what I'm supposed to do next.

So I let the restaurant consume me.

The new menu debuts in three days, and we're having a party to celebrate. It's not fancy or anything—just a celebration for all the people who have helped us with changes.

So many people have chipped in. Felix and I ripped up the remaining carpets in the dining room, and our sous chef refinished the hardwood floors. Silas painted over the red walls with fresh white. That's what we need.

Simplicity. The local florist sold us these things called "bud vases" for practically no money. Bekah stuffed them with wildflowers. Harvey Berman, our town electrician, switched out some outdated brass light fixtures with modern ones. He didn't even charge us for labor—only the parts. The whole kitchen staff collaborated on the new recipes, and Ellie designed the menus. The printing place gave us a huge discount.

And the reason everyone gave for helping us? My dad. I've heard it over and over again this week. When I thank people, they say things like, "It was my pleasure. Your dad was a good man." I start to say, "You didn't have to—" and they cut me off by telling me about my dad. About how he *was* Verona Cove. How they miss seeing him around. Mr. Hodgson told me that his wife was on bed rest for the last two months of her pregnancy. My dad delivered meals to them without being asked. "He always said they were 'leftovers,'" Mr. Hodgson told me, chuckling a bit. "But they were always warm and always her favorite meals, so somehow I doubt that."

Their son is ten now. I never knew. I accepted the long wooden planter the Hodgsons brought by for the patio. Mrs. Hodsgon built it herself, and Mr. Hodgson filled it with bushels of basil and cilantro and parsley and mint.

After the patio floor is clean, I water the planter. It takes me a second to notice someone waiting in the alleyway.

Ellie looks hesitant. I don't blame her. I'm sure I look like someone who's dangerously close to being unhinged. Welcome to Jonahville.

"Hey," she says. "Just wanted to let you know that Mr. Thomas is almost done installing the letters out front. Thought you might want to see."

"I do—thanks." Mr. Thomas has enjoyed our renovation more than anyone. He hasn't been able to stay inside his hardware store next door. He's over here every day, lending us supplies and jumping in to help.

The letters were a special find, and we needed an expert to get them onto the brick front of the restaurant. Silas went to an antique place a few cities over where they specialize in old architectural stuff from building demolitions and estate sales. He took Isaac with him, and they brought home letters to spell out *BISTRO*. They're all wrought iron, some of them a bit rusted.

Out front, Isaac and Bekah are standing with Silas and Felix. Isaac actually chose to spend his morning cleaning—baseboards, bathrooms. Bekah tore lettuce and mixed salad dressing with the prep cooks. The universe feels very disturbed.

Mr. Thomas is perched on the ladder, using his leveling tool to make sure the "O" is straight. He calls down, "Look okay?"

"Looks good!" Felix yells.

When Mr. Thomas starts down the ladder, I can see the new letters clearly. The fonts don't match, but they look great beneath the *TONY'S* letters. Ellie was right. Adding *BISTRO* gives a new feel, a casual sophistication. The antique letters are perfect because they're not *too* perfect. That's how my dad liked his restaurant and his recipes—inventive but classic. Real, never precious.

Silas drapes his arm over Isaac's shoulders. "Those letters were a great find, bud."

Isaac looks silly with pride.

"You did good," Felix says quietly, squeezing my arm.

"Silas and Isaac found the letters."

"I know," he says. "I meant . . . all of this. It's not so easy for a rigid old tree like me."

"Tree?" I ask, surprised. Has Vivi been talking to him, too, about past lives?

Felix laughs. "Yeah. A rigid old tree like me—it snaps in a raging storm. The pliant tree bends in the rain and survives."

We stand there for a few beats, and I'm frowning. Since I'm still not getting it, he claps me on the back before heading back to the kitchen. "You made us bend, Maní."

I thank Mr. Thomas and help him carry his ladder back to his store. When I return to the outside of the restaurant, everyone's gone back in, and it's just me here.

But it's not just me here. And that's the point.

∞

The sky is perfect blue on my way to see Vivi, and the long drive is good for me. My mind feels like an envelope that is too overstuffed to close. So I take some of the stuff out. I think about if my dad would like the restaurant changes, about how the party will go, about the things that might go wrong. I think about Vivi. About how hard the injuries and hospital stay must be for her. How I should be when I see her. If things will be different once she's released.

None of these things feel *good* to think about. But it makes room in my brain.

I pause outside the hospital and take a few deep breaths. A lady at the front desk gives me a visitor's badge. My hands shake a little as I buy some flowers at the gift shop. I should have thought of something clever. Something creative, like Vivi would have. I should have made her a black-cherry cobbler, like the first night she came over to my house. *Should have, should have, should have.* I'm sick of those words biting at my ankles no matter where I walk.

Once I'm outside her room, I can hear my own breathing. No other sound.

I step in. She's propped up in bed, poking at a tray of globby preservatives that the hospital calls food. There's a blue sling on her left arm. A bandage covers up part of her collarbone and sneaks under the hospital gown. Barefaced, she looks younger. I'm so relieved to see her moving around that I could drop to my knees in the doorway.

She glances up. I can see her lower lip trembling even from across the room.

"Jonah?" Her voice is shaky.

"Hey," I say, stepping forward with a smile.

And Vivi, she recoils. "What the *fuck* are you doing here?"

I blink, frozen. Okay. Not what I expected. *Stay calm.* Does she blame me for what happened? The plastic wrap around the flowers makes a crinkling noise as I tense up.

Her eyes flood with tears. "I could have *killed you*, Jonah. That night—you were on the Vespa with me. You should be furious with me. You should have my face on a dartboard. You shouldn't be here. What is *wrong* with you?"

It takes what feels like five full minutes for me to understand. She blames *herself* for this? I step closer to her. I just want to touch her hand, to feel that she's real and okay and here. "Nothing is wrong with me. God, Viv—I'm not mad. How could I be mad at you? I'm so sorry about what happened and that you got hurt."

Her eyes widen, almost wild. "I don't need your pity! Why would you even come here? *Why?!*"

I open my mouth to say something, but she cuts me off before I can begin. Tears dribble down her cheeks. This is going so wrong. So wrong.

"Get *out*." She hurls an empty plastic cup at me, and I dodge it. Good *God*. "I can't stand to look at you. GET OUT GET OUT!"

She stabs at the red button by her side, and it's only seconds before a nurse hurries in. I'm covered in a cold sweat.

"Make him leave!" Vivi sobs. "Make him leave, please."

"C'mon, son," the nurse says, motioning for me. I follow into the hallway because I don't know what else to do. I'm shell-shocked, guilt-ridden. The nurse shuts the door behind us. The stupid flowers are in my hand, and I just don't understand. The nurse looks so sad. "I hope you won't take it personally. The first few days are so volatile."

"It's all right," I mutter, more to myself than to her.

At the nurses' station, I leave the flowers and tell the woman at the desk to thank everyone for taking care of Vivi.

Vivi's words stick with me long after I break back out into the daylight. *Why would you even come here?* she asked me. *Why?*

Because I've been having a hard time since before the day we met. She never walked away from me because of it. Her feelings for me weren't contingent on how easy or hard it was to be in my life. She doesn't have to be sunny for me. That's not how it works.

At home, my siblings know better than to speak to me while I stir ingredients. I pound the dough onto the counter, pressing the rolling pin too hard. I ball it up, flatten it again.

It turns out like a picture. I'm covered in flour as I put it in a box from the restaurant. I press too hard on the paper as I write the note.

> Why? Because you once told me you aren't afraid of the dark places. I'm not, either, Viv. You know that. If I were, I think we both know I would have bailed on my family months ago.
> 
> You also told me to ask what people need and listen. This is me asking. I'm listening. In the meantime, here's a pie in case that's what you need. That hospital food looked disgusting.
>
> -Jonah

## CHAPTER TWENTY-FIVE
## *Vivi*

"Jonah was over at our house last night."

"I *know*," I say, irritated. New hospital but the same food. The starchy blobs are making me lose my damn mind in a new, different, and miserable way. I've been hospitalized for five days now, and I measure them by the most horrible parts—two days since I got my catheter out, and one day since I transferred here and screamed in Jonah Daniels's sweet, confused face. But my mom doesn't know the second part. "You told me. He's taking care of Sylvia."

My mom frowns. She wasn't in the room when Jonah stopped by, thank Gaia. "Well, yes. But when I came home, he was painting your ceiling. He taped everything off, and he was filling in all the edges you didn't get around to."

I literally threw something at Jonah when he tried to visit, and his response was to spend the rest of his day finishing a project I lacked the patience for? I resent him for it—I really do. What kind of monster resents a boy who would painstakingly finish the loose ends of her fancies? ME.

"That's nice." There is no inflection in my voice to suggest that it is actually nice.

"Chickie, you should really call him. He's so darling, he just—"

"Stop, okay?" My tone turns sharp, but she should know better by now. I know Jonah is so darling, and that is why thinking about him makes me feel like I could sweat through my hospital gown. Because he is just so goddamn nice to me, and I want him to react like a normal person and stay away from me. I'm the riptide, and he's a moon-eyed fool. Honestly, that kid has no sense of self-preservation. "Can you just help me get dressed? I'm not going to my appointment in hospital garb."

My mom brought me a few of her dresses. They're loose caftans that go easily over the cast and don't touch the bandages on my leg, and she helps me into my favorite one, pain shooting down my collarbone where the stitches are. There's no mirror in my room, but the dress feels good, at least.

It swishes against my legs as a nurse walks me down the hallway. I hate that I hobble a little, but my left leg is so stiff and scabbed.

The therapist is older than I expected—dark skin and a white beard and a sweater. He looks pleasant but no-nonsense, like an aging fisherman.

"Hi, Vivi," he says, shaking my hand. "I'm Dr. Brooks."

"Hello." I glance around for biographical information. The degree on the wall says his name is Malone Christopher Brooks.

He smiles as we sit down, but I'm still looking for—I don't know. Pictures of kids or even a dog. I hate that he has a file on me and I know nothing about him.

"So. Tell me how you're feeling."

Trapped, guilty, embarrassed, foggy from painkillers. "I'm fine."

"Good," he says, not buying it. "So, let's get to it. Your doctor in Seattle diagnosed you with bipolar II disorder last March. Do you accept that?"

What the heck kind of question is that? I wonder for a moment if he's going to officially change my diagnosis to bipolar I. "I don't really want to."

"Accept the diagnosis? Or have bipolar disorder?"

"Both. But before you say it, I *know*. Depression, hypomanic episode in March, depression *after* the hypomanic episode, then new medicine and manic again the past"—I almost say *week*. Two weeks? I don't even know—"time. So I know I have it, okay? Classic symptoms."

"Well," he says, setting his file down. "There are baseline symptoms, but it varies so much from person to person, and I'd like to know what it means for you. So can you talk about what your hypomanic episode in March was like?"

I take in his kind, open face, and something slithery in me wants to shock him.

"Oh, *can* I. Well, let's see! I went to a concert where I felt high even though I actually wasn't, until I was, and I went home with a girl I met there—a tattoo artist. I dreamed up a watercolor lotus the next morning, and she inked it onto my side. My mom was working all hours at her studio, but we got into a throw-down screaming match when she realized I hadn't come home." He's still nodding solemnly, jotting this down. Just wait, doctor. I'm only getting started. "I somehow managed to get myself to my friend Ruby's birthday party after buying her a three-hundred-dollar purse on a whim. I did shots and smoked with near-strangers. And then I slept with my friend Amala's ex-boyfriend in her bedroom. There was another guy, too, that night."

He isn't nodding anymore. His hand stops writing.

"Everyone just figured I got really drunk. And, well . . . you went to high school." I give him what I hope is a sardonic smile. "You can imagine what people called me after that. The next day, I told my mom that I needed to turn myself into the police, raving that I was a terrible person who didn't deserve to be free. And surprise! My mom took me straight to Dr. Douglas after that."

It takes him a few seconds to recover. "That must have been horrible for you. How did you feel?"

Mortified. Violated. Which doesn't necessarily make sense because I wanted to do all the things I did at the time—more than wanted. Needed. That's what it felt like.

"Dr. Brooks, I would wear a *potato sack* for the rest of my life if I could erase the hurt I caused people while . . . hypomanic." Is that the right word, even? I apparently have this thing, and I don't even know the language for it. "You don't know me, so you don't understand how much it would pain me to wear the same thing every day—let alone burlap."

"What about the hurt this has caused *you*, Vivi?"

After the first day back in therapy, Dr. Douglas sent me for an emergency contraceptive and an STD screening. And I was so depressed—so fucking depressed—that I didn't even feel relieved when the tests came back negative.

I got medical leave from school. If I want to finish high school on time, I'll have to do summer classes next year.

When I don't respond, the doctor inclines his head toward me. "Did you tell people? That you were experiencing hypomania? That your actions were affected by bipolar disorder?"

"No. I . . ." I didn't really believe, at the time, that I had bipolar disorder? That saying I did would have felt like an excuse that even I didn't believe? Amala was so humiliated, and I ruined Ruby's birthday party, and I have this perfect mental image of Amala sobbing, screaming at me on the front lawn, while Ruby had one arm wrapped around her shoulder. I walked miles and miles away from Ruby's house, all the way back to my house. "I didn't."

Dr. Brooks doesn't push me for more. "And, after that time, you were put on a mood stabilizer in addition to the antidepressant. How did that work out?"

I gesture widely with both arms, like, *Well, here I am! How do you think it worked out?*

"You stopped taking the mood stabilizer?"

"Yes."

"Why is that?"

I narrow my eyes. He knows why. "Because I felt . . . off."

He nods, scribbling down a note. "But that was only one medication at one dosage. There are plenty of options that will regulate your body into a healthier—"

"Regulate?"

"Yes." He pauses, as if reconsidering his choice of word. "Don't you think it's fair to say that's necessary at this point? You've now had a depressive episode that ended in self-harm. And so did this episode."

My temper snaps like a rubber band inside my aching chest. "Oh, Jesus Hullabaloo *Christ*. I wasn't trying to kill myself either time—*how* many times do I have to tell you people this shit?"

He backtracks, palms raised to show me he's unarmed. "I'm sorry I implied a suicide attempt. I meant that you were physically injured in both instances. But, Vivi, I really do think that medication at a good dosage for you will help more than you can imagine. I also think continued therapy will help you work through everything you've experienced and how bipolar disorder affects your identity."

And, partially because I prefer to be the one lobbing the questions, I ask, "You're a therapist, right? Can't you help me with that now?"

"In this brief time today? No."

"Why not?"

"Because I'd encourage you to communicate openly. But that takes practice. I'd want you to realize that bipolar disorder is just one facet of a multidimensional life. That takes a lot of thought about what you want that life to look like. And, beyond medication and therapy, I would counsel you to accept your diagnosis. That? Comes with time and experience."

"Oh, just *accept* bipolar disorder?" I almost push off this chair and walk out the door. He's sounding like Officer Hayashi. *But that's life. Gotta deal with what you got.*

Dr. Brooks is unfazed by my scorn. "Yes. I hear you when you say you don't want to have bipolar disorder. It's very trying and can be frustrating to manage. But you've got a loving family and a home and access to health care." His smile is tentative—warmer and less professionally clinical now. "And you've got a lot of fight in you. That much I can tell."

Ha! Fight and art and entire swirling galaxies, doctor.

"Let's say I do try another medication," I say, "and it doesn't feel right—"

"Different options will be discussed. You'll be heard. I know Dr. Douglas. That is a promise I will make and she would, too."

I sit back in my chair, settling in for negotiation. It feels like getting comfortable in the driver's seat, as if I could reach for the gearshift to my right.

"I think the only way this will work," I say, leveling my gaze at him, "is if I have some choice in this."

Dr. Brooks leans forward, letting me in on a secret we'll share. "I couldn't agree more."

"Lithium." I still like the word. "A different dosage. What about that? Or do you think I need the antidepressant and lithium and something else?"

"Let's talk about that." He opens his desk drawer. "Would you like to see the literature for yourself?"

I'd like to see everything for myself, doctor. The whole world. "Yes, please."

Later, in my room, I lift up my dress and twist to see the rainbow splotch of lotus on my side. And it occurs to me, what if I stopped hating it? What if the tattoo and the scar and this summer's freckles are my patina? *Wabi-sabi* says rust and faded paint hold beauty. So what if I let these marks be passport stamps from where I've been— ones that don't determine a damn thing about where I'm going next? What if I apologized to Amala and Ruby and didn't give a shit what people at school think about me because I know the truth? What if I was honest with Jonah and let him make his own choices and stopped feeling so goddamn ashamed? What if I dealt with what I've got?

∞

When I open my eyes again, there's someone moving toward my windowsill, holding a basket in both hands. At first I assume my mom's back, but this person has long black hair. Ellie. She glances over at me and freezes in place.

"Oh my gosh," she whispers, noticing me. "I'm so sorry. I figured you'd be asleep."

"You . . . drove here?"

"Yeah."

That does not make sense. I scoot up a little on my pillow, even though it hurts my shoulder and collarbone. "What's in the basket?"

"Oh, um. Just some, like, comforts from home, I guess. Sorry, it looked nicer but the front desk had to inspect it. Leah and Bekah and everyone helped me put it together."

I'm eyeing her suspiciously—I know I am—but I can't help but be curious. "Like what?"

She sits the basket down at the end of my bed. "Like some, um, dry shampoo. I know it's not the same as being in your own shower at home, but . . . thought it might be nice."

"Can I have it?" I ask.

"Now? Sure." She walks the bottle over to me and doesn't seem uneasy approaching me at all. "Want me to spray it in for you?"

I nod. I'm not sure why, but I'm oddly drawn to Ellie in this moment. I was *not* nice to her. And here she is. Why? She steps close to me and shields my eyes, holding her hand over my brow as I feel the spray against my scalp. It smells powerfully of pineapples. She massages the powder into my hair with the heat of her bare hands. I look at her even though her eyes are on my hair. They're so dark, her eyes, the pupils barely discernible from the irises, and her skin is as copper and smooth as a penny. I'm sure she was a mare in another life—elegant, with panels of shiny hair and long legs. Powerful but choosing to be gentle. Even to me, who was wretched.

I'm starting to think I'm a troll in this life.

But my hair does feel better. Less stuck to my scalp.

"Why are you doing this?" I stare at her dead-on. She's wiping her hands with a paper towel. "I was a total bitch to you, and don't act like I wasn't. And somehow I get a gift basket?"

"Yeah, you get a gift basket," Ellie says. "Because depression fucking sucks."

I thought Ellie was what I call a Lovely. I don't tend to like Lovelies because there's a lot of posturing and holding back of real human emotion. So hearing Ellie say the f-word so casually feels completely out of place, like if

Princess Kate booty-danced or flicked off the paparazzi with both hands.

"I don't know much about bipolar disorder," she continues, "but my brother stayed here a few years ago when his depression was at its worst. Well, not here. He had to stay in the actual psychiatry wing. But I figured I'd at least stop by and tell you the best vending machine is on the second floor near the emergency-exit stairs."

"Your brother was here," I repeat.

"Yeah. He'd probably stop by himself—tell you insider info—but he's doing a study abroad this summer. I figured I'd be his proxy."

"So . . . he's better. He's in college."

"Yeah, he's doing really well," she says. "And now he wants to be a doctor to help other kids. He does all this stuff on campus for mental health education and visibility."

"Did anything happen?" I ask, sitting up. "To trigger it for him?"

It's not a polite question, but I don't care. She considers my question, gnawing on her lip. "I don't think so. He has a great life and a great family, but he started feeling . . . not even sad. He felt *nothing*. The doctors said it could be, you know, hormones, serotonin receptors, who knows?"

I press my eyes shut, trying not to cry. "Same for me. It's like when the dentist numbs your mouth, and you can bite your lip or tongue without even realizing it. At first, it was almost funny, like—*Ha-ha, look at this! I can't feel anything.* But then the sensation stayed gone, and I thought it might be forever, and I got desperate to feel anything."

She nods. "Diego kept saying he felt like he should be able to control it. Like, he wanted to reason his way out of it. Because it's your own mind, right? But of course it doesn't work that way. Sometimes you just need medicine."

Her words make me want to cry but only out of relief to have someone *get* me—without pity. Everyone else seems to feel so sorry for me, and also like they're so glad that they're not me. No one settles inside my shoes—inside my towering, beautiful shoes—and dances around, not even for a minute. No one else looks me right in the eyes and says it like the simple fact it is, depression fucking *sucks*.

Ellie takes a breath to keep talking, but then makes a little gasp. "Oh gosh, listen to me babbling. I'm so sorry. I didn't mean to put words in your mouth, I—"

"No. Don't be sorry. Everyone else comes in here trying to be so polite. My mom, even the nurses, they give me these ridiculous, flowery platitudes, like they're reading straight off a sympathy card. But what I really need is to fucking *scream* because this feels like a war that I got thrown into, and I don't know how I can be so tired and mad at the same time . . ."

My eyes fill, warm and brimming over. It's an everything-finally-bursts cry. The kind that wrings out your spirit—a cleansing.

Ellie climbs onto the bed next to me, and I don't stop her. This should feel awkward. I'm fairly certain Jonah Daniels will eventually love this girl in a way he doesn't understand yet. But it feels like a strange kind of sisterhood—one that you find only when the masks are off and you realize that what's behind yours doesn't scare the other person. She offers one of the pillows to me. "Do it. Scream."

Without hesitation, I press my face into the pillowcase and tear my own throat out.

I scream for every time it's felt impossible to get out of bed, for every time it's felt hopeless, for every time I've felt out of control and terrified, for the guilt and unfairness.

When I'm done, my ears are ringing—my face hot from the pillow, throat raw and pulsing. I sit back and try to slow my breathing.

Ellie unloads more supplies from the gift basket. She puts mascara on my lashes and coral gloss on my lips. Then she paints my nails with hot-pink glitter polish.

"Did Bekah pick out the color?" I ask, admiring the now-shimmery right hand.

"No, actually," Ellie says. She doesn't look up from her brushstrokes. "Naomi did."

I didn't see that one coming. Ellie twists the bottle shut and pronounces the manicure complete.

"I'm the brightest, sparkliest thing in the whole joint," I say. My voice sounds flat. Even though I feel better inside, I can't seem to summon the energy to sound it.

"You already were." Ellie smiles. "Here, last thing. From Jonah."

She sets a white box on my lap, the size and weight of a cake. God, of course he'd make me food after I screamed at him. Maybe it says *Congratulations, Vivi! (You're a Real Bitch)* in icing.

I snap the box open, revealing golden cross-hatches and perfect red cherries. I know the careful hands that cut the dough, and I know that he'd rather cook than bake. I can see him in the kitchen, pressing the crust's edges into perfect little crimps. In my mind, his brows are pulled down, still frustrated by me even as he works.

The note trembles in my hand. God help him, Jonah Daniels can stand his ground even when his knees quake. Cherry pie, with a side of devotion and forgiveness.

"What is it?" Ellie asks, peering in.

"Everything," I whisper, lower lip quivering, and I press the note into my hand.

# CHAPTER TWENTY-SIX
## *Jonah*

There's a happy buzz through the restaurant that I haven't felt in months. We open the windows, and the cool breeze kicks up the smells of all the food. Ellie drew fancy letters on the sandwich board out front:

NEW MENU—OPEN HOUSE: 6–9. COME ON IN.

I'm in my kitchen gear, and I've actually kept my white shirt clean so far. I keep finding excuses to peer out the kitchen window. Normally I only want to be behind the scenes, in the kitchen. But tonight? Tonight I need to watch it all play out.

Some people are seated, but many are milling around. Our waitstaff is carrying the last of the passed appetizers, and soon we'll start in on the entrées. Most of the crowd is made up of townies—the very ones who helped make the restaurant changes possible. Everyone looks so relaxed. I was worried about that. Like, hey, come to my dead dad's restaurant, but try to have fun. They *are* having fun, though. Ethan, Naomi's friend and fellow environmental engineer, is making Leah laugh about something. Silas is chatting with Carol Finney, who graduated from the same college he's leaving for this month. Betty is standing next to her wife and regaling a group of people with some story that makes her light up.

"Go on," Felix says, flicking the end of a dish towel at me. "Take a lap. We're good here."

It's hard not to feel overwhelmed. As I walk through the restaurant, I'm bombarded. It's a lot for me to handle. I'm not good at it, the small talk. I try to smile. I nod politely. I take the hearty slaps on the back. The praise makes me happy, but I don't know how to react. I'd rather people scribble down their nice comments on a piece of scrap paper. I could read them later without anyone waiting for my awkward response.

I keep thinking I see my mom out of the corner of my eye, but I know she's not coming. And that's okay. I've shown her printouts of the new menus and everything. It's the most excited I've seen her in months. But being in the restaurant with everyone—it would be too much to handle right now. She's not there yet.

I'm not even disappointed. Because we *talked* about it. She told me that she couldn't come and why. She told me that she spoke to her support group about it, and they encouraged her to go with her instincts. I didn't have to assume she wasn't coming because she was tucked into her room. She told me, like I'm an adult who she trusts with the truth. She knows I can take it.

On my way back to the kitchen, I sneak one of my favorite appetizers off a tray—grilled-cheese bites. I made them with Ellie's homemade rosemary bread, melted Gruyère, and fig compote.

"*Mmmph.*" I grunt this to myself in the helpless way you do when something is just so damn delicious. Yeah, I made it, but . . . what can I say? I'm good.

"Sneaking some of the product?" Ellie asks, nudging my arm. She's in her waitress attire, hair in a ponytail. "I'm surprised they let you out of the kitchen."

"Eh, I made a break for it. We're all set for the entrée, and I've got a few minutes before dessert prep."

"I'm glad. I wanted to borrow you guys for a second."

She tugs me by the arm as she rounds up the rest of my brothers and sisters. They're all here—Silas brought Isaac and Bekah early to help and Naomi brought Leah a little later, so she wouldn't be bored. I'm hesitant to be with all five of them at once, here at the restaurant. It makes the absence obvious. It wrings my stomach, the missing him.

"What're we doing?" Leah asks.

"Just ducking outside for one minute," Ellie says.

Leah turns to me. "Jonah, I love the pizza! It's my favorite thing!"

"Me too!" Isaac says.

Pizza? Isaac notices my confusion. "Ya know . . . the one with the cheese. It has, like, apple slices on it?"

"The flatbread?"

Isaac and Leah shrug.

Huh. It's a Brie flatbread with apple slices and onion jam. And here I thought Leah would hate every new item except the desserts. I was prepared for four choruses of "This tastes like barf."

We're standing outside the restaurant, and Ellie motions for us to get together. I make eye contact with Naomi, wondering if she knows what this is about. She shakes her head.

"I just want a few pictures, okay?" Ellie calls. "My dad made me swear."

Naomi, Silas, and I all look at one another. We're already here. We might as well.

We cram together, the six of us. Silas picks Leah up, and Isaac leans against Naomi. At first I think I'll have to force a smile, like I normally do with pictures. But then Bekah, who has one arm around my waist, gives me a little squeeze. I know we'll be back to business as usual tomorrow, all of us talking over one another and breaking up fights among ourselves. But tonight is a good night.

"Smile!" Ellie says as she holds her phone up to us. She takes a few before we break apart. Silas sets Leah on the ground, and Bekah releases herself from my waist. I catch Naomi's eye again. My sister and brother and I don't hug. That's just not how we are. But Naomi puts her arms around me and Silas, and we stand there in this weird three-person huddle that doesn't actually feel weird at all. The littles join in, too, Leah hugging her arms around my leg.

I know Ellie's camera isn't pointed at us. It's too private. And something a picture couldn't really capture anyway.

We pull apart quickly because the moment starts to feel too solemn.

"Are you *crying*?" I ask Naomi, whose eyes look a little watery.

"No!" She swats my arm, smiling. "Shut up."

We go back inside like it never happened.

Since January, I've been trying to believe that we'll survive. And here, tonight, is the first time it occurs to me: I think we'll more than survive. I think we'll be good. Maybe even great.

I know the restaurant is not my dad. I know that his legacy is more than the bricks and mortar. I know that making oatmeal for my family isn't going to single-handedly save them from heart disease. And I know that making Vivi pie isn't going to fix what she's going through.

But the point is that trying to make things better sometimes makes us better, too. The point is I'm trying to create good things in the midst of the bad. Grief or no grief.

And in my case, it's still somewhere in between.

∞

After the last guest has left, I wipe down the patio tables. The white candles have melted to stubs, flickering out. This whole night, I've felt close to my dad. It aches—and somehow eases the pain, too.

But someone really is behind me now. The presence comes over me like a whiff of ocean water and something else. Wisteria. I sense Vivi right before I hear her voice.

"Hey."

She's standing in the alleyway, wearing a dress and flat shoes. It's a tame outfit by Vivi standards, and her lips are very pink instead of red. The arm sling eclipses half her upper body. Her left leg is half-covered in large square bandages. She's freeze-in-place beautiful—it's like my eyes forgot these past few days. Like I'm seeing her for the first time and like I've known her my entire life. Like the first day and the last. "Hey."

I put the rag down and turn all the way toward her, but she doesn't move any closer. She's keeping distance between us, hesitant of me.

"I'm sorry I missed the party." She runs her hand over the wall of the hardware store that faces the patio. It's something to do so she won't have to meet my gaze. "I couldn't be around everyone so soon, and—"

"Viv. I know. It's okay."

"I'm sorry about that day in the hospital, too. I didn't mean to lash out . . . I just . . ." She sighs. "I've always loved *The Wizard of Oz*, you know? Every girl wants to be Dorothy Gale or maybe Glinda. I never wanted to be the tornado."

I open my mouth to say that it's okay, that I'm just so glad to see her. That if she's the tornado, it's not because she's cut terror through a tiny town. It's because she's swept us all up into a place where there's color everywhere. But she starts up again.

"You did a beautiful thing here, Jonah." She finally makes eye contact, locking in.

"Thanks. I still have some food left. Do you want cheesecake or something?"

"No, thanks. I'm coming from breakfast with Officer Hayashi." She smiles a little at my confusion. "Breakfast for dinner."

I take a step closer to her because that's my impulse—to be near her. I'm not sure why she's hanging back. "Are you feeling okay? Are you in a lot of pain?"

"I'm okay. The pain meds help." She gestures toward the wall nearest her. "You should do something with this blank wall. I bet Mr. Thomas would let you."

"He suggested it himself, actually. Just haven't gotten around to it yet."

"Yeah. You've had a lot going on." She raises her chin to eye level again. "Do you want to take a walk with me? Can you leave?"

The cleanup detail can wait till tomorrow. Everything can wait when it comes to Vivi. "Of course."

I open the gate so that I'm standing in the alleyway with her. Normally, I'd take her hand. But this is not normally. I'm not sure if I should act the same way. I'm not sure if she'll still like me the way she did before. I'm not sure of anything. We fall into step down Main Street, and she stays quiet.

"So . . ." I try to begin. I've got nothing. The awkwardness trips me, and my brain takes a painful spill onto the cobblestone streets. "What's . . . new . . . ?"

She stops dead. I wish I could contort my body to kick myself in the face. *What's new?* What the hell kind of question is that?

But then Vivi starts to laugh. It's that wind chime sound at first, and then she's doubled over on the sidewalk, *ha-ha-ha*-ing. It makes me laugh, too. Hesitantly, at first. And then more and more. We stand across from each other, unable to stop. Vivi looks up, covering her mouth. Our eyes stay on each other as we shake with laughter.

Once we calm down, Vivi wraps her arm around my waist, still giggling to herself. Just like that, we're us again. A different us because I know more now. But that's good.

There are no cars out so we walk in the center of the street. The streetlights guide our path.

"Oh, Jonah. What a week." I want to put my arm around her shoulder, but I can't because of her cast and sling. I repress a cringe, thinking of the bone sticking out after her crash. "Was the party tonight everything you wanted it to be?"

"Yeah. It was. It felt like the right thing. If that makes sense."

"It does."

"So, um. How are you really?" I glance down at her, and she looks up in return.

Her eyes crinkle a bit at the sides when she smiles. "Pretty good, actually. I mostly just watched TV and slept and let nurses change my bandages. But I also went to some therapy appointments—even a family session with my mom. It felt . . . I don't know. Like a relief."

We're talking about really serious stuff. But—I can't explain it—the pulse of our conversation is steady. This almost feels casual. Or, at least, like us.

"Counseling with your mom—was that good?" I ask. "Just curious because, uh, my mom went to a grief support group twice this week. Officer Hayashi told her about it, actually. I guess he goes."

"Yeah." She smiles, clearly already aware of this. "Family therapy was really good. My mom and I are usually pretty good about talking, but it helped to talk in a different setting, I think."

"My mom's already trying to talk the rest of us into going. I'm glad she can go, but . . ." I glance over. "I don't know."

There's a pause, and I start searching for something else to say. Vivi bails me out. "My dad's wife sent me a letter. My mom gave it to me today."

Holy shit. "Oh yeah? Wow. That's big."

"Yeah. I haven't opened it yet." She reads my expression and smiles. "I know—it surprises me, too. I mean, if I had been around when Pandora got her hands on that box, I would have been on the sidelines, like, just *open* it, already, girl. But this letter is . . . a lot for me."

"Do you think you'll open it eventually?"

"Oh yeah. I have a lot of things to work through, and I want to give myself some time. With all of it. But I just keep thinking I didn't lose anything, with him. And I still have my mom, always have. And someday, maybe I'll even get to meet my half siblings."

We're out past the edge of town. I've known where we were headed this whole little walk. It's the edge of the coastline that Vivi likes the most. She keeps her arm around my waist as we step through the high grass. I can hear the water sloshing below as we dodge the stalks of yellow flowers.

The moon glows overhead, the way it did the night we ran into the ocean. It feels like a lifetime ago. A lifetime but not enough. She stops about five yards away from the drop-off.

"Let's sit down," she says. "This is the perfect spot."

## CHAPTER TWENTY-SEVEN
## *Vivi*

We sit side by side on this patch of earth that cuts into the ocean, and the wind tells itself secrets as it slithers through the tall grass. The moon pets Jonah's beautiful hair with the glow of his light. He's taunting me, questioning my will, but I'll still press forward the way we must when we know we are being true.

I'd already felt called back to the mountains, back to the rain and sunshine, back home. But my last shred of doubt was crushed when I got a text from Ruby while I was in the hospital. A picture of a pretty girl I've never seen before, dark skin and round cheeks, smiling across the table at Ruby's favorite coffee shop. *Her name's Kara*, the text said. *I'm falling in love, Viv. Wish you could meet her.* I held the phone to my chest, crying and crying and knowing where I belong. You can ache for where you come from, and it's homesickness. A relationship, and it's heartbreak. But is there a word for missing your friends like that?

So I've never felt stronger than when I was packing up my room at Richard's place. Using one arm to pack up the present, to face the past, to embrace the future. I've also never felt sadder. Sad but strong. You can be both. And I am.

Inhale and exhale and here goes nothing. "We're going back to Seattle."

The silence becomes a third party between us, swirling in and out and changing shapes. Finally, Jonah sighs. "I was afraid you were going to say that."

"In two days."

"Two *days*?" He looks sick with loss, with frustration, with confusion, with everything. I hate doing this to him, even if there's a part of me that is glad I could make him feel so much. "Your mom can't make you leave that soon—that's crazy."

I swallow hard, almost embarrassed now. "I asked to go back as soon as possible, actually. It was me."

"But . . . why? I mean. I know why, I guess. I just . . ." He winces like this is physically painful—and it is, really. "I don't want you to go."

I reach over for his hand. "I know . . . but it's like your party tonight. It just feels like the right thing."

He rubs at his jaw, where stubble has appeared since the last time I saw him. Jonah sighs again—a mile marker

I should have expected from this conversation. This is not any easier for me than it is for him. I am just more sure.

"I guess that means we're breaking up?" he asks.

The term *breaking up* is so bourgeois. The idea of it simply doesn't fit my notions of relationships and their fluidity. I sigh, too, because I'm very uninterested in devoting precious time to defining or undefining who people are to me. But maybe this is what he needs from me, and I want to give him anything that he needs—anything but myself. That's not something I can give. "We'll be twelve hours apart. I don't see how we could be together."

"We could still . . . text. And visit." He glances over to gauge my reaction.

I squeeze my eyes shut, and I can't imagine seeing Jonah Daniels casually. We'd meet up for coffee while he's in Seattle on a college visit, and it would be so quotidian, just two former flames sitting across from each other. But all I'd want to do is crawl across the table and into his arms, desperate to transport us back to this summer. It would hurt too much, I think.

Besides, there are other girls in his future, and each will change Jonah in little ways that push him along. More stepping stones in our paths. I want him for myself, but I want adventure for him, too—and for me.

And heaven knows texting wouldn't be enough. "Oh, Jonah. You're the roots, darling. I'm the clouds. Our love will always be from afar."

I expect him to smile, but he looks so stricken that I give it to him straight. "I need to get things right for myself."

"I know, and I *want* you to. And I'd support—"

"I know. But I have to do it in my time, for me. I know you would never rush me, but I think *I'd* rush me. If we planned visits, I'd want to seem better for you."

He opens his mouth to say something, but I climb into his lap before he can. He's sitting with his knees bent, and I sit exactly the same way, only facing him. It takes me a minute to situate myself because of the sling on my arm and the broken ribs that ache throughout my side. Once I'm settled, I stare right into those brown eyes of his, and they almost liquefy my resolve. The coastal wind whips our hair, a chill rushing through me. I imagine what we must look like from a distance—two little specks interlocking, sitting on a cliff over the seas with a backdrop of ocean and stars. What I mean is, there are worse places to break someone else's heart. And your own.

But finding each other was celestial, and this is how it must be.

"Maybe we were dying planets, Jonah, being drawn into the darkness." I hold my right palm against his cheek, and I wish I could touch him with both my hands. "When we collided, we bounced each other back into orbit. And now we have to do that—we have to return to our own paths because that's what we gave each other."

"Sounds lonely." He gives me that self-deprecating smile.

My heart bangs into my rib cage, screaming at me, *Traitor! Traitor!* "A little lonely, yes."

Jonah tucks a lock of wild hair behind my ear. His smile doesn't hide his own aching chest—I can feel it. "Can we say 'someday'?"

I lean in, touching my lips against his. He smells like him, like shampoo and oregano and everything I want to keep even though I know I can't right now. "Someday, Jonah. Someday."

When I sit back, we stay there with our foreheads pressed together. Jonah Daniels, my sweet boy with his rumpled hair and khakis and heart, handed me so many things that I needed. And his beautiful, boisterous family, they gave me something I've never held before in my life: the desire for that kind of love. Maybe I'll grow up and fall in love and have half a dozen kids. Or maybe I'll buy a little house with a big dining room table and a deck, and I'll have a group of friends who come over all the time to drink wine and laugh our way even through the hard times.

I've always fixated on the *things* I want in my life—paint palettes and sumptuous fabrics and star-flecked skies and dancing on my tiptoes and the smell of jasmine. But I usually imagine myself alone or falling in love with all kinds of different people. These days, I've started to daydream of the permanent relationships I want to have. Friends who stay in my life forever. People who I trust to love me even if I'm wobbling—the way I trust Jonah. And if that's what I want, then I have scorched earth to till and replant. I love Ruby and Amala too much to not try.

I have a Japanese maple seedling, and I have seen how beautiful a rooted life can be. But I have miles to go before I decide where to plant us.

"I want to tell you something," I say. I wish I could explain everything to Jonah. But *bipolar disorder* is an untranslatable term. I could tell him that sometimes it feels like being on a carnival ride, so fast and dizzying and fun at first. Then it goes on for too long, and you can't stop. I could tell him how I hurt friends without meaning to. I could tell him that depression made me feel like a husk, empty and lifeless. Those comparisons might help, but bipolar disorder is so complex, and it's mine. My feelings have back rooms and trapdoors, and I'm still learning them. I can't quite articulate what bipolar disorder is for me, exactly, but I can articulate who *he* is to me, and so I take a deep breath.

"I want you to know that I wouldn't have done anything differently this summer. Well, that's not true, obviously." I give a breathy laugh, and I let myself start over. "That first night we went to the beach, I wore my nightgown because why not? That's me. But the day before I crashed the Vespa, I wore *that* nightgown all over town without even caring that everyone could see . . . and well, I wouldn't have done that. But there still would have been picnics and writing plays and making scavenger hunts. I would have loved you the same."

"I know that," he says. But he closes his eyes for a split second—relief that he can't hide from me. His hand is on my cheek, looking at me so admiringly that I almost can't believe I'll walk away from this. "It doesn't change anything for me either, Viv. You know that, right?"

My own eyes blink closed. Yes. I already knew that, but I treasure the words.

"And thank you for the pie, Jonah," I whisper, even as the first tear rolls hot down my face. "I'll never forget it."

"Me neither, Viv." God knows—and so does Jonah Daniels—that I don't just mean the pie. We know there are three little words branded inside my heart: *Jonah was here.*

I'm bogged down in my realities: money gone, friends I've hurt, medications I haven't taken and the ones I have and will, a way forward that will be hard to navigate. I feel a little emptied out, but not exactly hollowed. Sometimes I feel empty like a new canvas.

I almost try to explain another untranslatable word—*śūnyatā*—to Jonah. The idea has Buddhist roots and several meanings, depending on context. I think *emptiness* is the closest word, but, in English, we infer emptiness as a void, a lack. *Śūnyatā* is open with possibility, a meditative space.

But Jonah's lips are warm on mine, and so I savor this kiss like the last bite. That's the thing they never tell you about love stories: just because one ends, that doesn't mean it failed. A cherry pie isn't a failure just because you eat it all. It's perfect for what it is, and then it's gone. And exchanging the truest parts of yourself—all the things you are—with someone? What a slice of life. One I'll carry with me into every single someday.

I lie down in the cool grass beside him as planets collide above us, and we stay like this for a long time, down to every last crumb. My cheeks are wet, but oh, my heart—it is so full.

## CHAPTER TWENTY-EIGHT
## *Jonah*

"Hi," a little voice says. "Hi, hi, hi. Guess what! Waffles!"

I peek one eye open. Leah's grinning back at me, bouncing at the edge of my bed. I was up till sunrise with Vivi two nights ago, and I've had a pounding headache since.

"Jonah, come *on*," Leah says. She pushes all her weight onto the bed, jostling me. "You're the only one who's not up."

"Okay, okay." I sit back against my elbows. "Your hair looks nice."

"Thanks." Leah's hands move to the ends of her braids. They're the fancy kind. I can't even fathom how to bend hair like that. "Mom did it."

I trudge downstairs with Leah traipsing in front of me. Something stops me in the kitchen doorway. And it's not just the smell of hot waffle batter.

Naomi is manning the waffle iron. Isaac is trying, and failing, to juggle three oranges. Bekah's tongue is sticking out in concentration as she slices up strawberries. Silas is stuffing his face with the first batch of waffles, piled high with whipped cream and powdered sugar.

My mom is putting water in the coffeemaker. She's in her pajamas, but then so is everyone but Silas, who's wearing his work polo.

My family is everywhere, busy with individual tasks and reaching over one another. But, somehow, doing it all together. It's such a familiar scene that part of me expects to turn the corner and see my dad. I know he won't be there. But it feels like he's in the kitchen all the same—in Naomi's determination and Silas's easy humor and Bekah's sensitivity and Isaac's precociousness and Leah's everyday excitement. In my . . . well, I don't know what. But I hope something. Something good.

Silas's plate clatters in the sink, and he sees me as he turns back. "Hey, Sleeping Beauty."

I grunt. He swats me with his apron as he passes by.

"Silas," my mom calls over her shoulder. "Before you go off to work, leave the dorm packing list out, okay? The one from the website? I'll see where we are with it."

"Okay," he calls, hurrying up the stairs.

"Jonah," Bekah says. "What toppings do you want?"

"Um. Strawberries and chocolate syrup." I sit down on a stool. Leah grabs the whipped-cream canister and sprays it into her mouth. My dad used to do that with us. We'd all shriek with joy. It was too good to be true, eating straight whipped cream.

"Hey," my mom says to Leah. "No spoiling your breakfast with pure sugar, missy."

"*Swrry*," Leah says, with her cheeks puffed out. She's clearly not sorry.

My mom shakes her head but in an *oh-you-kids* kind of way. "Morning, pal. You want some coffee?"

"Yeah. Thanks."

She pulls another mug from the cabinet. Naomi slides a waffle to Bekah, who tops it with whipped cream and strawberries and passes it to Leah. They're an efficient assembly line, like the kitchen staff at the restaurant. My dad would be proud.

"Isaac," my mom says. "Put the fruit down and eat your food."

One of the midair oranges hits the counter with a thud.

When the coffee is ready, my mom fills up the mugs and hands one to me. She sits down at the kitchen table with a plate of waffles. Bekah and Isaac sit on either side of her. I stay seated at the island between Naomi and Leah.

I have to find a way to tell Leah that Vivi's leaving today and probably won't stop in to say good-bye. I wait until she takes a bite, so she'll have a second to process it. I use a calm, quiet voice.

"I'm going to see Vivi today, before she has to move. Do you want to draw her a picture or something?" I texted Vivi yesterday, to see if she needed help packing. She said no. I was so disappointed that I almost went over anyway. But then she told me to meet her at the park today. Of course—it'd be a dramatic farewell, with a meeting time and anticipation. I'm half dreading it. I'm half desperate for it.

Leah shakes her head. "I already gave her one. She came over yesterday morning, and we played."

"Vivi came over while I was at the restaurant?"

"Yep! We played ponies and stuff."

I glance at Naomi for more information. "Were you here when she came over?"

Naomi nods, not looking up from her waffle. "We all were."

In a quieter voice, I ask her, "Why did she come over? To say good-bye?"

She chews a bite and swallows. "She came to pick up something of Sylvia's, she said. I think she actually said 'seeya' as she was leaving. She was just . . . I don't know. Being Vivi."

I turn it over in my mind. I'd understand if she wanted to slip out with the shadows, after all she's been through. Instead, she came over here, when she specifically knew I wouldn't be home. To spend one more happy day with my brothers and sisters. My throat aches. I don't think it's the too-big bite of waffle I just tried to swallow.

Leah swings her feet below the island ledge. "I wish Vivi didn't have to leave. It makes me sad when I think about it."

"Yeah," I say. "Me too."

Naomi shakes her head. There's something ironic in her smile. "You know what? Me too."

∞

I shower and shave and try to make my hair look presentable. There's a sailor's knot in my throat. I'm supposed to walk to the park, toward Vivi, and that part's fine. It's the walking away from her that I can't imagine.

On my way, I think about how Isaac is obsessed with archaeology. I get it. The dinosaur bones and ancient artifacts and excavated graves—it's cool. It comes to mind because Vivi climbed into my life with her fossil brush, and she swept away the dust. She rediscovered me under all that rubble, and that means I'll always be a little bit hers. How am I supposed to say good-bye to someone like that?

I'm still yards away from the park when I realize she's not here. You can feel a girl like Vivi. She shifts the ground under your feet. And I don't sense them, the tremors beneath me.

There's a note pinned to the oldest tree in the park—a tree scratched with her name. So this is how it will be. She gets to say good-bye. I don't. I should have known.

Dear Jonah,

I lied. "Good-bye" is my least favorite word in my entire vocabulary, much worse than even "squish" or "protuberance," and I just can't say it to your handsome face. Give your family kisses from me, will you? I think I fell for all seven of you a little more every day. But mostly you, Jonah. Mostly, madly, beautifully you. Won't tell Isaac, okay? He'd be crushed.

Maybe in my next life, I'll be a wave in the ocean, and you'll be a mountain, and we'll spend years and years brushing up against each other. You'll shift so painfully slowly, and some days I'll crash right into you and other days I'll approach gently, licking your sides. That sounds like us, doesn't it?

Or maybe we'll meet in this same life. Maybe I'll be working as a costume designer for a movie that's filming in a city where you're the chef of your own restaurant, and our eyes will lock in the middle of a busy street, and I'll whisper, "It's you." Maybe I'll sneak into your little bungalow house while your fiancée is out of town on business, and we'll make love like we have in past lives and in this life. That doesn't sound like something you'd do, but a girl can dream.

*Either way, Jonah, I simply cannot wait to see who you become.*

*Until someday,*
*Vivi*

*P.S. I left something for you on the restaurant patio. Took me all night. I call it "How We Say Good-bye."*

I blink, taking in the sharp lines of her name and, next to it, a red lip print, kissing me good-bye. Of course she'd make a dramatic exit, even without being here. We can't keep each other—I know that. But I wanted to see her one last time. I wanted to say thank you; I wanted to make one last attempt at memorizing her.

I hurry to the restaurant, clutching her good-bye note. What would she leave for me? What would take her all night?

I don't even bother going into the restaurant itself. I cut through the side alleyway to the patio, and I stop dead in my tracks. I expected that she left something for me on the picnic table. But it's not that.

On the wall opposite the patio, she painted me a mural.

My heart beats like tripping feet. I try to imagine her, balanced on a ladder all night with a sling on her arm.

The patio lights are on—I never leave them on—so she must have painted by the light of them. She did this for me. *How We Say Good-bye.*

The Verona Cove lighthouse is in the right foreground. Beyond it, there are ships in the harbor—seven of them—all with white sails. I'm not sure how she gave a flat wall so much movement, like each sail is flickering. I can almost hear them beating against the wind. There's one bigger boat in the distance, sailing toward the upper left corner. The horizon, gold and blue, looks inviting and limitless. The lone boat's sails puff out in pride, a pioneer to the unknown. The seven boats in harbor seem to be waving good-bye, cheering *Bon Voyage!* Vivi crammed all her vivification into this one painting, right down to the nautical flags on the biggest ship.

I learned the letters associated with nautical flags when I was a kid. The first is a "D." The second, blue and white: an "A." Wait. My eyes skip down the mast. They spell out D-A-N-I-E-L-S. It strikes me like whiplash—there are also seven little ships in harbor. One for every living member of my family.

This is not a painting about Vivi and me saying good-bye.

The large boat sailing away for new adventures . . . it's my dad. Oh my God. She painted a family portrait. She painted us as sailboats. I see it now—how could I have missed it at first?

My eyes fill, hot with tears. Because, apparently, casual crying is just something that I do now. My chest caves in with missing my dad.

I touch the horizon line, skimming my hand over the still-tacky paint. Gold melts into every color of blue where the ocean dips off into nothing. *Do you believe in heaven?* Vivi asked me once, and I told her the truth: that I want to. In one painting, she gave me something I've needed for months now: happiness even in uncertainty. What's past that horizon line? And how many of us get our somedays? I don't know.

But just because I don't know doesn't mean it can't be great.

It takes me a second to notice the small letters painted in the bottom corner. But I knew they'd be there like I know they'll be all over the world someday.

*Vivi was here.*

# AUTHOR'S NOTE

Here's the truth: I wasn't sure if I should write this author's note because *When We Collided* is just a love story in a world that looks a lot like mine. Some of us go to therapy, some take medication, some have to carefully balance exercise and sleep to stay in a good place mentally. There are bad days. There are also best days: dinner parties, art galleries, vacations, and sunlit, sideways-laughing happiness. They can coexist. They *do* coexist. This is my normal.

But that's the thing, isn't it? I didn't always see this as normal, and I worry that we're not talking about mental health enough. And if we're not talking about it enough, how can we possibly shine enough light into places that can feel very dark and very lonely? So I'm going to talk about it here.

This is what I would like to say. The experiences in this book are of course fictional, but depression—whether clinical, spurred on by trauma or grief, or as a component of bipolar disorder—is so very real. If you, like Vivi, are trying to navigate your own mental health or, like Jonah, are grieving or supporting a loved one, I truly encourage you to talk to someone you trust. Reach out to a parent, teacher, counselor, or therapist. Visit the resources I've listed for you below. People out there are waiting to be on your side. But first you have to tell them where you are so they can come stand with you. I know verbalizing what you feel—what you need—can be intimidating if you've never done it before. But using your voice is a kind of strength that makes you powerful. And while I can't tell you what will work for you or if that path will have setbacks, I can tell you I believe prioritizing your health is important, undervalued, and something you deserve.

I can also tell you that you are so, so not alone. The CDC statistics about bipolar disorder and depression are staggering, but it can be easy to see those as just numbers. I keep a mental list of all the people I know in real life or people I admire who live with mental illness. People who have faced difficult battles and gone on to thrive. Sure, it takes management, but those friends and family members are my visibility. They're my list. When I'm having a rough anxiety day, I go over their stories in my mind, like a prayer, like a chant. I see that a diagnosis isn't a destination a doctor sticks you in but a road you walk—with agency, with travel companions if you wish. That journey can bring you closer to the people beside you and take you as far as you want to go. I believe this.

Sometimes it seems like the portrayals of mental illness we see—in movies, in the news—are primarily tragic ones. Please hear me: there are thousands upon thousands of other stories. One is that it's hard sometimes, and maybe the path isn't perfect, but you get there. Some difficult weeks in wonderful lives. That's Vivi's story and mine.

Keep talking. Because, even when it does not feel like it, more best days are always ahead. Claim them.

Resources
- NAMI.org: National Alliance on Mental Illness. NAMI is an amazing hub for support, education, and advocacy for mental illness, including resources for families, vets, and diverse communities. They have chapters in many, many cities and a helpline: 1-800-950-6264.
- AACAP.org: American Academy of Child & Adolescent Psychiatry. The AACAP includes family and youth resources, from learning the basic vocabulary/facts of mental illness and seeking help to speaking up for yourself and others through advocacy. The AACAP website also has a specific Bipolar Disorder Resource Center, which includes their clinical resources, book recommendations, and facts for families.

- DBSAlliance.org: Depression and Bipolar Support Alliance. The DBSA site contains educational materials, wellness information, peer support through personal stories and art, and more.
- AFSP.org: American Foundation for Suicide Prevention. The AFSP website has a wealth of information and support. Here's their Lifeline: 1-800-273-8255.

# ACKNOWLEDGMENTS

First thanks to Bethany Robison, dear friend to me and Vivi, equal parts critique and partner. I love you and I like you.

Taylor Martindale, my trusty agent and navigator. No matter which direction I want to go, you steer with enthusiasm and confidence, and it has never been truer than with this book. Thanks for traveling to deeper waters with me.

To my editor, Mary Kate Castellani: Thank you for taking on this story with tremendous insight and care. I'm particularly appreciative of your incredible ear for these characters' voices and the unflagging support you've given me throughout revisions and additional reads.

Team Bloomsbury—Erica Barmash, Amanda Bartlett, Hali Baumstein, Beth Eller, Lili Feinberg, Cristina Gilbert, Courtney Griffin, Melissa Kavonic, Linette Kim,

# ACKNOWLEDGMENTS

Cindy Loh, Donna Mark, Lizzy Mason, Cat Onder, Emily Ritter, Nick Thomas, Ilana Worrell, Brett Wright: I'm so lucky to be on the receiving end of your hard work, fierce minds, and creativity. Thank you for giving my books a home in this house.

I'm eternally grateful to those who shared their personal experiences before and during the writing of this book. In particular, to the key readers who shared valuable insights along the way: Thank you for showing me a part of yourself and letting me do the same. But beyond even that, thank you for making me feel shoulder-to-shoulder with such good people.

I'm hugely indebted to Dr. Martine Lamy for fielding my early questions and for picking through the final manuscript with a lens of knowledge I am so grateful for. Martine, thank you for the resources, for the thoughtfulness with which you guided me, and especially for the incredible work you do every day.

Thank you to my family for supporting and inspiring me with their love and strength. I won't name you all because there are so many, and that is one of the great blessings of my life. I wouldn't trade for a small (or normal) family in a million years. Special thanks to my mom and dad and aunts, who have been incredible supports when I've needed to talk about this story. Love forever to my uncle Todd, whose humor, everyday zeal, and devotion to his family I held close while writing.

To my friends, thank you for keeping me laughing, inspired, and borderline annoyed by your wit and good looks. For Alyssa, Janelle, and Kristen—because you wait till the end of events and I just scribble in your books quickly so we can go eat dinner, here it is in print: you are the reasons I write friendships as the real love stories of high school.

I write this on a plane returning from a book festival, and I don't know if there's a word for the hugeness of my YA community love. To borrow from Viv: spectacularity, burstsomeness. Readers, educators, librarians, booksellers: thank you for the energy and passion you bring to this world. My writer friends, thank you a million for talks about life, art, craft; for so many laughs; for being my people. Particular thanks to Kate and Jasmine, who have picked me up from literal and metaphorical/creative flat tires this past year.

Finally, to J, painter of my edges, mountain to my sea: thanks for sharing your work, your life, and your goodness with me.